FOR RICK

Thank you for always believing.

*There is a way that seems right to a man, but in the
end it leads to death.*

PROVERBS 14:12

THE NETWORK

CHAPTER ONE

JACK LOGAN HAD DITCHED HIS CATHOLIC UPBRINGING but kept the guilt. He hadn't planned on blowing his entire afternoon listening to the woman he was interviewing talk about her dead daughter, but he didn't have the heart to tell the grieving mother that he already had enough for the story. So instead, he bought her lunch *and* dinner, listening as she painted a picture of the girl she had loved and had failed to save. Now he was behind schedule and would have to work all night. Man, he hated the pieces involving kids. The parents got to him every time, and his attempts at comforting them were as effective as a Band-Aid on a gunshot wound.

It was after eight by the time he got to his East Village apartment. He sprinted up the three flights of stairs and heard his landline ringing as he approached the door. Jamming the key in the lock, he pushed the door open, rushed over, and snatched the phone, upsetting a bottle of Bass Ale and spilling the dregs on the table. He grabbed a towel to sop it up before it dripped onto the hardwood floor.

"Great." He clicked the green button. "Yes?"

"Could you sound any more annoyed?" It was his editor.

"Sorry, Max. What's up?" Jack sank into his worn leather sofa and ran a hand through his hair.

"Tried your cell. Went right to voice mail."

"I was interviewing one of the mothers."

The sound of papers rustling came from the other end of the line. "You already did your piece on the decision. What's the angle on the follow-up?"

"The fallout from the decision to let the show go on."

A sharp intake of breath. "You're not saying the Supreme Court should have censored it?"

"No, no. Of course not. But the voices of the bereaved deserve to be heard." He wasn't much of a television watcher, but when the class action suit against the network behind *Teenage Wasted* had reached the Supreme Court, he'd tuned in. At first it looked just like the setup of any of the other reality shows jamming the airwaves—an eclectic group of teenagers allowing the cameras behind the scenes into their world. Within the first five minutes of the show, though, Jack had sat open-mouthed while a young man retrieved paraphernalia from under his bed, pulled up a porn site on his computer, and began doing what your average adolescent boy did behind closed doors. It was filmed so that there wasn't any actual nudity, but it was obvious what he was doing. It wasn't until the young man put the noose around his neck that Jack's shock turned to horror. So that was what erotic asphyxiation looked like up close and personal.

The internet went nuts the following day and homemade videos of other kids demonstrating their own secret hobbies began to appear all over video sites. When kids started turning up dead, it really hit the fan. A class action suit was filed against Omega Entertainment Inc., the entertainment giant responsible for the new show, by the grieving families whose children had been inspired by *Teenage Wasted* to engage in dangerous experiments that had cost them their lives. The Supreme Court decision had been handed down a few weeks ago, to the great shock of the plaintiffs, and the show went on—more popular than ever. Omega had won the case under freedom of speech protection, which Jack couldn't argue with, but he was disgusted by how the company executives were perverting the First Amendment for their own profit. He was happy to do his part to help tarnish Omega's reputation.

"All right, email it when you're finished. You still coming tonight?" Max asked.

Jack grimaced. Sally Goldman's retirement party. He had forgotten.

"Wish I could, but I'm too jammed up with this." Sally was a great gal. He was sorry he'd have to miss it. He'd send her some flowers tomorrow.

He'd better get to it. He opened his laptop and began to organize his notes. He was starving; he'd barely touched his dinner earlier. He picked up the phone to call Joe's and order a pizza and was surprised to hear a knock at his door. He made no move to answer it. The knocking continued, louder now. Who the hell would just show up uninvited? Once again, he regretted moving into an apartment with no doorman—someone must have held the main door open downstairs. He slammed the phone down, jumped up, and strode to the door, ready to tell whoever it was to beat it. The words died on his lips when he opened it. Probably best not to piss off a US senator. Without waiting for an invitation, Senator Malcolm Phillips walked right in.

From the first time he'd met Phillips, something about him struck Jack as off. He couldn't put his finger on it exactly: the guy's manners were impeccable, his background impressive. Phillips was perfect. A little too perfect. Everything about him was so well-rehearsed that Jack could almost believe an invisible teleprompter fed him his lines. What surprised Jack most was how Phillips's wife, Taylor, failed to see he was all wrong for her. Of course, he kept this to himself. His opinion didn't mean anything to Taylor anymore.

Going no farther than the apartment foyer, Phillips started speaking in an uncharacteristically nervous rush. "I won't waste time with pleasantries. I need your help." His voice shook, and his face was ashen.

"What is it?"

"I scuttled the vote. It was supposed to be a good thing. But he snuck something else in the rider. He has to be stopped."

Jack had no idea what Phillips was talking about. "Whoa, slow down. Who has to be stopped?"

He ignored Jack's question and handed him an envelope instead. "Take this. You'll need it to convince Taylor. I didn't believe it. He told me he would do it. I didn't believe him but . . . they'll kill me."

This was insane. He hardly knew Phillips, yet here he was in Jack's apartment rambling like a crazy person.

"I'm sorry, but I have no idea what you're talking about. Can you slow down and start from the beginning?" Jack asked, trying to sound calm.

"No time. You're the only one I trust. You've got to find Jeremy. Get Taylor to him. They won't hurt her now, but later . . . I was so stupid . . ."

Phillips had moved into the living room, where he was pacing, sweat breaking out on his forehead.

"Who's Jeremy? You're not making any sense," Jack said.

"Go to Taylor and show it to her." He pointed to the envelope. "It's all in there. Get Taylor and take her to the cabin."

How did he know about the cabin? Jack wondered, but he had a more pressing issue.

"I'm the last person Taylor wants to see. She's not going to go anywhere with me."

Phillips moved closer to Jack and grabbed his arm.

"They own me. And Brody Hamilton, too. You'll see when they kill me. Then you'll know."

"When who kills you?"

Phillips let go of his grip and backed away.

"Promise me you'll get her to Jeremy." He handed Jack a remote control. "This will get you into our garage. I've taped our address to the bottom." He wiped his forehead with the back of his hand. "Remember, Jack, no matter what it looks like, I'm not suicidal or prone to accidents." Suddenly, the senator ran past him and was out the door before a flabbergasted Jack could respond.

Jack shut the door, began to walk away, then turned back and engaged the extra deadbolt. His eyes narrowed as he looked around, half expecting a phantom to appear.

What was Phillips talking about? Did someone really want him dead—someone powerful enough to own two senators? His head began to pound, and he leaned forward to massage his temples. What had Phillips done? Maybe he'd gone nuts, or this was early-onset dementia. Jack could only hope.

He would do some digging. Try to make sense of what had just landed in his lap. He threw the envelope on the coffee table, opened his laptop, and set a Google alert for "Malcolm Phillips." Then he looked at the envelope Phillips had pushed into his hand, marked with Taylor's name. *The hell with it*, he thought, as his thumb slid under the lip and he tore it open.

CHAPTER TWO

MALCOLM PHILLIPS WAS 110 FEET UNDERWATER. HE checked the metrics on his dive computer—five more minutes before he was in danger of getting the bends. He had spent too much time in one room of the wreck and now would have to forgo exploring the rest of it. Scuba diving was the only time he truly relaxed, and wreck diving was his favorite. He loved the history and mystery associated with these old Japanese ships.

It was the first time since he'd scuttled the vote that he hadn't felt the target on his back. After he had landed in Guam, he had called an old friend and borrowed his private plane to get here. Part of the appeal of this remote Micronesian island was his ability to blend in with the other tourists—nobody knew who he was or paid him any extra attention. He wanted to be as far away from Taylor as possible to be sure she wasn't caught in the cross fire. Who would have thought that he would be willing to make such a sacrifice? Before he met Taylor, he had never done a single thing out of concern for another person. As some would say, miracles never cease.

Satisfied that he could count on Jack to look after Taylor, Malcolm intended on making the most of whatever time he had left. He wasn't foolish enough to believe he'd be able to elude his enemies for long, but in the time he had left, he was going to do what he loved most. He rented the equipment from a dive shop he knew well and checked it over carefully before heading to the dive boat. He'd been here more times than he could count, and the divemaster knew him well enough that Malcolm convinced him to make an exception and take him out alone. He needed to think, and he never thought better than when he was gliding along a coral reef.

The water caressed his skin, and he surveyed the visual feast surrounding him. Angelfish painted in vibrant blues and yellows floated by, oblivious to their glory. The soft whooshing of his regulator filled his ears, and the lack of conversation added to his pleasure. Closing his eyes, he relished the feeling of floating through the ocean. He checked his dive computer and saw it was time to go up. He began ascending, making a concentrated effort to exhale as he rose, but was surprised when he heard a warning tone from the device. *Beep . . . beep . . . beep. What was wrong?* He looked at his wrist—the ascent warning. He was going up too fast. Swimming back toward the wreck, he grabbed the rope dangling from the boat above. Now he would need to hang for at least ten minutes. He continued checking his gauge while he held on to the rope, then began a slow ascent when it indicated he was clear to go up. At last, he broke the surface and felt the warmth of the morning sun on his face. After climbing aboard the boat, he slipped the heavy tanks off his back and discarded his wet suit. He was looking forward to a well-earned lunch.

When he reached the outdoor restaurant, a young man showed him to a table overlooking the sea. He inhaled deeply. Salt and diesel combined to make a surprisingly pleasant aroma. He ordered a Hammerhead Amber, one of nearby Yap Island's newest microbrews, and made notes in his diving log. His waiter returned with the beer and smiled at him.

"We have nice fresh fish, mister. You want same as yesterday?"

Malcolm nodded. "Let the chef know it's for me. He knows how I need things prepared."

"Yes, sir." He bobbed his head and left.

The tuna was delicious, and he devoured it. Leaning back with a satisfied sigh, he debated whether to order another beer. Deciding a nap would be even better, he paid the bill and walked the quarter mile to the small hut he was staying in. On the way, his throat started to feel funny. He tapped his pants pocket to see if it was there. *Deep breath, don't worry.* Maybe he was coming down with a cold. When he reached the hut, he had to steady himself against the door as the scratchiness in his throat intensified, and he became dizzy. The realization that he was definitely having an allergic reaction hit him, and he pulled the EpiPen from his pocket. He snapped open the case, removed the safety, and plunged the pen into his right thigh. *Relax. It'll kick in soon.*

But it didn't. The tightening around his neck increased, and he managed to croak out a dry, wheezing cough. Staggering to the dresser, he felt around for another Epi and stabbed it into his other leg. The face looking back at him in the mirror wasn't his, the swelling so exaggerated it rendered him unrecognizable. This couldn't be happening. Not yet. Dread filled him. Someone had tampered with the food—and his medicine. His shellfish allergy was in his medical file. Grasping the dresser, he pulled the hotel phone toward him as he fell to the ground. When he lifted the receiver to his ear, there was only silence.

CHAPTER THREE

JACK HAD REALLY THOUGHT PHILLIPS WAS OFF HIS nut—on drugs, anything but serious. Especially after he'd read the letter Phillips had left for Taylor, which sounded like the ravings of a lunatic imagining conspiracies everywhere. But when he got the Google alert that morning, he realized with a sinking feeling that Phillips *had* been telling the truth.

Dead. Phillips had been standing in this apartment less than a week ago. A chill ran through him as he grasped the full implications of this news. Phillips had made a powerful enemy, and if Jack decided to get involved, he would be turning himself into a target.

After Malcolm's visit, he'd done some quick research on the bill Phillips had been ranting about. It was the last vote Phillips had cast, and he'd voted no. It seemed fairly innocuous, just broadening the range of vaccines that received federal funding to help those who couldn't afford them. Sure, maybe people felt strongly about covering the cost of the vaccine, but to kill over it? He really hadn't known what to make of Phillips's visit other than to think that he was going through some sort of mental breakdown. But as soon as he got the alert, he knew he had to get to Taylor right away. It was too coincidental. Phillips *was* dead—reportedly, from some kind of accident while on a diving trip. He remembered Phillips's last words to him with a shiver.

Throwing a few things into a duffel, Jack then opened his safe and took out his SIG, making sure to pack extra ammo. He went to the hall closet and grabbed his go bag. This would take care of Taylor and him for a couple of weeks. Now all he had to do was figure out how to get Taylor to leave with him. He had a few hours to think about it on the drive from the city to her house in McLean, Virginia. He was relieved as he pulled his '66 Mustang out of a nearby garage that his car was too old to have GPS.

O O O

The winter sun was setting when he pulled up to the property. The massive black iron gates were locked, as he'd expected, and he had to get out of the car to swipe the card reader to open them. He had never been to the house Taylor shared with Phillips, and as he came up the long driveway to the enormous, French colonial–style manor, his eyes widened. There were five exterior stone arches, illuminated from above by large, round light fixtures. A second-story balcony ran across the entire front of the house. This place cost serious money—clearly, Phillips's Senate salary wasn't covering the mortgage and upkeep on it. He remembered reading about it a while ago in *Town & Country* one night when he'd had a few too many and started googling Taylor. It had its own basketball court, indoor pool, and home theater. It suited Phillips perfectly, but Taylor? Maybe she had changed over the years, from that little girl he'd grown up with who'd hated ostentation to a senator's wife overseeing a grand estate.

He followed the circular driveway past the front door and around to the four-car garage, per Phillips's instructions. Using the remote, he opened the garage doors. Three cars were parked inside—a navy blue Aston Martin Vanquish, a black BMW 7 Series sedan, and a green Range Rover with a dog rescue bumper sticker that must belong to Taylor. He parked the Mustang in the only open spot, got out of the car, and pressed the intercom. Malcolm had given him the code to get into the house, but he didn't want to spook her.

A wary voice answered. "Who's there?"

Hearing the strain and grief in her voice broke his heart. "It's Jack." He heard a dog growling in the background.

A click and then the door opened. She was standing on the other side, a ghost. They looked at each other.

He pulled something from his pocket. "Gummy bear?"

A forlorn smile appeared then vanished just as quickly. He crossed the threshold, and they stared at each other for a long moment. He'd forgotten how beautiful her eyes were—like sparkling emeralds. Even now, red-rimmed from crying, they were arresting. He shook his head to clear his thoughts.

Now was not the time to be thinking about things like that. A golden retriever came up to him and began to sniff and wag his tail.

"What are you doing here? How did you get into the garage?" she asked.

"Malcolm gave me the remote."

Her brow furrowed. "What?"

"I'll explain everything." He followed her into the huge kitchen and took in the marble countertops and the ornate chandeliers hanging above a center island that could easily accommodate twenty people around it. He'd have bet she and Phillips could've walked around this house for days and not run into each other.

The dog jumped up and nudged Jack's hand with his head.

"This is Beau." Her voice was wooden.

Jack crouched down and ruffled the fur on the dog's head. Beau's tail thumped wildly.

"Nice to meet you, Beau." He looked up at her. "Malcolm came to see me last week and told me that if anything happened to him, I was to come straight here."

"I can't believe he's d-dead." She stumbled on the word.

"Taylor." Jack took a breath. "It wasn't an accident." There was no easy way to say it, so he just came out with it. "He was murdered."

She shook her head. "No, no. What are you talking about? He died of an allergic reaction. He's allergic to shellfish, there must have been some in his sauce. The medical examiner ruled it an accidental death."

Jack persisted. "He warned me that someone was after him."

"I don't understand. Why would he come to you? You hardly know him."

"He said I was the only one he trusted. He's seen me around the Hill, knows my reputation." Jack hesitated for a moment before asking, "And I assume he knows our history, that I'd want to help you?"

At this she glared at him. "Yeah, well, he should have gone to someone else." Her eyes filled with tears and she swiped them away with the back of her hand. "I still can't believe it."

"Did he say anything out of the ordinary before he left?"

She shook her head. "No. But . . ." She stood up, pacing. "Well, he *was* preoccupied, distracted. I just figured he was stressed from work. The trip was a last-minute thing, just to blow off some steam. I don't dive. It's something he does alone."

Jack sighed. "He told me he would be killed, that I had to get you. You're in danger. We have to get out of here tonight."

"Are you crazy? I'm not going anywhere. I have to plan his funeral."

He tried a different approach. "Let's just back up a minute. What do you know about this vaccine bill he voted on before he left?"

She shrugged. "Malcolm was for it. It was going to help a lot of families that couldn't afford the vaccine. RSV infection is horrible in babies, and the vaccine is costly."

"So why did he change his mind?"

She frowned. "What do you mean?"

"He voted no."

"That doesn't make any—"

She was interrupted by the buzz of the intercom.

"Are you expecting someone?" He didn't like this. It was almost ten o'clock—late for visitors. He walked over to the window. Even with the outside lights on, the thick hedge of boxwood in front of the driveway made it impossible to see anything.

"See what they want, but don't buzz them in."

She gave him a skeptical look, then pressed the button on the speaker on the wall. "Yes?"

"Mrs. Phillips?" a gravelly voice asked.

"May I help you?"

"Sorry to disturb you, ma'am. We're from the Capitol Police. We need to speak with you."

She hit the buzzer before Jack could stop her. "Come in."

"Why did you do that? How do you know they're legit?"

"It's the *police*. They must have news. What's wrong with you?"

A few minutes later, the flash of headlights shone through the curtains briefly and a car door slammed. A low growl came from Beau and he padded close behind Taylor.

Jack followed her into the hallway, and as she opened the front door, he stood behind it, unseen, but could hear what was going on.

"May I see some ID, please?" Taylor said. "What are you doing?" she asked, her tone rising.

Jack heard the exterior storm door being rattled, then Taylor slamming the front door shut and engaging the deadbolt.

The sound of broken glass made them both jump, and Jack

grabbed her hand and pulled her out of the hallway. Beau was barking and jumping up and down now.

Her eyes were wide as she said, "When I asked for ID, he tried to open the door."

Jack flew into action. "We have to leave. Now. Get in my car—it's in the garage." He pulled out his gun just in case there were any surprises waiting for them there.

"I have to get my stuff."

He could hear something ramming against the door. They'd be in the house any second.

"No time. Let's go."

"But—"

"Taylor, please!"

The dog whined as they all ran to the garage.

He started the car, not turning on the headlights, and opened the back door for the dog, who jumped in. Turning to Taylor, he said, "I don't know how we're going to get past them."

She pressed her index finger onto the fingerprint reader pad on the alarm panel, grabbed a key ring from the hook on the wall, then got in the passenger seat. He watched in shock as the ground in front of the car opened into a black void that ultimately revealed a downward ramp.

"What the—"

"It's an underground tunnel. Installed by the previous owners."

This was something new. He pressed on the gas and slid the car into the dark opening. A dimly lit tunnel led them about a mile from the house, still her property apparently, until they came to what looked like a solid concrete wall that was stained red from years of groundwater rusting the concrete's rebar.

"Now what?"

She took the key ring, which had a small LED flashlight attached, and illuminated the wall until she found the oval embossed star on the face of the concrete. As she held the proximity sensor on the key chain against the star, the muted sound of mechanical movement commenced. The wall slowly opened as if it were a garage door.

Jack drove through and cast a sidelong view at Taylor. "Seriously? Was the previous owner regularly hunted by assassins or something?"

"She was a former head of state. It's one of the things that drew Malcolm to the house. He thought it was cool. Like the Batcave or something." She bit her lip. "I always thought it was ridiculous. Never thought *I'd* need to use it."

Jack was relieved to see that theirs was the only car on the road and that they'd make a clean getaway.

"Who do you think was at the door?" she asked.

"I can only assume they're connected to whoever killed Malcolm."

"So it's really true? He was murdered?"

"Looks that way. Right now we need to put some distance between us and them—whoever they are. Let's get out of the state, and we'll stop somewhere for the night. I'll show you everything when we get there."

She ran a hand through her hair and looked at him.

"This is surreal. I cannot believe I'm actually in a car with *you* running off into the night." Then her hand flew to her mouth.

"Oh no."

"What?"

"I forgot my progesterone shots."

"Your what?"

She was quiet a moment then sighed. "Jack. I'm pregnant—I'm high risk. I need to take these shots for two more weeks. Without them, I could lose the baby. We have to go back."

Jack shook his head. "We can't. It's too dangerous."

Pregnant! Phillips had left that little tidbit out. The idea of her carrying another man's child upset him more than he wished, and he swallowed the lump in his throat. Rubbing his temples, he gave her what he hoped was a reassuring smile.

"Don't worry. I'll figure something out."

CHAPTER FOUR

THE LIMOUSINE CAME TO A STOP, AND AS DAMON CROSSE waited for his driver to get out and open his door, he admired the massive stone facility he had commissioned. He'd purchased the two hundred acres in upstate New York over twenty years ago, but this newest compound had been recently completed. Towering iron gates, which surrounded the perimeter of the property, served as a deterrent to the curious; guards stationed in towers and twenty-four-hour video surveillance ensured that he was informed of all goings-on at all times. He divided his time between this building and one much more secluded and secret, where the important work was being done. But today was the start of the new fellowship program and he was curious to get a look at the newest recruits. Before getting out of the car, he removed a long white hair from his pant leg. He would have to speak to his housekeeper about brushing Peritas more often. He normally kept the Great Pyrenees with him, but today his schedule was too packed to give his pet the attention he deserved.

The latest group had just arrived. He took the long hallway to the west elevator, entered, and pushed the button, tapping his foot on the descent to the basement level. He emerged and walked down another cold, bare corridor before entering the room adjoining the barracks, where he could observe the new group through the two-way mirror. They sat on their bunks, awaiting further instruction. Their excited chatter and delight at the novelty of their circumstances had been replaced by an apprehensive awe due to the formidable surroundings. Every group reacted the same way. A knock at the door made him turn.

"You may enter," he said.

"Sir, is there anything else you desire?" Jonas, his longtime estate manager, spoke.

"Everything is as it should be?"

"Yes, sir. The dossiers are on your desk. The medical records on all the recruits are attached to each folder. Everything so far is unremarkable."

"That is all then."

Jonas cleared his throat.

"He's waiting in your office, sir."

"Very well."

Damon watched as the heavy door closed, then observed the recruits for half an hour. Deciding he had let the visitor wait long enough, he rose and returned to the main level, and to his study.

He stopped before opening the door, pulled out his cell phone, and watched the man on the screen. Dwarfed by the enormous wing chair he sat in, the visitor waited. Despite the chill in the air, perspiration had discolored his thin white shirt, and beads of sweat glistened on his brow. He muttered, "We'll find her, sir. Not to worry. Not to worry." His head bobbed as he repeated the mantra to himself over and over.

Damon frowned, put the phone in his pocket, and opened the door.

"So good of you to come." Damon's smooth, deep voice resonated in the room. "I trust you have good news for me?" He seated himself behind the large mahogany desk and looked at the visitor with pursed lips.

The man swallowed. "She got away, sir."

"How?" Damon pressed in a soft voice.

"We don't know. Her car and Phillips's cars were still in the garage. We checked the records, and there are no other cars registered to either of them." The man hesitated. "I don't know how she did it. It's like she disappeared into thin air."

Damon said nothing.

The man in the chair flinched and hurried on. "We'll find out who it is. We will. We've got a lot of men on it, it won't be long. I'm sure, sir—we'll fix it. Stupid, stupid, I know but—"

"Enough," he said. His left hand moved to a small box that sat on the corner of the desk, and with deliberate calm, he pressed the red button. He looked up and studied the visitor for a full minute before he spoke again. "You have failed."

As Damon stood, he nodded toward the back of the room, and the three men who had entered silently surrounded the visitor. They didn't need to use any force to subdue him. Everyone in Damon's employ understood the consequence of failure.

He pressed his intercom. "Jonas."

The door opened. "Yes, sir?"

"Send a team to the Phillips house. Have them retrieve the video footage. I want to know who's with his wife. There's no way she did this alone."

CHAPTER FIVE

TWO HUNDRED AND FIFTY MILES LATER, JACK PULLED OVER at a run-down motel in Pennsylvania and got them a room. The rumpled man behind the desk looked annoyed at having to tear himself away from his phone, which Jack could see was playing a video not meant for anyone under eighteen. In response to his request for a credit card, Jack slapped two hundred-dollar bills on the counter. They disappeared into the man's pocket and a room key appeared in their place. No one else was around, so it was easy to sneak Beau from the back seat of the Mustang into the room.

The stink of stale cigarettes wafted over Jack when he opened the door. He flipped a switch, and a dingy bulb in a cracked lamp illuminated a modest room. He threw his bag on one of the two orange Naugahyde chairs next to the small, round wooden table.

Taylor looked around the room, her eyes resting a moment on the double bed, then back at Jack.

"One bed. You should have gotten two rooms."

He shook his head. "Don't worry. I'll take one of the chairs."

She pulled the comforter off the bed, folded it, and placed it on the floor. Jack didn't even want to think what kinds of stains would show up on it under a black light. Sitting on the bed, she called Beau over and patted the mattress until he jumped up next to her.

Jack handed Taylor a protein bar, but she shook her head.

"You have to eat. Think of the baby."

She took the bar, opened it, pulled off a small piece, and put it in her mouth. "I don't even have any clothes with me," Taylor said, as she watched Jack put his duffel bag on the table.

"We'll pick some things up tomorrow." Rifling through the bag, he brought out a pair of faded blue sweatpants and a Boston University sweatshirt. "In the meantime . . ." He held his breath as he handed them to her, watching her expression carefully.

Her mouth dropped open. "I can't believe you still have these." She held the shirt at arm's length, looking it over, then shook her head. "You kept them all these years?"

He shrugged. "Couldn't force myself to get rid of them."

She got a faraway look for a minute, pressed her lips together, then stood up and walked into the bathroom without another word.

He turned on the TV and flipped channels until he found CNN.

She returned, having changed, and sat down at the table. "Tell me again about what Malcolm said when he came to your apartment."

"He was clearly agitated and wasn't making much sense. He mentioned someone named Jeremy that we need to find, said now that he'd voted against the bill, they would kill him. He said Brody Hamilton is involved somehow, too. He gave me an envelope for you. Then he left."

"Senator Hamilton? The majority whip?"

"Yeah."

"Let me see the letter."

Jack went to his briefcase, pulled out the letter and gave it to her, then sat back down.

She looked at Jack with suspicion. "Why is it open?"

He cocked an eyebrow. "You didn't really think I wouldn't have read it, did you?"

She opened it and read it, her face paling. She brushed a tear from her cheek, then handed it back to Jack who scanned it again.

My dearest Taylor,

Let me begin by saying how I am sorry and how painful it is to know that nothing I can do will fix the mess I've made. No matter how it started, in the end, I did love you. If you believe nothing else, believe that. You will find things out—things that will make you hate me. I need you to understand that what we've gone through in the last four years to create this life you carry, it changed me. Brought

*us closer and gave me a glimpse into real love—
something I'd never known before you. It was your
love and the love I already feel for our child that gave
me the strength to stand up to them. To finally do the
right thing.*

*There's so much more at stake than meets the
eye. For reasons too complicated to explain in this
letter, I have changed my vote. Look into the rider. It
opens the door for untold evil. And look into Brody
Hamilton's record. Once my vote is cast, they will
know that I have deserted, and they will kill me. I
can't tell you how it will happen, or when, but you
must know that, when you hear of my death, it was
not of my own doing. They are excellent at making
things appear as they want. They fabricated my entire
background and made up a new identity for me to
serve their purposes.*

*Trust no one. Not the press, not the enforcement
agencies. They have people everywhere. Disappear.
Go deep. I have already arranged your first stop.
Jack knows where to go. Once you arrive, you will
find instructions for your next one. Don't waste
time.*

*You must find a man named Jeremy. He is the
key to all this. He has been in hiding for the past
year and has, over that time, built up a network
of allies and advocates. I've enlisted the aid of Jack
because I know he will do everything in his power to
keep you safe.*

*I don't deserve your forgiveness, but I pray that
one day you will find it in your heart to grant it.
All my love,*

Malcolm

Jack was watching her, wondering how she was handling
all this. "Do you have any idea what he was talking about?"

"Of course not! What does he mean, his identity was
fabricated?"

"I don't know. But he told me that he was in the pocket of
a powerful man. Hamilton, too."

Taylor looked shocked. "No. That's impossible. You must
be wrong."

"Look, Taylor, I know this is hard to take in, but you need
to think. Who else could be involved? What about other politicians in DC?"

Jack could see the wheels turning in her mind. Grabbing
the cheap, plastic motel pen from the table, she rooted in her
bag and brought out a small pad of paper.

"Number one: the rider. Two, Brody Hamilton, and three,
a man named Jeremy. You said he told you to go to some cabin—
where is it?"

"In New Hampshire. It belongs to a friend of mine."

She looked confused. "Why would Malcolm know anything about your friends, and why would he be keeping tabs
on you?"

"I don't know."

"How can his identity be fake? How did he get through
the background checks?"

"That's what I'm trying to tell you. Whoever he works for is powerful enough to build him a bulletproof identity."

The voice on the television got their attention.

"US Senator Malcolm Phillips was found dead in his room while vacationing in Truk Lagoon, a small island in Micronesia. The senator apparently died of anaphylactic shock from a seafood allergy. In a bizarre twist, his wife, Taylor Parks Phillips, is missing. Funeral services are on hold until Mrs. Phillips is located."

Jack changed the channel again. Fox News was discussing the implications of Phillips's death.

"On a more personal note, Bill, what do you make of the wife's disappearance? Seems a little strange, don't you think?" A picture of Taylor flashed across the screen.

The news anchor's eyes widened, and he turned to his coanchor.

"It seems there is a new development in the disappearance of Taylor Phillips. She may have been abducted. Look at this. A man was captured on video by the security camera. He's been identified as Jack Logan, an investigative journalist well known in DC circles. Police are asking anyone who's seen either of them to report it immediately."

The footage showed Jack holding a gun as Taylor was rushed into the front seat of his car.

Jack cursed and turned the television off. "How did they get that?"

"We've got cameras everywhere."

"Everyone will be looking for us. There's probably already an APB out. We've got to get moving, and we've got to dump my car. We have to change our appearances. I'll run out in the morning and get what we need."

"What about my shots? We need to go back."

She didn't get it. "We can't. I'll figure something out. Trust me."

As soon as the words left his lips, he regretted them. Her expression said it all—trust was the last thing she would bestow on him. He would earn it back. Somehow. He would figure out a way to make things right.

o o o

The next morning, the sliver of light through the motel curtains woke Jack, and he stretched, trying to work out the kink in his neck from sleeping in the stiff chair. He glanced over at the bed and saw that Taylor was still asleep. He watched her and smiled when he noticed that she still favored lying on her side with a pillow clutched tightly to her chest. It was hard to believe he hadn't seen her in almost fifteen years. If it was possible, she was more beautiful now than she was back then. He knew he should wake her, that she'd be furious to know he was sitting here, staring at her, but he wanted a few minutes more to really take her in without being met by her accusing gaze.

Beau sprang off the bed, nudged Jack with his nose, and barked, indicating he wanted to go out.

"Beau." Taylor sat up, a look of confusion flickering across her face, as if she was trying to remember where she was. She slid from the bed in a single motion and put her feet into the loafers waiting on the floor.

"He needs to go out. I'll take him," she said.

"I'll go with you."

"Honestly, Jack, I don't need a bodyguard. If you don't give me some breathing room, this is never going to work."

He put his hands up and backed away. "Okay, okay. Just let me do some quick surveillance to make sure no one found us."

"By then we'll have a puddle to clean up. Excuse me." She pushed past him, grabbed Beau's leash, and opened the door. "I won't be long."

Jack followed immediately behind her. He didn't care if she got annoyed.

After Beau was finished, they returned to the room. Jack was mentally assessing what he needed to accomplish before they hit the road again. He pulled out his laptop, wanting to see how many outlets had picked up his story. He typed *Manchester v. Omega Entertainment* into Google and his name. This was interesting. Not many papers had run the story. He typed in *Teenage Wasted* to see what other journalists had said about the ruling on the show. The page was full of links— mostly to YouTube. He scrolled down, clicked the first link, and was taken to a video.

It had an adult content warning and he clicked play, then watched in horror as a young man demonstrated the most efficient way to build an autoerotic asphyxiation room. He gave a tour of his room, a list of supplies, suggestions on where to hide them, where to set them up, and promises of a live demonstration to come.

"What are you watching?"

He paused it.

"I did a story on *Manchester v. Omega Entertainment*. You know the case I mean? The class action suit about the kids' reality show that went to the Supreme Court."

"Of course. It's been all over the news. Disgusting. I can't believe Omega won."

"Take a look at this. There are hundreds of them."

He hit play again, and they continued watching the video until it ended with the noose around the boy's neck and him winking. Then the screen went black.

Taylor shook her head. "Unbelievable. I wish Omega had lost."

He arched an eyebrow. "A surprising stance coming from a journalist."

She looked at him. "It's not so black and white, Jack. There was an analogous case out of California a few years back, *Brown v. EMA*. The state banned certain violent video games from being sold, and the gaming company fought back claiming protection under free speech. The gaming company won, but only because there wasn't enough proof that the games incited violence." She raised her eyebrows and gave Jack a long look. "I think we can safely say that's not the case with this show."

"Listen, Taylor. It wasn't an easy call. I gotta say, it worries me when we start fooling around with constitutional liberties. This case came dangerously close to censorship. On a personal level, I agree with you, and would like nothing more than to shut that show down. I've talked to those parents; they're heartbroken."

Jack thought about the mother from his last interview. He'd seen a lot of grief covering war zones and natural disasters, but the abject agony in her eyes haunted him. What could he say to this woman who had saved her daughter from the grips of death years earlier, only to have her succumb to it in a misguided attempt to get high? Her words echoed in his mind.

She spent years working with therapists. She was throwing up every day to look like those airbrushed models in the magazines. Finally had gotten the bulimia under control. Was happy. And then . . . gone. Copying those foolish kids. Gone in seconds.

How do you comfort someone like that? Did he want Omega to pay? Absolutely—but there had to be a way to do it without screwing with the First Amendment.

"I read your articles." She pursed her lips. "Your follow-up did a good job giving the parents a voice. It's just that Omega's behavior gives all the media a bad name. I mean, exploiting vulnerable teenagers for ratings with no regard to the consequences. It's unconscionable."

"Agreed." He stood. "I'm going to run out and get the hair dye, et cetera, before we hit the road later. I'll be back as soon as I can."

She opened his laptop. "What's your password? I'll start digging and see what I can find out about the bill and the rider while you're gone."

He took a deep breath, looking at the floor as he answered. "Koukla."

Her eyes shot daggers at him. "Really?" She looked back at the screen and stabbed the keys with the password.

He didn't bother trying to defend himself. He had no answer as to why his old nickname for her was his password when he'd left her behind for another woman a lifetime ago.

CHAPTER SIX

CROSBY WHEELER, CEO OF OMEGA ENTERTAINMENT, looked at the men gathered around the table. He pushed the sleeve of his black cashmere sweater up and admired his new Patrimony watch, which he'd added to his collection just that morning. Not one to waste money on expensive suits or designer clothes, his Bohemian style defined him, and he never felt the need to try to impress others. A simple wardrobe of black pants and turtleneck was his signature look. But he allowed himself this one indulgence and didn't flinch at the six-figure sum the watches commanded. In his mind they were works of art that one happened to wear.

He was in a good mood today, pleased by his recent win in court. It was unfortunate that the parents of the kids who had died had gotten together so quickly and organized the class action suit, but it was ridiculous to pin the blame on his show. That was the problem with society these days—no one wanted to take responsibility for their own actions. They should have been more involved with their kids, known what they were doing, maybe looked in a closet or checked their cell-phone texts. His job wasn't to parent America's children. His job was to entertain and keep his shareholders happy.

He had jumped on the streaming bandwagon early. Omega had started small but was now the uncontested leader in this space, made popular by his original programming. He made shows that no one else dared make. He was criticized widely by some, adored by others.

He'd never had any doubt that they would prevail, but it had been an inconvenience having to put a hold on the show until the verdict came in. Luckily, the forced hiatus had only increased interest in it, and he was certain that the losses incurred over the past several months would be made up in no time. He looked at his executive producer.

"Do you have an update?"

The man nodded. "Yes, I just got the latest figures."

"Any fallout?" he asked.

"Parents are outraged. They can't accept that they've lost. The other networks are using it to their advantage, hosting parent interviews. We've lost a handful of sponsors."

His new executive in charge of advertising, Adrian Winters, cleared his throat and spoke. "But we've got a long line of others waiting to take their place. I've replaced them at double the price."

Crosby looked at him with interest. He took a sip from his bottle of mineral water. "Do tell."

Winters picked up a mint from the crystal bowl in front of him and unwrapped it. "The media frenzy has caused the ratings to skyrocket. Internet channels are jamming from the traffic. It's an advertiser's dream." He popped the mint in his mouth.

Crosby spoke. "Good work. Email me the list and the new production schedule." He addressed his producer again.

"The kids on the show okay?"

"Mostly. They were pretty upset, but the counselors talked them down, gave out some anti-anxiety meds. They've been compensated."

Crosby nodded. "Good. They need to understand that they are not responsible for the deaths of those kids who imitated them. Make sure their contracts are all up-to-date. We don't need any more lawsuits." He stood and left without another word.

Back in his office, he reviewed the newest script. It was going to make the other episodes look tame.

He opened his email and input the addresses of his top ten YouTubers. He wrote a short note, letting them know what he had planned for the next show and telling them to be ready to imitate it on camera, then post their videos after the show aired. It never hurt to give the public a little extra guidance on how to behave.

CHAPTER SEVEN

TAYLOR HAD BEEN READING THE BILL FOR OVER AN HOUR, and her vision was starting to blur. It must be the pregnancy—before it, she'd been used to working well into the night on deadline. She moved over to the bed, stretched out, and patted the space next to her. Beau jumped up and nestled against her legs. His warm body was comforting, and she stroked his head.

"You're wondering what in the world we're doing here, aren't you, baby?" She sighed.

The enticement of sleep became stronger, but she resisted. *Oh, Malcolm, what did you do?* How could it be that she would never again hear his soothing voice or feel his strong arms around her? That he wouldn't be there with her to raise the child they'd worked so hard to conceive? He'd been her best friend these past few years, the one she'd confided everything in. And now she found out everything she thought she knew about him was a lie. She picked up the letter again. All he'd given her to go on was that one cryptic line in his letter: *They fabricated my entire background and made up a new identity for me to serve their purposes.*

She thought back to the evening she'd first met him. She had just returned from a trip to Greece and was having dinner at her father's house. Evelyn and he hadn't mentioned inviting any other guests. She'd heard the deep laugh before she walked into the living room and wondered to whom it belonged.

"Ah, there you are. Come have a drink and meet Malcolm Phillips. Future senator," her father called over to her.

She looked up to meet Malcolm's eyes as he clasped her hand in his. Was this some kind of setup? She'd recognized him right away. He was running for one of the Virginia Senate seats and her father was a major supporter and contributor to his campaign. Prime son-in-law material. When would her father learn that Taylor's priorities were not the same as his? She gave Malcolm a tight smile. She'd lived near DC long enough to know the type. Polished, powerful, and political. No thanks. "Nice to meet you." She sat down in the chair farthest from him.

"You as well. Evelyn tells me you've just returned from Greece. It's one of my favorite diving spots. How did you like it?"

She hadn't been in the mood for small talk, tired from the flight and jet-lagged. But she was polite and smiled when she answered.

"I've been many times. I'm half Greek. But this wasn't a vacation. It was a trip to support a children's ministry my mother started there. They live a very simple life on the island, but they are grateful for everything they have."

He nodded. "They have so little, yet they have so much."

"Exactly. Here we're so caught up in ambition and impressing others. It's easy to forget how most of the world lives."

Her father patted Malcolm on the shoulder and turned to Taylor. "Malcolm's well traveled. You have that in common." Her father and Evelyn exchanged glances.

"Let's go into dinner, shall we?" Evelyn linked her arm around Taylor's dad and Taylor and Malcolm rose and followed them out of the room.

Malcolm stopped to look at a photograph on the mantel. "Is this your mother?"

Taylor took the picture and wiped the dust from it with her hand. "Yes. She died when I was fourteen."

He put his hand on her arm. "I'm so sorry. I know how hard it is to lose a parent. Both my parents were killed in a car accident when I was fifteen."

"Oh, Malcolm. That's so awful."

At that point in the evening, something in her softened toward the guy with the slick exterior. They began seeing each other every weekend, and by the time he took his place on Capitol Hill, Taylor was his wife.

Hot tears wet her cheeks, and she hugged Beau closer to her. The familiar ache returned. Being with Jack after all this time brought it back: the heartache, the betrayal. She needed to clear her head.

"Come on, boy. Let's take a walk." She got up and attached his leash, grabbed her purse, and left the room. Her father would be beside himself with worry after the news report. She had to let him know she was okay. She pulled out her phone and dialed him on his cell.

He answered on the first ring.

"Taylor?" A deep voice came over the line.

"Dad?" Her voice broke with emotion.

"Thank God you're alive! I've been out of my mind. Where are you? I've just run your picture on the front page of my paper. What the hell is going on? Why was Jack at your house?"

Her father, Warwick Parks, was the editor of the *Washington Daily News*, second only to the *Post* in circulation. "Oh, Dad. I don't know where to begin. Jack showed up at my house last night. He said Malcolm told him to come and get me, to keep me safe. It's all so mixed up; I don't know what to believe."

"Listen to me, Taylor. I don't know what in the world he's thinking—whisking you off like that, but the police think he kidnapped you. He's in a lot of trouble."

"He *didn't* kidnap me. Some men came to the house, and we had to leave. I can't explain it all now. I just wanted you to know I'm okay. We're trying to figure it out." She heard a long sigh on the other end of the line.

"Taylor, you need to come home. You haven't seen Jack in years. You have a funeral to plan. Everyone's looking for you. You can't just run off . . . I don't trust Jack."

"Dad. Stop. You have to trust *me*. I have to see where this leads. Jack is not going to hurt me." What did she expect? That the bad blood between her father and Jack would just disappear?

"Tell me where you are."

"At a motel in Pennsylvania, but we're leaving shortly."

"Where are you going?"

"We're following clues Malcolm left in a letter to me, trying to find someone named Jeremy."

"Are you crazy? This makes no sense. Come home!"

She had to hang up. "I love you. I don't know when I can call again, but I will as soon as I can. Try not to worry." She pressed end.

Beau sensed her mood and jumped, putting a paw on each shoulder, and gave her face three quick licks. Laughing, she rubbed his head.

"No matter what happens, I've always got you to cheer me up." She took a seat on the bench by the motel's front office and lifted her face to the sun. Beau curled up on the ground and rested his head on her foot.

The first time she had seen Beau, he had been a mess. Abandoned on the side of the road, his coat mangy, and with sores all over his legs, it was impossible to see what a beautiful dog he was, but Taylor had loved him from the instant his soulful eyes locked upon hers. After a visit to the vet, he began to look better. But Malcolm had been less than thrilled.

"How do you know where he came from? He could be rabid for all we know."

Taylor had been floored. "The vet's checked him out, and he's fine," she'd said fiercely. "All he needs is a little TLC. Please, Malcolm. He needs me." Her voice broke. "And I need him."

He'd softened. "All right, but at the first sign of any aggression, that dog goes."

She had cupped Beau's head in her hands and lowered her face to his.

"No one will ever hurt you again. I promise," she'd whispered and kissed him on the nose.

Beau had turned out to be a loving, gentle, and loyal companion. It was his calm and nurturing presence that had gotten her through all her days of disappointment and devastation month after month, year after year, when it looked as though she would never achieve her dream of becoming a mother. Despite his teddy-bear nature, he had also turned out to be a fierce guard dog and was particularly protective of Taylor. She had discovered this one day when the cable repairman had shown up unexpectedly at her door saying there was a downed cable. Before she could let him in, Beau had gotten between her and the door, a deep growl rising from his throat. She had tried to calm him, but he'd been immovable. He began to bark ferociously, and, no matter how hard she tried, she couldn't pull him away from the door. Finally, she had to call through the intercom and ask the man to come back later. When she'd phoned her cable company to reschedule, she had been shocked to discover that they had no record of any repairs being done in her area. She wondered then who'd raised Beau the first few years of his life, and after that she'd never doubted his instincts again.

The wind kicked up and Taylor stood. "Come on, let's walk around a bit and find a place for you to go potty." Beau walked close beside her as she walked him around the parking lot toward a grassy section near the back. She knew better than to hurry him, and at least twenty minutes passed before he finally did his business. She'd brought a bag with her from the room and cleaned it up. "Come on, let's head back." Beau didn't move as she tugged on the leash but stared across the lot and began to growl. Following his gaze, she saw a dark car idling. The skin on her arms turned to gooseflesh, and she pulled the leash harder, suddenly anxious to get back inside the room. As she began to run, pulling Beau with her, the car accelerated and raced toward them. Before she knew what was happening, a man jumped out of the back seat and grabbed her, tearing the leash from her hand and throwing it to the side. "What are you doing?" she screamed, but his hand clamped over her mouth as he struggled to push her into the car. She kicked at him and bit his hand, but he was too strong for her and she couldn't break his grip. Just before he could slam the door shut with her in the back, Beau jumped in next to her, his jaw snapping as he tried to bite the man's hand.

The man jumped in the passenger side and yelled at the driver. "Go!"

CHAPTER EIGHT

THE INSTITUTE, MAY 1975

I LOOK STRAIGHT AHEAD AS THE SEDAN CLIMBS THE LONG
hill, and the stone building comes into sight. It is immense
and imposing and makes me think of knights and maidens
from a long time ago. The building is surrounded on all sides
by forest. Thick evergreens everywhere increase the sense of
isolation and secrecy. A chill runs through me, and I have the
urge to scream: *Go back! Let me out!* Then I think, *Get a grip.*
My overactive imagination is at it again.

The moment I learned about this fellowship, I knew I had
to apply. The program is a three-month postgraduate fellowship into cutting-edge medical research. Out of the thousands
who apply, only one hundred are accepted. The faculty list is
impressive, boasting thought leaders in every endeavor from

all around the world. During the program, we will be completely isolated from the outside world. This is necessary, we are told, to help us to focus on our goal—to get into the top 20 percent of the program and prove we are worthy of the one-year fellowship, all tuition paid. There is no time for distractions from family, friends, or lovers. I said my good-byes to my parents and my dear sister with the assurance that the months would fly by, but they were still upset to see me go. Greek parents don't like to be away from their children for so long. I would miss the weekly Sunday dinners at their house, but a part of me was eager for the break. No matter how much I loved them, I felt suffocated at times. I was ready to spread my wings.

As I got ready to leave after dinner on that last Sunday, my mother looked at me with tears in her eyes. "We can't even speak for three months? That is too long." I hugged her and told her that before we knew it, we'd be celebrating my elevation into the full-year program. Because, of course, I intend to win. It's my only chance to work under Dr. Strombill, the bioethicist I've admired for years. Now that I am actually going to meet him, to have the opportunity to impress him, I am feeling awestruck and giddy, and I'm never awestruck and giddy.

The car comes to a stop, and the driver walks around and opens my door. I smile at him, but he looks right through me.

"Please proceed to the front steps."

I grab my backpack, throw it over one shoulder, and walk the cobblestone path to the immense structure. I wait for the others to fall in line, and while I do, I study the ornate carving on the door. I've never seen anything like it before; it's a crest featuring a dragonlike creature. The beast is otherworldly and grotesque but beautiful at the same time. I am oddly drawn to it and reach out to trace the lines of its head when a voice behind me makes me snatch my hand back.

"Put your belongings on the ground next to you. You will have no need of them."

There is an instant outcry of protest from everyone, and I clutch my purse to my side as my heart pounds in indignation. But then the door opens, and when I look inside, my indignation turns to awe.

CHAPTER NINE

J ACK RUSHED DOWN THE AISLE AT WALGREENS, THROWING hair dye, scissors, makeup, and some local maps into his basket. He glanced over at the newspaper shelf by the cash register and swore to himself. The pixelated picture of him and Taylor in her garage was on the front page of the *Washington Daily News*. He pulled his baseball cap down lower and hoped no one would notice him, jiggling his keys nervously while the line moved at a snail's pace. Why were there never enough cashiers? Biting his lip, he tried to stay cool as the elderly woman in front of him fumbled with a stack of coupons. At last, she was done. As she moved away, her foot caught on the rug, and she went tumbling. Jack lunged forward and caught her before she hit the ground.

"Oh my goodness. I don't know what happened."

The contents of her purse went flying. He collected them and handed her purse back. "Are you okay?"

"Thank you, dear. I *am* a little unsteady."

"Let me help you to your car." The blood pounded in his ears, but he maintained an air of calm. The poor woman looked like she was in pain. He was worried that she might not be well enough to drive. It took them ten minutes to cross the asphalt lot to her battered sedan.

"Do you want me to call someone for you? Are you going to be okay driving?"

"I'm fine, dear. Have a sore hip, that's all. Doctors keep trying to convince me to have it replaced, but I'm not a fan of surgery. I manage okay."

"Are you sure?"

She nodded. "Yes. Thanks. You're a kind young man," she said as she smiled at him. Before taking a seat behind the wheel, she leaned in and opened the center console. "I want you to have this." It was a Saint Christopher medal on a chain.

He shook his head. "Thank you, but I couldn't possibly take it."

She pressed it into his hand. "I won't take no for an answer. There aren't too many young men like you, who would stop and help an old lady. Please, he'll look after you." She put a hand on his and held his gaze. "Saint Christopher is on your side."

He doubted that, but he closed his hand around it anyway. Seeing the earnest look on her face, he said, "I *could* use a little help." He gave her a warm smile and waited for her to drive away before running back to the store. The line was five people deep again. He picked up his basket from the counter and got back in line. *No good deed goes unpunished*, he thought with a sigh.

When he was finally done, he threw his purchases on the passenger seat, put the medal in his jacket pocket, and pulled out his cell phone. Finding the contact, he pushed send.

"Hello?"

"It's Jack. I need you to leave Kyle's truck unlocked with the keys in it. I have to borrow it for a while."

"When?"

"Tomorrow night. I'll text you when I'm close. Also, can you get your hands on some progesterone oil?"

"What?"

"It's a long story. I need fifty milligrams, and needles, too."

"Is there something you want to tell me?" she asked.

"It's for a friend. Don't ask."

"I'll see what I can do. And Jack?"

"Yeah?"

"Be careful."

"Love ya, sis." He hung up and got back into his car to head to the motel. As he pulled into the lot and got out of the car, he looked toward their room and cursed. Their door was wide open. Jack broke into a run.

CHAPTER TEN

Brody Hamilton watched from the bed as Rita Avery rose and hurried to the bathroom and the steaming shower. He admired the view as she walked away, the perfectly rounded buttocks with the creamy skin, unblemished except for the tiny scorpion tattoo on her left cheek. He knew she was eager to wash away his touch. He found it amusing—the depths to which she was willing to sink to achieve her goals. He grudgingly admired her tenacity and determination, which had made her the most admired and sought-after lobbyist in the business. Hamilton knew all about her shabby beginnings, her mother's insistence that she attend an upscale school, blind to the fact that their trailer park existence made it impossible for Rita to fit in. Yes, he knew all that and more, but not from Rita—Brody never let anyone get close to him without having them thoroughly investigated. No one would have ever suspected she had grown up in poverty. She carried her Birkin bags like badges of honor—a different one for each season.

She came out of the bathroom in a beige Chanel suit, her Christian Louboutin alligator pumps clicking on the marble floor.

"Thanks for the tumble, darlin'." He liked rubbing it in her face. Hamilton snorted, and his naked belly shook with his laughter.

She smiled tightly.

"I'll go on ahead and meet you at the Blue Duck. Everyone will be there soon."

He swung his legs over to the side of the bed where they barely reached the carpeted floor. Grabbing his robe, he put it on and stood. He was all business now.

"Go down the back stairs and out the side entrance."

She nodded and left.

o o o

Hamilton was the last to arrive. Two other men on Rita's team were seated at the table with her.

Rita pulled out a folder from her briefcase and laid it on the table.

"I want to talk about ingredient labeling. The health nuts are pumping out more propaganda about the vaccines. People are asking for ingredient lists. We want to make the lists unavailable."

Hamilton raised his eyebrows. "Do you now? And why, pray tell, should I support a bill that would do that?"

"The ingredients need to be proprietary, to keep other companies from copying our formulas."

"Don't people have a right to know what they're putting in their bodies?" Hamilton asked. He didn't give a whit about the people's rights, only that the public believed he did.

Rita smiled. "Well, of course we'd label the main ingredients, especially those that are a potential allergen, like eggs. We don't want to have to specify everything included."

Hamilton took a sip of his Johnnie Walker Blue, licked his lips, and then took another long swallow. "Metals?"

"Aluminum, formaldehyde, mercury, silicon, polysorbate 80—they've been in there forever without hurting anyone, but people may opt out if they see all the ingredients."

"Can't blame them," Hamilton said. Let her work for it.

One of the men jumped in. "Look, these are preservatives and bonding agents that are necessary to make the vaccines shelf stable. Sometimes there is a small downside to accomplishing a greater good. We don't want children not to receive lifesaving vaccines because their tree-hugging parents are freaking out over a few metals. And no one wants a resurgence of diseases that we've successfully eliminated."

Hamilton, his eyes mere slits, leaned in close and spoke so softly that everyone else had to lean in to hear him.

"Don't give me that true believer crap. You don't want to lose any money, pure and simple. And you don't want to invest any money into replacing those so-called bonding agents with something safer. Let's not kid each other here." He leaned back in his seat and looked at Rita.

Rita sat up straighter and looked at Hamilton with what

he had come to recognize as her *let me stroke your ego so you don't notice I'm full of crap* look. He indulged her.

"Thoughts, Miss Avery?"

"Well, Senator, I respect your devotion to your constituents and your desire to look out for their best interests. They are indeed lucky to have someone like you representing them. Now I respectfully point out that there is no proof that these metals are dangerous, and to replace them with something that is only presumed to be safer would cost the company millions in research, development, and implementation. They would then have to pass those costs on to the consumer, thus making these vaccines unavailable to a large portion of the population. Additionally, my company would have to cut back on the vaccines they donate to developing nations. So, in effect, by changing these bonding agents, we would be causing great harm to many children, in the US and around the world."

Hamilton stroked his chin, pretending to digest this last bit of baloney. After a few more moments, he said, "Well, my dear, as my grandpappy would say, your tongue is more silver than a tree full of tinsel. How are you going to position this?"

"We'll list the organic materials and then we will put a statement like, 'Could include a combination of minerals all within US defined safety standards.'"

Hamilton's belly shook as he began to laugh. "Minerals. I love it. Honey, as my grandma used to say, you could sell ice to an Eskimo. I think I may have a solution that will suit all our needs."

The three of them leaned forward like little birdies waiting for their mama to give them a worm.

"You know that my vaccine bill was unexpectedly scuttled, and I have to go back to the drawing board and make some revisions before we submit it again. What say I add your little secret-ingredient-list law to it? In the meantime, I need you to start lobbying my colleagues to support the bill. Wine and dine 'em. Tell 'em stories of dead babies who could have been saved if only they'd gotten the RSV shot. I want a lot of people on it."

Rita smiled. "Of course, Senator. Consider it done."

Hamilton had been in Washington forever. The Senate's longtime majority whip, he held a seat on the most important congressional committees and had the ear of the president. His hillbilly colloquialisms belied a mind sharper than a grizzly's claws. There was nothing he enjoyed more than the look of shock on the face of some poor fool who had fallen for the hokey southern charm and failed to recognize the power he wielded—which is why he was furious that Phillips had voted against the Vaccinate All Children Act. Did the fool really think he could stop them? What had gotten into Phillips anyway? One minute he had been completely on board, the next he'd killed the very bill he'd sponsored. Well, he'd gotten what he deserved.

Hamilton got up from the table without another word. On the way to his office, he pulled out his iPhone and opened the Twitter app.

No child should die of a preventable illness. Support Senate Bill Vaccinate All Children Act #VACA

CHAPTER ELEVEN

A s Damon sat puzzling over how Jack Logan had
reconnected with Taylor Phillips, Peritas came over to him
and nuzzled his hand.

He held out a dog biscuit, and the Great Pyrenees sat and
waited for the treat.

"Good boy. Down." The dog took his place next to his
master's feet just as there was a knock at the door. Peritas
growled deep in his throat and sprang up.

"Down." The dog obeyed immediately. "Come in."

Jonas escorted a woman in and seated her.

"Evelyn, I appreciate your making the long drive."

"Of course, sir. I know how important this is to you."

He drummed his fingers on the mahogany desk. "You
heard from your stepdaughter?"

"Warwick has. Taylor called him. As you've seen on the

news, she's with Jack Logan. She told her father that Malcolm had sent Jack to help her."

Damon's jaw clenched. How had he missed this?

"I'd have thought that Malcolm's pride would have prevented him from going to Logan. Do *you* have any idea why he changed his vote at the last minute?" If anyone understood Malcolm's psyche, it was Evelyn. Until she'd married Taylor's father and moved into his Chevy Chase home, she'd lived on campus and been Damon's most valued psychologist; she could detect a vulnerability long before it became a liability. No one advanced in the programs here without her approval. Her consulting services still served Damon well.

"There can only be one reason, sir."

"And that is?" He was losing patience now.

"She mentioned a letter Malcolm left. He told them they need to find Jeremy."

"Jeremy got to Malcolm?"

"It appears so, sir. Jeremy must be very angry to try to sabotage your work."

"That phone call led my men right to her. Logan left her alone and they were able to grab her. She will arrive shortly. For the sake of the baby, I want her to feel safe, especially after what she's been through. That's why I summoned you. She'll feel less threatened if she sees you." He pushed his intercom and summoned Jonas.

"Jonas will take you to wait," he told Evelyn.

Evelyn was about to leave when his phone buzzed, and he put a finger up to stop her.

He grabbed it from the desk and swiped. The color drained

from his face as he listened to the man on the other end. "You lost her?" Damon demanded.

"Logan must have had some training," he told Damon. "They got away."

Damon ended the call and looked at Evelyn, the fury building in his chest. "She and Logan got away. You know her. What will she do next? Will she call Warwick again?"

She shook her head. "I don't know. Maybe Jack won't let her." She opened her mouth as if to say something else, then seemed to think better of it and waited for him to speak again.

If Jeremy had indeed told Malcolm the truth about the bill, and he had passed the information on to Taylor and Jack, they would follow the story to its conclusion. They were news hounds, after all. So Damon needed to find them before they got to Jeremy. He didn't share this with Evelyn, instead leveling his gaze at her. "Figure something out. Use your talents. Find a way to make her call home."

"Yes, sir." She got up and left.

Damon's phone flashed, and he saw a Twitter alert for Brody Hamilton's latest tweet. He picked up the phone and dialed Catherine Knight.

"Good afternoon, Mr. Crosse." Her Texan accent was strong.

"I want you to put out stories on why the Vaccinate All Children Act is important. Find pictures, children who've suffered from RSV, parents who've lost children to it—flood all the outlets."

"I'm on it."

"I want print and broadcast, too."

"Done."

"And keep up the heavy coverage on Taylor Phillips's disappearance. I want you to dig into Jack Logan's background. Find something we can use to make him look dangerous. Make sure by the end of the week Logan's face is more recognizable than the president's."

CHAPTER TWELVE

TAYLOR WAS GONE. HE SAW THE LAPTOP SITTING ON THE bed and grabbed it before he ran out of the room. He ran around to the side of the motel. She was being pulled into the back of a brown Dodge, a snarling Beau still on his leash, clutched in her hand.

"Stop!" He flew toward them.

Dropping the computer, he pulled out his SIG and aimed at the right front tire, shot, then did the same to the left.

The driver scrambled out of the car.

"What the—"

"Drop your weapon," Jack yelled.

The man didn't move.

Gun pointed at the man's head, Jack spoke again. "Do it."

The man reached in his pocket and slowly pulled his gun out and threw it to the ground.

"Kick it away from you."

The man complied.

Jack bent forward to retrieve it, keeping the gun trained on the man, and his gaze level. "Now get back in the car and no one gets hurt."

The man put his hands up and backed away.

Taylor's face was white as she ran toward Jack.

"Grab the computer, and get in the car." Taylor and Beau jumped into the Mustang.

They tore out of the parking lot as a black SUV rounded the corner and started gaining on them. Jack floored it, navigating around traffic expertly, and sailed up the on ramp to the highway. His eyes darted to the rearview mirror. The SUV was still behind them.

Jack jerked the wheel all the way to the left. The tires squealed as they did a 180 and headed into oncoming traffic. Horns blared as cars swerved to avoid colliding head-on with them.

"What are you doing?" Taylor screamed as she turned and kept a hand on Beau to keep him from lurching forward.

Jack expertly wove in and out of approaching traffic, swerved onto the shoulder, and turned the car around.

"Saving our lives!" he yelled above the din of screeching tires and screaming horns. In the rearview mirror, he watched as two cars collided trying to get out of the path of the SUV that was racing to catch up with them.

"Hold on." He pushed the gas to the floor and changed lanes, clipping the back of the car next to him. They were on top of an overpass now. He had to get rid of them. He swerved again, until they were in the left-hand lane, against the low Jersey wall. He slowed enough for the SUV to catch up. When the SUV was two cars back, he tapped the brakes a few times quickly. The car behind them slammed on his brakes, causing a chain reaction behind him. The SUV was sandwiched between a truck and a four-door sedan. Jack veered to the right again and sped up until the crash was no longer visible in the mirror.

"You okay?" He looked at Taylor.

She shook her head. "I'll let you know when I can feel my face again. Where did you learn to drive like that?" Her voice was shaking.

"I took one of those evasive driving courses a few years back. Long story."

"I guess you passed with flying colors."

After another ten miles of checking his rearview, Jack was satisfied that they were in the clear. "We should be in Boston in a couple hours. We'll switch cars, then keep going."

He didn't understand how anyone had found them so soon. He turned to Taylor.

"Did that guy come to the door?"

"No. I was walking Beau, and he just pulled up and grabbed me."

"I don't understand how they knew where we were."

Her hand flew to her mouth. "I think I know."

"What?"

"I used my cell phone to call my father."

He felt the blood rush to his face. "Oh, Taylor, I told you not to call anyone."

"I had to let him know I was okay. Besides, we were using

your computer; it didn't occur to me that these people were that sophisticated."

He took a deep breath. "I installed a VPN, a virtual private network. No one can track it. I didn't know what we'd be dealing with, so I took precautions. You need to take the SIM card out of your phone and give it to me." He shook his head. "I should've thought of it before."

"How do I do that?"

"Oh right." He grinned. "I suppose you haven't become any more tech-savvy?"

"Ha ha."

He pulled off at the next exit and into a gas station, where he removed the SIM card from her phone and inserted a different one. Then he stuck the old card deep into a trash bin while she used the bathroom. The last light was fading from the sky as they got back on the road.

"Anything in the vaccine bill that looks strange to you so far?" Jack asked.

"Nothing suspicious. It was just about adding RSV to the list of illnesses receiving federal assistance for vaccines—a good thing."

"Tell me more about RSV."

"Well, it's a respiratory illness that preemies are especially vulnerable to. I have a friend who had twins and one of hers wound up in the hospital for a month. The treatment is expensive, and the preventive vaccine costs hundreds of dollars even after insurance."

"So why wasn't the vaccine a part of the inclusions in the first place?" Jack asked.

She shrugged. "RSV is not that common. It's only indicated for a certain subset of children, preemies and those at
high risk. But it can be fatal, and it's certainly better to prevent
it than to have to treat it. I don't understand why Malcolm
would oppose the vote."

Jack wondered the same thing. Obviously, there was more
to it. "He said it had to do with the rider. Hamilton sneaking
something in it that had nothing to do with the main bill. We
need to read all of it—see if there's anything else. How many
children get RSV every year?"

"I'll check. Let's hope the laptop didn't get damaged when
you threw it on the ground," Taylor said. She unclipped her
seat belt and reached back to get it.

Jack got a whiff of her hair as she moved past him. Lav-
ender. He heard the twang of the Mac turning on. "Seems to
be working." Her fingers tapped the keys. "Well, someone's
certainly pissed."

"What are you talking about?"

"I googled RSV, and the entire page is populated with
article after article from today. From every news outlet."

"Strange, considering the bill hasn't even been in the
news," Jack said.

"There's a segment on *Newsline* tonight, too, about a
family who lost two of their triplets. From what I can tell,
it looks like the whole Knight news outlet is covering it: in
print, internet, and television."

Jack was stumped. This wasn't the type of do-gooder bill
the power players cared about. Catherine Knight's holding
company owned television stations all over the world, over

thirty magazines, twenty-five major newspapers, myriad radio stations, and the second-largest social media platform. Why would she expend resources to make a bunch of noise about something that affected such a small portion of the population? It's not like most people wouldn't already be in favor of increasing funding to make vaccines affordable to children. Someone was trying to stir up a public outcry. But why? And against whom?

"We need to read every line of that bill."

"I'll keep reading. But it's over four hundred pages with the rider," Taylor replied. "I'll see how far I can get before we reach Boston." She pulled it back up on the laptop and Jack was quiet as she continued to read.

○ ○ ○

After an hour, Taylor leaned back and massaged her neck. Night had fallen, and she glanced out into the darkness. Finally, she spoke. "I never really knew him at all, did I?"

Jack shifted in his seat. What could he say?

"He was fighting his own demons, Taylor. His heart was in the right place at the end."

"I think I knew deep down that he was holding back, that things weren't as they should be, but it was all so intangible. We were both so busy those first few years. Between my hours at the network and the traveling I had to do when working a new story, we hardly saw each other. And then when I couldn't get pregnant, he was so wonderful, supportive. It was like we were finally in a real partnership, but now I don't know what's real."

"I'm sorry, Taylor. That must have been tough."

"That's the funny thing. All—and I mean all—the women I met in the infertility support groups complained about how insensitive their husbands were, how they couldn't relate to how devastating infertility is. Some of their marriages fell apart over it. But it brought us closer together. He was suffering just as much as I was, and he never said the wrong thing. I wouldn't have gotten through it without him."

Jack didn't feel like hearing what a saint Phillips had been. He drummed his hands on the wheel. "Try to get some sleep. You've been through a lot."

"There's no way I can sleep with all this going round and round in my head."

"Just lean back and close your eyes anyway. We'll be in Boston soon and we can switch cars there. My brother-in-law has a truck registered to his business that we can use. It shouldn't be on anyone's radar."

"I'll keep reading," Taylor said.

"Okay." As long as they didn't talk anymore, he thought. Every turn of their conversation had been rife with minefields. He didn't want to discuss her marriage or her pregnancy. She was supposed to have married him. That had been the plan. She would finish her last year of college, and they would be married the following fall. He'd gotten an apartment in New York and a job with the Associated Press. Taylor used to come down from BU on Friday afternoons, and they'd spend the weekends together exploring the city. They were going to live the life they'd always dreamed of—two journalists in the most important city in the world, the future at their fingertips.

He had never seen Dakota coming. A flash of red hair that framed a face defined by angles and contours, her blue eyes flashed with an intensity he'd found irresistible. He might never have met her if not for his sister Sarah. Their father had died a month earlier, and Jack had still been grieving. Sarah had come into town to visit friends and had insisted he join them for dinner. After, she had talked him into accompanying them to an art exhibit in Chelsea—not typically his thing. Once they arrived, Jack went straight to the bar, grumbled that there was no beer, and grabbed a plastic cup of wine. Nails with chipped red polish reached out and took the cup from him.

"You don't want that rot. Come with me."

Taken off guard, he went along. She grasped his hand in hers and led him to the back of the gallery and to a small kitchen. Picking up two crystal wineglasses, she held a bottle of pinot noir in her other hand and showed it to Jack.

"Much better, no?" She smiled.

"It's lost on me." He grinned. "I'm happy with a cold beer."

She stared at him and bit down on her plump bottom lip, her white teeth showcased by the soft pink hue. He found himself wondering how her lips would feel on his.

"Time to change that. You have no idea what you're missing." Moving toward him, she lifted the glass to his lips.

He took a sip then shook his head.

"Sorry. Still rather have a beer."

The full lips puckered in a pretty pout. "You're a terrible boor." A smile lit up her face, and she put a hand on his shoulder. "No matter. I've decided I like you, and I'm going to keep you."

Jack frowned. "Keep me?"

"Oh, don't worry, silly. I'll keep you as a friend. Come on, let's see if any of my paintings have sold."

"You're . . . ?"

"Yes, I'm Dakota Drake." She took a bow. "Welcome to my world."

"Stop. Stop. Jack! Beau needs to go out," Taylor shouted.

Jack glanced at her, startled out of the memory. "Sorry. I'll pull over."

He steered the car to the shoulder and put it in park, then turned on the interior light.

"You stay here. I'll take him. Where's his leash?"

Jack held the leash while Beau sniffed in the dark for a place to relieve himself.

When he had finished, he loped up to Jack and licked his hand. Jack envied the dog his uncomplicated existence. He shook his head and wondered how he had managed to screw up his life so badly.

CHAPTER THIRTEEN

THE INSTITUTE, MAY 1975

T HE ENTRANCE FOYER IS ENORMOUS, AND WARDROBE RACKS are lined up on the marble floor, each tagged with a sign bearing a name. Clothes hang from each of them—*uniforms* is perhaps a better word. Shiny black jumpsuits. I take one and hold it up in front of me. It appears to be a perfect fit. There are slippers, too, and scrubs, cotton shirts, blankets, and pillows on a shelf below. I notice a Dopp kit and pick it up. Inside are toiletries—toothbrush, mouthwash, shampoo, and soap. I look around at the others. Everyone has the exact same provisions. Our hosts have thought of everything.

Our driver clears his throat, and we all turn to look at him.

"You may follow me. Pull your rack behind you. We're going to your quarters."

His face is as expressionless as it was when he first picked us up, and I wonder at his lack of affect. I have an urge to reach out and poke him, try to provoke a reaction. But of course, I don't. I make my face a mask and follow along with everyone as if this is the most natural thing in the world. We are led to an elevator and line up to go down in groups. No one speaks while we wait our turn. I have to pee but am too embarrassed to ask. He comes for my group, and we descend six floors, and when the elevator opens, we are faced by a steel door. A woman stands next to it, in a black jumpsuit, and smiles.

"Good evening, students. Welcome." She is pretty, not much older than me, and her eyes look kind.

Gratitude rushes through me at her warmth, and I feel myself relax.

She opens the door, and we push through with our new belongings.

There are beds lined up on each side of the room, army barracks–style, and others have already staked their claims and are sorting their things.

"Marianna, you're over here." She turns to me and puts a hand on my arm, then leads me to a bed at the end of one of the rows.

"Please, call me Maya."

She tilts her head. "Maya?"

I smile. "My sister couldn't pronounce Marianna when she was little, so she called me Maya. It stuck."

"Maya it is. I'll make sure to let your instructors know. I'm Evelyn. I'll be your coordinator for this session. Anything that you need, any problems you have, you can come to me."

"Thank you," I manage, my voice cracking. I look around. "Are we *all* staying in here?"

"Part of being here is learning how to think differently. Does it matter, when you treat a patient, if the person is male or female? Certainly male doctors examine females, just as female doctors examine males. Would you refuse to examine a male patient?"

I shake my head.

"Of course not," she says. "And you would find it absurd if a male patient refused to let you examine him because you are a woman." Her hand sweeps across the room. "It is no different here. This is where you all sleep, no matter your sex." Then she laughs. "Trust me, at the end of the day, the only thing that will be on your mind is sleep."

o o o

Today is the first day of classes. We are awakened early, though I don't know the exact time, as I no longer have my watch. There are about thirty of us in the room, and I dress silently in my black jumpsuit and slippers, averting my eyes to avoid looking at the other half-naked bodies in the room and hoping they are doing the same. Despite my conversation with Evelyn, I am still unnerved to be quartered with the men and didn't sleep well last night. I whisper to Amelia, the woman assigned to the cot next to me. "Don't you think they should separate the men from the women?"

She doesn't turn to look at me but casts a glance in my

direction out of the corner of her eye and answers, her words barely audible, "Shh. They'll hear you."

I bite back my retort, disappointed to realize that she's a rule follower, and that I won't be finding any companionship in her. We were told during initiation to keep to ourselves and focus on one thing only—being chosen as one of the final twenty. The competition is going to be fiercer than anything we'd experienced at medical school. Our ability to display a singular focus and to shut out everything around us is one of the things we will be judged on. I can see that Amelia is as serious as I am about being admitted to phase two.

The bell rings, and we walk single file behind our training coordinator to begin a day filled with lectures. I am excited, wondering when I will get to meet *him*. We are taken in groups of five to the elevator and back up six floors, where we are ushered into a classroom. It is nothing special, could be any classroom in any high school, with a large screen at the front. But then a man walks in the room, and I bite my cheek to refrain from gasping. It is him—Dr. Strombill. He is shorter than I expected, almost diminutive, and I wonder if this can be the man who has written with such passion and brilliance. He stands in front of us, silent, assessing, and seems to examine each of us before he finally opens his mouth to speak. When he does, all my doubts dissolve, and his passion is so palpable I almost believe I can reach out and touch it.

"Welcome. The fact that you are here is evidence of your extraordinary talent and dedication." His Austrian accent is slight, melodic. "But more will be required. Innovation.

Three-dimensional thinking. You must be able to see into
the future and stride into the unknown. You have spent years
being indoctrinated into the established way of viewing medicine. But we are to revolutionize the face of medicine, to
see the big picture and make the difficult decisions that will
advance medicine and treatment far above where it is today."

He walks from the front of the room, pushes a tape into
the VCR and presses play. Without another word he turns off
the lights. The screen comes alive, and we are looking at an
older man lying in a hospital bed. I watch as the man on the
screen gasps and wheezes in a vain attempt to get air into his
lungs. His sallow skin is stretched tautly over his skeletal face,
and his pained grimace reveals brown teeth. He croaks out a
hoarse request.

"Nurse." It comes out as a whisper.

His bony fingers press repeatedly on the call button as a
look of distress fills his face. When there is no response, he sags
backward, and his head hits the pillow in despondent resignation. The nurse finally appears, then frowns when she sees that
the sheets are wet. She sighs.

"Let's get you cleaned up, Mr. Smith. Lemme get some
help in here."

Two medical aides appear with another bed, and together
they move the frail body into it. The man she called Mr. Smith
grimaces in agony as they jostle him, and he cries out.

"Leave me in peace! Why can't someone make the pain
stop?" His anguished cries are punctuated with bouts of
coughing and gasping.

The screen goes black, and light floods the room.

"What you have just seen can be prevented." Dr. Strombill leans forward and peers over the dais at the students in the front row.

His voice rises. "You must be the voice of that poor man. It is up to you to make sure that a human being does not endure that kind of suffering. It is your moral imperative, your sacred duty as doctors, as purveyors of mercy, to spare your patients from this degree of pain and indignity."

He scans the faces and looks pleased. "Who of us wants to spend our last days on earth filled with pain, fighting in vain for every breath? No. It is indecent. We cannot allow people to linger indefinitely until their disease-ridden bodies finally give up and free them from their torment and anguish."

A timid hand waves.

"Yes, you." He points at Amelia.

"What is the alternative? If we don't give any treatment, the patient will still suffer from the effects of the disease."

He looks at her, and a frown pulls at his mouth. "I assume you have heard of euthanasia?"

A look of shock appears on her face. "Are you suggesting that we actually kill people? Put them down like dogs?"

"And are *you* suggesting that a dog has more right to compassion than a human being? What is the benefit in prolonging the life of someone who will be left with nothing but pain and indignity?"

I hold my breath. Can't she see she's making him angry?

Her cheeks are flushed. "But it's illegal."

He walks toward her. "It is *now*. But that is changing, and we must lead the charge."

"But sometimes a terminal patient *does* recover. How are we to know which are hopeless cases and which are not?" She looks around the room, waiting, I think, for someone to come to her defense. No one does.

Dr. Strombill's cheeks grow red, and a vein throbs in his forehead. He shakes a finger at her.

"That is what is wrong with this country. Overindulged children who grow up to be spoiled adults. The world does not have at its disposal the resources to squander on lost causes. Have you considered the financial and emotional toll on the family? Do you have any idea how difficult it is to watch someone you love wither before your eyes until they are nothing but an empty shell?" Spittle flies from the corners of his mouth, and his eyes are slits.

Every eye in the room is on her. With tears streaming down her face, she stumbles to her feet and runs to the door, leaving her notebook on the desk.

Dr. Strombill turns back to the class. "She won't be needing this anymore." He knocks the book to the floor. "I trust no one else has any questions?"

CHAPTER FOURTEEN

JACK TOOK BACK ROADS TO HIS SISTER'S HOUSE IN NEWTON and they arrived at eight o'clock. They stopped behind a pickup truck parked in front of a Cape Cod.

"That's it?" Taylor asked.

"Yeah. Time to ditch the Mustang."

"Aren't you going to at least go in and see Sarah?"

He shook his head. "We need to keep moving. And I don't want to involve her any more than necessary." He hesitated a moment. "She did ask me to give you her love." Taylor and his older sister had always liked each other growing up.

They quickly moved everything from the car to the white Chevy pickup truck; then Jack told Taylor to get behind the wheel of the truck. Beau jumped out of the Mustang and went with Taylor.

"Follow me," Jack instructed.

She drove behind him until they reached the Charles River, where they pulled into a secluded clearing set back from the road, and she put the truck in park and got out.

"What are you doing?" she cried at the sight of him positioning his beloved Mustang on the precipice of the hill, aimed at the river below.

"Got to get rid of it or they'll know where we are. I can't very well leave it at my sister's and implicate her."

"Oh, Jack! You love this car. You've spent hours and hours working on it and now you've got to get rid of it because of me."

"It's not your fault."

"If Malcolm hadn't involved you in this, we wouldn't be here right now."

"Don't blame yourself" was all he said. He couldn't bring himself to admit what he was really thinking: she would never have married Phillips if Jack hadn't been such a fool.

She turned around and placed a hand on the roof of the car.

"I still remember when you brought it home. Your father had a fit, said it was a death trap." She laughed. "By the time you were finished with it, he loved it almost as much as you did."

He swallowed the lump in his throat. His best memories with his father, whom a heart attack had taken right after his fiftieth birthday, were because of this car. Their Saturday mornings working on it were the only times the two had really connected.

Taylor looked at Jack. "Do you really have to get rid of it? Can't we hide it somewhere?"

He shook his head. "No, it has to be this way." He stood straighter. "It's just a car. Step back."

Taylor took a last look, squeezed his hand, and stood back.

He leaned down and pushed. The car ran slowly down the hill until it reached the water. Jack held his breath as it began to sink, and when it was no longer visible, he opened his mouth and exhaled. *Time to keep moving.*

"Keep an eye out while I do one more thing." He walked to the front of the truck and opened the hood. After a few minutes, he returned, holding a small chip.

"What's that?"

"A device placed on all cars made after 2000. It's an internal GPS, so that the car can be located. The government's been installing them on cars ever since 9/11. Of course, the dealers have turned it to their advantage. They sell it as a way to find your car if it's stolen. What they don't tell you is that it's automatically on every car anyway."

Taylor studied Jack. "And you know this how?"

He shrugged. "If I told you, I'd have to—"

"Not funny," she interrupted.

"A few years back, I took a break from life and did a piece on the cartel kidnappings in Colombia. I got a job as a bodyguard, made some connections with some other guys who worked in security. One was ex-military intelligence. Let's just say I learned a lot."

She was looking at him like he'd lost his mind.

"You took a break from life by going to Colombia and protecting people from drug lords? Don't you need training for something like that? Why would they hire a journalist?"

"Aw shucks. Thanks for the vote of confidence." He gave her a wry smile.

"You know what I mean."

He didn't want to get into all of it with her. "I do have a black belt, and I took one of those civilian training courses."

"To train as a bodyguard?"

"Something like that. I needed to do something different for a while." He didn't tell her that it was what saved his sanity, that if he hadn't been able to get out of the country, away from everything and everyone he knew, he probably wouldn't have made it.

Her eyes widened. "Was this after . . ." She couldn't bring herself to say it.

He looked away and started the truck. "Let's hit it."

After an uncomfortable silence, Taylor finally spoke. "How long till we get to the cabin?"

"Maybe three hours."

She ran a hand through her hair. "I hope there's running water. I'm in desperate need of a shower."

Jack nodded. "It'll have everything we need."

"Jack, listen. I really need to get word to my dad that we're okay."

"There'll be an untraceable phone waiting there for us."

"Good."

"But, Taylor, I'm not so sure anything you say to him will make him feel okay about your being with me."

She raised her eyebrows. "I'll make it clear that it's temporary. He knows I would never be *with* you again." Her tone was sharp, and she turned in her seat toward the window, as if she couldn't get far enough away from him.

An hour later, Jack realized they were low on gas and

pulled into a rest stop. His sister had probably been so busy with the arrangements for Taylor that she'd forgotten to fill up the truck. Sarah had tucked the progesterone oil with a supply of alcohol packets and syringes in the glove compartment, though, and now Jack followed Taylor into the cramped bathroom, arousing looks of curiosity and a few disapproving glares, so that he could give her the shot. The thick viscous liquid necessitated a large-gauge needle, and Jack cringed looking at the size of it.

"I'm used to it, Jack. It's no big deal."

She winced as the needle went in, and he slowly plunged the needle into the area right above her buttock. She rubbed the spot, then gamely smiled and thanked him for helping her.

They grabbed some bottles of water and granola bars and got back on the road. Jack reached into the bag behind him and took out two canisters of Mace, which he handed to Taylor. He wished Taylor knew how to use a gun, but there was no way he could bring her up to speed that quickly.

"Keep these with you. You never know when they'll come in handy. Maybe if I'd given them to you sooner, that guy wouldn't have been able to grab you."

She took them and put one in her purse, the other in her jacket pocket. "Thanks." She went back to reading the bill on the laptop, but after a while, he saw she'd leaned her head back and fallen asleep. She was snoring, and he chuckled to himself. She would die of embarrassment if she knew. His attraction to her was still strong, and though it had made him feel like a heel, he had enjoyed the glimpse of her slim hips when he gave her the shot. Being with her again made him wonder, for the thousandth time, how he had ever walked away from her. He had sacrificed her happiness as well as his own, and he hadn't even had the guts to tell her himself. It still shocked him to remember how selfish he'd been.

After the art show, he had gone home and berated himself for flirting with Dakota. What was wrong with him? He was in love with Taylor—she'd been the only one for him from the time he was old enough to think about girls that way. Their relationship was storybook—next-door neighbors since childhood, high school sweethearts. So when there was a buzz on his intercom at 3:00 a.m., he should've known better than to answer it. Half-asleep, he pushed the button, and her throaty voice floated into his room.

"Hey, Jack. Whatcha doing?"

"Sleeping," he'd mumbled.

A laugh came over the speaker. "The night is young. Buzz me up, I have champagne."

Against his better judgment, he had. He'd intended to tell her that he was involved already, then send her on her way.

She'd walked into his apartment, gone straight to the kitchen, opened the cabinet, and gotten two glasses, all like she'd lived there forever. She poured them each some champagne, leaning against his counter, her full lips shiny with gloss, just begging to be kissed.

He took the glass from her and threw it back in one gulp.

"Listen, Dakota. I like you, but I'm—"

She moved toward him and put a finger on his lips. "Shh." He caught a whiff of her perfume, something spicy, musky.

And then they were kissing, and he was lifting her shirt off.

The whole thing felt like a dream, and he half expected to wake up in the morning alone. When the bright light of day shone through the curtains, he'd realized with a sinking feeling that he'd screwed up. Seeing the long, red hair fanned out on the pillow next to him—the pillow where Taylor's head should have been resting—made him sick with guilt. He'd never been with anyone but Taylor before that night. Dakota had rolled over and looked at him, the expression in her eyes taking his breath away. There was something in those eyes that said, *I know you—you belong with me*, and he was torn in two, paralyzed by confusion. She closed the space between them, folding her body into his, and he felt himself respond. Like a drug, he had wanted more, needed more, and there was no turning back.

After that, he and Dakota became inseparable. He was bewitched. She was fascinated by everything Jack had to say, loved to read his articles, would look at him like he was the only person in the world.

After a month, he still hadn't told Taylor. He didn't know how. For the first time in his life, he lied to her and told her he would be away on assignment on the weekend of her next planned visit. He knew he had to break the news, but how?

He had planned on going up to Boston on Friday and telling her in person. Dakota was cooking dinner when he mentioned it.

"I need to tell Taylor about us."

She'd turned from the counter and sat down across from him, taking his hand in hers.

"Of course. Do you want me to go out for a while, so you can talk in private?"

He rubbed her hand. "No, I have to do it face-to-face. I owe her that."

A frown marred her face, and her lips turned up in a tight smile. She withdrew her hand and stood, turning her back to him. "Oh. When are you planning on going?"

Jack came up behind her and wrapped his arms around her waist. "Don't be mad. We have a long history together. I can't just call her up and tell her I've fallen in love with someone else."

She turned around and pressed against him, cupping his face in her hands. "I know. But I can't stand the thought of losing you."

"You're not going to lose me. Not ever."

"Of course, you have to go. I was just having a moment." Her tone became light. "I would expect nothing less from you, my knight in shining armor."

He smiled, relieved, and she reached out and grabbed his hand.

"Dinner won't be ready for another half an hour. I know what I want for an appetizer."

They fell on the sofa together, limbs tangled, lips locked, and he could think of nothing else but the way she made him feel.

When Dakota got the phone call on Thursday inviting them to a last-minute anniversary celebration in Las Vegas for her aunt and uncle that weekend, he'd modified his plans and made arrangements to go up to Boston the following weekend instead.

They arrived in Vegas late Friday night and Jack wasted

no time in teaching Dakota blackjack. The party for her family wasn't until Saturday, so they had the first night to themselves. As the chips accumulated and the liquor flowed, a pervasive euphoria filled Jack. He looked at Dakota and his heart swelled.

Dakota's uncle Marcel walked over, clapped Jack on the shoulder, and gave him a broad smile.

"How're you kids doing?" He glanced at the pile of chips in front of Jack. "Looks like you're in the winner's circle. We're turning in for the night. See you tomorrow."

"Good night, Marcel."

Dakota got off her stool and, swaying, put an arm on Jack to steady herself. "Hey, handsome. Ready to call it a night?"

They walked arm in arm from the casino to the elevator.

She started to laugh.

"What's so funny?"

She pointed to the sign by the elevator.

"The chapel of love. I was picturing us standing in front of an Elvis look-alike getting married." She doubled over, laughing.

Jack chuckled and they both began to sing: "Going to the chapel and I'm going to get married. Going to the chapel and I'm gonna get maaaarried . . ."

They both stopped and looked at each other.

"Would it be too crazy?" he asked.

Dakota bit her lip. "Nothing seems less crazy."

He couldn't think of anything he wanted more. The truth was she owned him already.

"Let's do it," he said.

The rest was a blur. Say this. Sign here. Kiss the bride. And then it was done. They were married. They left the chapel and walked into the cool evening air. Suddenly he was sober. What in God's name had he done?

He looked over at Taylor again, who had shifted and was facing the window. "I won't let you down again," he whispered even though she couldn't hear him.

CHAPTER FIFTEEN

THE INSTITUTE, JULY 1975

AMELIA IS GONE AND DESPITE THE COLD SHOULDER SHE gave me, I feel a little bad for her. To get thrown out on day one is humiliating. She wasn't the only one who couldn't stomach Strombill's stance on euthanasia. Three others left later that same day. I see now that they intentionally presented the more radical ideas in the beginning of the program as a way to weed out the students who lack the ability to expand their thinking. It's not as though the idea of euthanasia doesn't give me pause. As a woman of science, I have left behind my childhood fancies about God and angels and saints. I leave that magical thinking to my mother. But while I have no religious ground to base my objection on, I do believe in the sanctity of life. The question is, what constitutes life? A pain-filled existence with no chance of recovery? I think what Dr. Strombill is trying to teach us is that we have to keep an open mind if we are to learn anything; otherwise, what is the point of being here?

It's been over a month now. I see my own exhaustion mirrored in the eyes of others. We are pushed beyond our limits each day, but not one of us complains. No one wants to look weak. Every month, we are sorted into three groups of thirty, rotating at the end of the month so that we have the chance to work with everyone. We are given a survey at the end of each day where we write two names—the person we feel has worked the hardest that day, and the person we believe cut a corner or didn't push him- or herself hard enough. To make sure we don't vote for ourselves, each survey has a number that corresponds to our name that they check later. When we finish our time here, the votes will be tallied and will factor into who makes it to the next stage.

It is the sixth and final lecture of the day. I am in the front row, where I always sit, waiting for him to take notice of me. I *must* be chosen for phase two. The desire to beat them all out consumes me. My identity has always been rooted in my accomplishments. A good strong work ethic has been drilled into me since birth. Both my sister and I are going to be doctors, and unlike with many siblings there is no competition between us. Although she never played favorites, my mother did sometimes tell me that she wished I would try to be a little more relaxed like my sister. She's the more balanced of the two of us. She wants work *and* family and I'm glad for that. She'll be the one to give my parents grandchildren. She's content to be good in what she does, but she doesn't have to be the best. But for me, being the best is the only thing.

Today Dr. Strombill leans on the desk and tosses a ball back and forth between his hands as he speaks.

"What if I were to tell you that we are making strides in gene therapy? That we are working to isolate the genes that cause diseases and replace them with healthy ones?"

There is a murmur of approval throughout the classroom. I lean forward in my seat, my body quivering with excitement. This is exactly the type of research project I'm dying to be a part of.

He looks up at the ceiling as he talks and spreads his fingers wide as he gesticulates. "Imagine. One day a world with no disease, no suffering." His face darkens. "But there are those who warn of abuses, of playing God. Why should we *not* play God? If we can improve on his flawed design, should we not?"

I raise my hand. He nods in my direction.

"They are afraid." My voice falters, and I clear my throat, trying again. "Of progress. There will always be those who stand in the way of progress."

He smiles. "Yes, Maya! And do we let these naysayers, these cowards, stop our progress?" He answers his own question. "Of course not. But how? How do we stop them?" He walks toward me, puts a hand on my shoulder.

"Maya?"

"We become more than scientists. We become persuaders, convince others who can help us—lobbyists, politicians. Find those who hope to gain from our research and use it to our advantage."

He claps his hands together and laughs. "Very good, Maya. You are learning fast."

His comment garners looks of jealousy in my direction. I smile at him, unfazed by the reaction of my classmates. The only opinion that matters to me is Dr. Strombill's.

o   o   o

We have just finished lunch and before I can return to the classroom, Evelyn approaches our table. Everyone goes quiet, and all eyes are on her. She looks at me.

"Maya, you're excused from the rest of your classes today. You've been chosen for a special project." I blush with pleasure at being singled out. My unwavering attention is paying off. I follow her from the lunchroom, down a long hallway I've never traveled before. She stops before a closed door and smiles at me. "You can wait here." She opens the door and I walk inside the room—a small space with only a sofa and a coffee table.

"What's the project?" I ask.

"I haven't been told anything. Only to fetch you." She turns and leaves before I can ask anything else.

My belongings are already here, so I take a seat on the sofa and wait, my stomach fluttering with butterflies. A few minutes later, the same driver who first brought us here escorts me out of the building and into an idling limousine.

"Where are we going?" I ask him.

"To another building on campus."

I lean back and look out the window, intrigued. We drive for over fifteen minutes, each mile seeming to take us deeper and deeper into uncivilized terrain, trees and branches obscuring the view of everything but the road in front of us. At last, we stop, and I gasp as I open the door and step outside. I am standing in front of a castle. A real castle! I crane my neck to look at the top where I count at least eleven turrets. It is something out of a fairy tale, and I hug my arms around myself, too enchanted to speak at first. Finally, I manage.

"What is this place?" I ask. The neo-Gothic architecture looks familiar to me. I've seen it somewhere, in a picture or postcard.

"It is a replica of Hohenzollern Castle," he replies.

"In Germany, right?"

He nods with a bored expression, as if we're discussing the weather. "Of course, on a much smaller scale."

I wonder again what I'm doing here and what in the world this has to do with my research fellowship.

"Follow me," he says, and I walk behind him up a steep hill that leads to an entrance and stop in front of the tremendous iron door, feeling as though I've traveled through time and am about to encounter knights in all their splendor waiting on the other side.

When we enter the cavernous hallway, there are indeed suits of armor, but they are empty, their owners long departed. My heart is pounding as I try to take it all in, when I am whisked down the hall by a woman in a nurse's uniform. She leads me into a room that has a doctor's examining table in the center and a counter littered with medical supplies. I am directed to sit on a table, which is covered with a paper sheet.

"What's going on? Where am I?"

She hands me a robe. "Congratulations. You've graduated to the next phase."

I look at her, dubious, wondering if I'm dreaming this. "I still have two months to finish my fellowship. This doesn't make sense."

She ignores my objections. "Everyone has to undergo a physical before moving on to phase two," she states.

I take a deep breath. This feels wrong, but I'm afraid to jeopardize my chances.

"What do you want me to do?"

"Get undressed and put this on." She hands me a paper gown and sits down in a chair by the door, and thumbs through a magazine. It becomes obvious that she expects me to change while she's still in the room. I sigh loudly but she doesn't look up. I quickly change and sit on the examining table, covered only by the thin paper. She continues reading her magazine, ignoring me. After a few more minutes, I can no longer contain my curiosity and clear my throat in an effort to gain her attention.

"Excuse me."

"Yes?" she says, not bothering to look up.

"Can you tell me why I need to be seen by a doctor?"

"It's just a standard physical."

I look up at the ceiling and try to distract myself while I wait. *What is taking so long?* My face grows warm as impatience gets the better of me. I am about to jump down from the table and put my clothes back on when the door opens. I smile at the man in the white coat, hoping to connect with him.

He doesn't smile back but simply moves his hand in a

shuffling manner to indicate I should lie back. He holds a syringe in the other hand.

"What are you doing?"

"Relax. It's something to calm you."

I inch away from him. "Stay away from me."

The woman is by my side in an instant. She takes my hand in hers. "It's okay, Maya." Her voice is sugar all of a sudden. "Look at me."

The distraction is enough. I feel the sting of the needle, and the next thing I know I am lying down with a pillow under my hips.

She is sitting in a chair in the corner of the room again.

I rub my eyes. "What happened?"

She pushes a button on the counter.

The doctor returns.

"What did you do?" I manage to croak out.

He looks at the woman.

"Make sure she doesn't move. He will be in to talk to her later."

I try to sit up but before I can, a strong arm comes down on my arms and holds me still.

"You heard what the doctor said. Do I need to strap you down or are you going to be a good girl and stay still?" There is no compassion in her eyes.

I drop my head back onto the table. What have I gotten myself into? All of a sudden, my ears are wet, and I realize I'm crying. I make no move to wipe away the tears. I won't give her the satisfaction. I lie still, staring straight ahead, and make my mind blank.

CHAPTER SIXTEEN

Senator Hamilton played solitaire on his phone while the clerk continued with the roll call vote. Knowing the outcome tended to make these bill votes even more tedious. Three more yeses and he could get out of here and enjoy the steak he had been thinking about all morning.

"How do you vote, Mr. Marin?"

"Aye."

"Mr. Marin, aye."

"Mr. Plomkin?"

"Aye."

"Mr. Plomkin, aye."

Hamilton didn't look up from his phone.

"Ms. Linway?"

Finally, last one.

"No."

Hamilton's head snapped up. He must have heard wrong. He turned around to look at her, but she wouldn't meet his eyes. The bill was dead.

He strode from the room and rushed to his office. Within minutes, four senators arrived.

Hamilton picked up the phone.

"Hold my calls."

Wheezing from the exertion, he took a long sip of water and wiped the perspiration from his forehead with his hand-kerchief. He looked at the man sitting across for him.

"Would you mind telling me what just happened? We engi-neered this to be a close vote. How did we lose Linway?" He was livid. First Phillips and now this—the second time in the past month that two of his bills had fallen apart at the last minute.

The only woman in the room, Senator Marcus from Con-necticut, cleared her throat. All eyes turned to the young woman.

"She's pregnant."

"So?" Hamilton's eyes narrowed.

"I think it colored her perception. She just got the news yesterday."

Hamilton glared at her. "When did you find this out?"

She gulped, her face red. "This morning."

His voice rose. "Why didn't you tell me? I would have found someone else for the swing vote."

"She's my friend, and she asked me to keep it quiet. Be-sides, she promised it wouldn't change her vote."

Hamilton wanted to strangle her. "And you believed her?"

A man on his left interrupted. "It's a minor setback. There is more than one way to achieve our goals. Remember how long it took to make prescreening mandatory? The rest of the bills have passed quickly and mostly unnoticed. The bioethicists have done their jobs well. Everyone wants healthy children. We'll make some minor modifications to mollify our constituents and get them on our side."

Hamilton exhaled and leaned back. Maybe he was right. On its surface, the bill was a win-win. It covered a wide spectrum of birth defects and chronic illnesses that were detectable in the first trimester of pregnancy. Any of the conditions included would qualify as a preexisting condition that would be excluded from coverage, thereby, in practical terms, mandating the termination of the pregnancy. Since prescreening had become mandatory, these birth defects had been reduced by 40 percent. The senators who had put forth the bill had garnered widespread support from special interest groups whose mission it was to optimize health care. It was the fervent belief of those supporting the bill that this was the path to eliminating diseases and freeing up resources to work on curing other diseases that were not yet preventable. They were on the forefront of a better, more perfect world. Hamilton didn't care a whit about any of that. His name was on the bill, and he'd be damned if some uterus with legs was going to be his undoing.

He pulled out his phone, clicked the Twitter app and typed:

Thanks to all who supported Senate Bill #healthy #children #bill. Unfortunately, no win this time. #HCB

CHAPTER SEVENTEEN

THE INSTITUTE, JULY 1975

IT FEELS LIKE I'VE BEEN ON THIS HARD, COLD TABLE FOR hours, but when I look at the clock on the wall I see it's been less than thirty minutes. The door opens, and the woman gets up from her chair and withdraws from the room without a word. When a man comes in right after, I feel a momentary flicker of hope. Surely someone this beautiful is not to be feared. His face is almost perfect, marred only by a small, round scar on one cheek. Otherwise, it is a face to rival any movie star's: chiseled cheekbones, straight Roman nose, full lips. My gaze moves to meet his and then my hope crashes.

I have never before seen what I see in those eyes. They are predatory and penetrating. Something intangible terrifies me when I look into them. There is a heaviness in the air, an invisible darkness that threatens to invade me, and I want to cover my own eyes like a child and pretend I am invisible. He looks at me as if we know each other.

I take a deep breath, affect a bravado I don't feel, and swing my legs off the bed, ready to stand.

"Don't get up." His voice is deep, pleasant.

"Who are you?"

His lips curl in a smile. "All in good time, my dear." His tone is mocking.

I take a deep breath and stare at him.

He pulls a chair next to my bed and sits. "You are a brilliant young woman. It's why I chose you."

"What have you done? Why am I here?"

He arches one eyebrow. "You have been chosen to bear my child."

His child? My stomach tightens, and I feel sick. I glare at him. "Did you rape me?"

A look of repulsion transforms his face, and the corners of his mouth point to the floor.

"Please, Maya. I am not an animal. There are other ways to impregnate someone."

"Why? Why would you hope to impregnate me?"

"We do not hope. We plan. I have your entire medical history; you have been monitored for the past month. I'm fairly certain that you are pregnant."

I jump off the bed and began to pace. "Why in God's name?" I scream. I don't understand.

"God has nothing to do with it. For now, you need know

nothing but this: you have been chosen from thousands. You should be pleased. You have not only made it to the top of the class, you have made it to the top of the world."

"I don't understand. I came here to learn medicine. Who *are* you?"

"Damon Crosse. I am the one in charge here. You were selected from a great many to come here—but not for the medical internship." He stands and walks to the corner of the room, picks up a folder, and opens it. After reading something inside, he closes it and returns to the chair.

"It was very close. I almost chose someone else. But your pedigree was better."

What is he talking about? "Pedigree? I'm not a dog."

He smiles again. "No, Maya, you are more like a brood mare."

"Go to hell, you bastard." Spittle flies from my mouth.

He looks at me with no change in expression.

"I'm getting out of here. I'm going home. This is insane!" I rant.

He withdraws from the room without another word, and then the men arrive. They push me down on the bed and strap me into a white vest.

"You're making this harder than it has to be," one whispers in my ear.

I scream until my throat is raw. I can no longer move my arms, and the more I struggle, the tighter everything becomes. I don't know when I finally fall into an exhausted sleep. When I awake, he is there again. Watching. Calm. Cold.

"The sooner you learn to accept things, the better."

"I'll never accept being held prisoner. Why have you done this?" I croak, my voice barely audible.

"In good time. In good time you will know the part you will play, but not quite yet."

"I need to move. Take these off."

He frowns. "You must learn the proper way to address me. You may request but never demand." He stands up and hovers over me. "Do you understand?"

My stomach tightens. I nod my head.

He sits back down. "Good."

"Would you please take this vest off me?"

"Not yet. When I believe you can be trusted, then I will have it removed."

I lie there still restrained, while he sits a few feet away staring at me. I fear I shall never see my family or anyone else ever again.

CHAPTER EIGHTEEN

THE ROAD NARROWED AND BECAME EVEN MORE BUMPY and pothole ridden. Taylor winced as the truck bounced up and down, and her head bumped against the roof.

"Sorry 'bout that. Almost there."

She winced and put a hand on her stomach.

He gave her a worried look. "Are you okay?"

She shook her head. "Just nervous. I've had two miscarriages, and so I need to be monitored closely. It's also why I need the progesterone shots for the first eight weeks—it helps decrease the chance of anything going wrong. This is not the best time for me to be stressed out."

His hands tightened on the wheel. "I wish Malcolm had told me."

"Yeah, well, I don't understand what was going on in his mind. Truthfully, if those guys with guns hadn't shown up,

I'm not sure I would have believed any of it was real. I just want to find Jeremy, whoever he is, and get some answers."

The scenery began to change as civilization faded away. Everything was a green blur. Never had she been in the middle of so many evergreens. As they crested the top of the hill, she saw what looked like a brown rectangle nestled in the patchwork of forest. As they got closer, a small A-frame log cabin appeared. The enormous trees dwarfed the dwelling, and Taylor shivered, thinking of old horror movies involving isolated houses. Jack pulled into the gravel drive.

They walked up to the door, and Jack took the key from his pocket and opened it.

Beau began running around the house in frantic loops. After about ten rounds, he bounded up to Taylor and prodded her to pet him.

"Poor guy, stuck in the car all that time. Maybe we can walk him a little later?" she said.

Jack looked at his watch. "Let's get settled first."

He seemed familiar with the place, as he walked over to a lamp with a base made of miniature canoes and turned it on. The amber glow made the room cozy and inviting, and she headed to a plush brown sofa and ran a hand over the velvety fabric. Large windows with sheer, white curtains on two walls looked out at the barricade of trees, and she suddenly felt safe and cocooned.

"Before we do anything else, we have to change our appearances. Our faces are all over the news." He pulled out the hair dye and scissors from his bag. "Come on."

She followed him to the bathroom and turned to him.

"May as well get it over with." She braced herself while he began to cut her hair. When he was finished, she looked at him with surprise. "It actually isn't half bad."

He took a bow. "One of my hidden talents. My mother taught me how. She thought paying for haircuts was wasteful."

She arched an eyebrow. "You didn't always have such a steady hand. Remember when you butchered your sister Megan's hair. I thought she was going to kill you. It was all uneven and spiky."

He laughed. "I had to sleep with one eye open for weeks." He took a deep breath and winced. "My turn." He made broad cuts to his blond hair, cutting it close to his head. Then he picked up the razor.

Taylor winced. "You're not going to shave it all, are you?"

He made the first swipe right down the middle. "Yup. Guess we'll get to see what I look like bald." He grinned. It didn't take him long to finish. Wow. Who knew hair made such a difference? He wondered what Taylor thought.

"Well?"

Taylor's eyes traveled the length of his head. "At least it will grow back."

"Not exactly a ringing endorsement." He shrugged. "We're not done yet." He grabbed the box of hair color from the drugstore. "I don't know how this will turn out." He paused and took a long look at her. "I always imagined I could see the reflection of the sun in your hair. I'm sorry to have to do this." He lifted a strand and held it between his fingers.

She flicked his hand away in obvious annoyance. "Just do it."

What was wrong with him? Just when the tension between

them had started to dissipate he acted like an awkward teenager rushing in for his first kiss.

"Here goes nothing."

When he was finished, Taylor was a blonde. They walked back into the living room and Beau started whining and turning in circles.

"Aw, baby, it's okay. It's still me." She knelt and called him over to her.

He approached her tentatively and began to sniff. Tail wagging, he licked her face until she was laughing and had to push him away.

"Good job, Jack. My own dog didn't recognize me."

He had to admit that her appearance was quite changed. Even with his hack job, she was still beautiful. The familiar longing returned, burning in his belly like a shot of Jameson.

"Are you hungry? How 'bout I fix us something to eat?" Jack said.

"We don't have any food."

He opened the refrigerator, which was filled to overflowing with a huge variety of meats, fruits, and vegetables.

Taylor's stomach growled in anticipation. "Where did that come from?"

"Let's just say I have resourceful friends."

"Good to know."

"How about an omelet?"

"Sounds good."

Not much later, Taylor sat down at a wooden table by one of the windows. She took a bite from the still-steaming omelet. "Not bad. What kind of cheese is this?"

"Goat. I also threw in some chopped dates."

She raised her eyebrows. "Impressive. Last time you made me a meal, it was a lumpy peanut butter and jelly sandwich."

"I seem to remember your liking those sandwiches." He laughed. "Remember in fourth grade, you would trade me your turkey and cheese for my PB&J?"

She had forgotten that. "They were good. My mother's never tasted the same. The bread was wrong, and so was the peanut butter. You always had Wonder Bread and Jif." She used to feel so bad that Jack's mom didn't get up with him before school and make him breakfast or pack him a lunch. He had been taking care of himself for as long as she could remember. He became such a regular fixture at their dinner table that, after a while, her mother automatically set a place for him.

"I'm happy to make you one any time you want."

After Taylor had finished eating, she pushed her plate aside and brought Jack's laptop to the table, opening it to bring up the VACA bill she had been reviewing. She had gotten through the rest of it last night and now looked at the rider again, peering in close at one line. "Jack, I think I found something."

He walked behind her and looked at the screen where she was pointing.

"Look at this. It's talking about a TB vaccine. Doesn't one exist already?"

He shrugged. "I've never heard of one. Don't know."

"Well, this rider claims that one is in testing now for widespread use in the US, and that once it gets FDA approval, it can be mandated in case of a national health emergency."

"Mandated for kids?" Jack asked.

She shook her head. "No, no. And this has nothing to do with the main bill. This would require all health care workers to get the vaccine if there was an outbreak, and the language defining what an outbreak is goes on for pages."

"So what? Don't they already have to do that with flu shots?"

Taylor thought a minute. That was true, but something was niggling at her. "Yeah, but I think that's more a hospital requirement. This would make it federal law. Right now states mandate those decisions." She kept reading. "Here. If the incident rate rises above .05, *everyone* would be required to get the vaccine."

"Define incident rate."

"The number of cases per one hundred thousand. The incident rate is now .03."

"I guess that's a significant increase, not sure if it's enough to justify forcing the vaccine on the entire population," he said.

She swiveled around to face him. "Jack. Why would Congress pass a law mandating a vaccine that doesn't even exist yet?"

He raised his eyebrows. "Well, you know the old saying— follow the money . . ."

"Good point. The company making the vaccine. Let's see who that is." She turned back around and started typing again. "Hmm."

"What?" Jack asked.

"There *is* already a TB vaccine. BCG. Says here it's been around since the 1920s but is not highly effective. Hold on." She typed in "new TB vaccine."

"So there's the Tuberculosis Vaccine Initiative, a nonprofit working together to find a better vaccine."

"Interesting. I'm assuming they partner with drug companies?"

Taylor clicked through the site. "There's no specific company listed. But nonprofits are required to file a financial report with the IRS and make it available to the public." She went through all the tabs on the site. "You can request it here. Should I fill it in?"

Jack shook his head.

"No. Don't put your email info there. We don't know if they could be involved with whoever is behind everything. We have to be careful not to tip anyone off. Let me get in touch with my pal Mac. He's a PI who's done some work for me."

"Okay." Taylor got up and took their dishes to the sink. "So in the meantime, what are we doing here?"

Jack walked over to the fireplace. He pushed aside the mesh curtain and reached inside. Taylor watched as he dislodged a brick and pulled out an envelope. He dusted off his sleeve and brought it over to her, holding it up.

"Our next set of clues."

"If I didn't just see it, I wouldn't believe it." She shook her head.

Jack opened the envelope carefully and took out a map and a note. He scanned the note then walked over to Taylor.

He handed it to her. "Does this mean anything to you?"

She read it aloud. "Taylor, go to the library in Claremont, New Hampshire, and find your favorite book. The one that has always spoken to you of resilience and fortitude. There, you will find the address. The number can be calculated by multiplying the number of letters in the protagonist's maiden name times 6 and adding 7. The town bears the same name as the town where her true love returns. The street name will be in the book." She smiled. "Malcolm is talking about *Gone with the Wind*."

Jack chuckled. "Don't tell me—your favorite part is when Scarlett throws a dish at Rhett Butler's head."

"Very funny. He meant the scene where Scarlett swears she'll never be hungry again." For a moment, she forgot about Malcolm's deception and remembered only the intimacies they had shared. She felt a wistful longing for him.

"You and Scarlett definitely share some personality traits," Jack teased.

She laughed and was surprised to find that the familiar mischievous look in his eyes lightened her heart. For a split second, it was like old times, before any of the complications, when they were just two best friends looking for their next adventure.

She pursed her lips. "And you have a lot in common with Charles Hamilton." That would fix him.

Jack fell back against the cushion and clutched his heart. "Ah, Scarlett, you have cut me to the quick."

She became serious. "So we need to go to Claremont and find the book to get the actual street name for Jeremy's place. We can figure out the number: her maiden name is O'Hara, five letters times six equals thirty plus seven means the street number is thirty-seven."

Jack nodded. "So, the town. He said where her true love returned. Where did Ashley go?"

Taylor shook her head. "Her *true* love. Ashley was only

who she thought she loved. She didn't realize until too late that she really loved Rhett and that's when he left to go back to Charleston." She was annoyed that she had to explain it. Everyone knew Scarlett never really loved Ashley. Even Malcolm understood that. She realized Jack was talking.

"What?" she said a little too snappishly.

"There's a Charlestown on the map, that must be what he meant. It's not far from here." He circled the two cities. "We're a little more than an hour away. Now all we need is the street name."

"We need the book. Let's hope no one's checked it out," she said. "I'll be right back. Need to use the bathroom."

She closed the bathroom door and took a deep breath. She had actually been acting like things were fine between them. What was wrong with her? They weren't away on vacation. She was angry at herself for letting her guard down so easily. *Remember what he did. He is not the Jack you used to love.* She pulled down her jeans and sat down on the toilet seat. It took a few seconds for her to register what she was seeing. Blood.

No. Not again.

She grabbed the counter to steady herself.

"Jack," she yelled. "Come here."

He raced in immediately to see her hunched over, her eyes full of tears.

"I think I'm losing the baby."

CHAPTER NINETEEN

CROSBY WHEELER GLANCED DOWN AT THE ALERT ON HIS phone and saw the tweet from Hamilton. He pressed the intercom for his secretary. "Get me Winters."

She buzzed back and let him know he was holding.

Crosby picked up the phone again. "We need to change the lineup on *Behind Closed Doors* Friday night. Slot in the episode of the family with the disabled kids."

He clicked off, took a sip of his water, and waited for the video to load. Red letters slowly appeared on his computer monitor until the title of the show filled the screen—*Radical Reality: Regrets, Recriminations, and Reflections.*

The camera zooms in on a stark-white kitchen with bare counters. A harried-looking woman stares at the camera, runs a hand through disheveled hair, and begins to speak in the voice of one battle weary and defeated.

"It's Friday morning, but it could be any morning. One day dissolves into the next, the same as the one before, our one and only goal to make it through until we have the blessed reprieve of sleep. I'm Monica. Welcome to my personal hell."

The camera follows her into the living room, where two children, somewhere between eight and nine, sit, strapped into their individual wheelchairs, heads tilted, eyes unseeing.

The woman holding the camera is an attractive woman in her fifties with warm, compassionate eyes. She reaches out to cover Monica's hand with her own. "Monica, I know this is terribly difficult for you. We so appreciate your giving us a glimpse into your life." She pauses and then continues. "Can you please share your story with our viewers?"

Monica wipes a tear from the corner of her eye.

"When the girls were in utero, everything looked fine. Their development was on track, and the ultrasounds showed two normal babies. Most people who meet them think that they were born prematurely, but that's not the case. It wasn't until they were born that it was discovered that they both suffer from a rare genetic anomaly. If the genetic testing had been done in utero, it would have been discovered before they were born, and all this could have been avoided."

The interviewer looks shocked by the statement. "Are you saying that you wish they had never been born?"

Monica returns her stare without flinching. "I am saying that I wish they didn't have to have a life of suffering. They can't see. They will never walk or speak or have any semblance of a life. I don't know what they are thinking or feeling. What kind of a life is that for them?"

"I am so sorry. Of course, I have no right to judge. Please go on."

Monica stands up and begins to pace. "What is going to happen to them when their father and I are gone? Who will take care of them then? All our money is tied up in caring for them now. We've spent a fortune making this house wheel-chair accessible, so that we can take them out occasionally. And when we do . . . the stares . . . you wouldn't believe how cruel people can be."

The reporter shakes her head. "That's why it's so important for your story to be told, so people can understand what it's like. We are so grateful to our sponsors for their support."

Crosby shut the laptop. The show was perfect—just the thing to get the public on the right side of the Healthy Children bill. He just needed to check one more thing.

He buzzed his secretary again and told her to get the executive producer.

"Louis, how are you handling the legalities surrounding the mother on the *RRR* show?" he asked once he had him on the phone.

"We have a disclaimer in the rolling credits stating that she is the stepmother. We were very careful with the dialogue, so that she never makes a claim that she was pregnant or is their birth mother."

"You've taken measures to ensure she won't abandon them in the middle of the season?"

"Yes, sir. Her contract is solid. She'd have to pay back all the money. But if for any reason she breaks it and leaves, we can use that to our advantage, show how this has devastated their marriage. By the time we reveal the entire story—that the mother died in childbirth and Monica is a latecomer to their care—it won't matter. Everyone will be invested in the story by then."

"Good." Crosby hung up.

He rose and grabbed his cashmere blazer from the credenza, slipping it on as he walked out the door. "Call my driver and tell him I'm ready," he told his secretary without breaking stride, and he inserted the key into his private elevator.

"Yes, sir. Before you go . . ."

He turned. "Yes?"

She tilted her head. "Would you like me to have dinner sent over for you and Mrs. Wheeler tonight?"

He didn't miss the look of sympathy on her face. After twelve years, they both knew no more about each other than they did on day one. She had never asked him what was wrong with his wife, knew only that she was confined to a wheelchair and under the daily care of nurses. She had tried to probe once, but he had cut her off. His personal life was none of her business. He'd made it very clear that any questions on that front were off limits and told her if she valued her job, she'd rein in her curiosity. She'd been a perfect assistant ever since, handling everything at the network with efficiency and professionalism.

"No, Millicent. I'll cook it myself this evening," he said briskly and entered the elevator.

CHAPTER TWENTY

THE INSTITUTE, AUGUST 1975

I AM BEING HELD PRISONER IN A BEAUTIFUL ROOM HIGH IN the castle, like a princess in a fairy tale, alone and forgotten. Maroon velvet drapes with thick, gold sashes adorn the floor-to-ceiling windows. Murals of kings and their ladies watch me from the walls. My wooden bed looks as though it was hand carved. The beauty in its detail would bring me joy if I were here under different circumstances.

Crosse has left me alone for three weeks. The only contact I have is the cursory greeting from those who bring me my meals and take me to the gym for my exercise, and from the doctor, whom I assume will be monitoring my pregnancy. I have missed a period. Still too early for a medical test confirming that I am pregnant, but I know. My body feels different.

He comes into my room, and the very air changes. I can barely breathe. He gives me one of his cold smiles and sits in one of the velvet-cushioned chairs next to the ornate, wooden table.

"You seem calmer, Maya. Are you beginning to settle in?"

"What choice do I have?"

"What indeed? To set your expectations, I will tell you what lies ahead. You will stay here during the entirety of your pregnancy. If you do as you are told, you will earn some freedoms. You will receive a menu and may choose your meals. And you may use my library—when escorted, of course. When you have delivered my child, you will be set free."

Does he really think I'm naive enough to believe he'll let me go? "And if I don't cooperate?"

He frowns. "If you don't cooperate, you will find yourself very uncomfortable indeed. Needless to say, you will enjoy none of the aforementioned privileges, and you will be moved to a padded room where you will be restrained in order to keep the child safe."

"I'll cooperate," I lie.

"Wise choice, Maya. I will return soon. I think you will be most interested to learn what awaits the child."

"Help me, God," I find myself saying aloud once he leaves, even though I have long ago given up any belief in a supreme being. I wish I still retained a kernel of that faith. But then again, I reason, what good would faith do me now, and why, if there was a God, would he allow me to be imprisoned here? No. The only one I can count on is myself.

o o o

I was taken to see the doctor five days ago. I didn't bother to engage him. He drew my blood and gave me a pelvic exam. I hope against hope that the test will be negative.

I hear Crosse's footsteps now, and I steel myself. The door opens, and he enters. His eyes find mine, and I am unable to look away. His gaze holds mine hostage—I am immobilized. It sears me, that look, and I want to scream, to tell him to let go, but no words come. I muster all my strength and squeeze my eyes shut, wishing with everything that I have that this has all been a bad dream.

His laughter causes my eyes to fly open.

"Maya, Maya. A bit childish, don't you think?"

He smiles that perfect smile, and I marvel again at the beauty of his features. How can someone so beautiful be so ugly?

"Please let me go. You don't need to do this."

He shakes his head. "I can't let you go. You are carrying precious cargo."

So it's been confirmed, then.

The violation is overwhelming, and I break out into a cold sweat. I don't want his child inside of me. "There must have been any number of women who would have been willing to give you a child. Why me?"

He sits down on the leather chair across from where I sit.

"I chose you for a specific reason. Your family has something I want."

"What do you know of my family?" My heart skips a beat.

"Much."

His smug manner infuriates me. I want to reach out and scratch his face until it bleeds. I must know. Has he been following me? My parents and my sister? Are they safe?

"My family has nothing to do with this. What is your interest in them?" I demand.

A frown mars his face, and his voice is stern. "I'm the one who will ask the questions. Have your parents ever mentioned any valuable treasures or relics they brought with them from Greece?"

My mind races. "I don't know what you're talking about."

He leans back and pours himself a glass of water from the glass pitcher on the tray on the table. Taking a long sip, he stares at me the entire time, then sets the goblet back down. I have to tear my gaze away from his again.

"Your parents grew up on the island of Patmos, and they left right after World War II."

How does he know this?

He continues. "Patmos is the island where Saint John lived for many years."

"So?" I say in a voice more rebellious than I feel.

"There were a great many religious relics hidden there. The Germans found most of them, but not all." He stands and turns his back to me, as if he's weighing whether to continue.

"That is all I will say for now," he finally says. "Think,

Maya. Think about your family stories. What has been handed down. Try to remember so that I don't have to pay a visit to your parents and ask them." He lets the words sink in, then adds, "That would be unfortunate for them."

He has to leave my parents out of it. I have no idea what he's asking for, but I try to get more information.

"Then tell me, if you are to be the father of my child. You know about my family. What about yours? Where is your family? Your parents?"

He seems to consider my question, looking off into the distance. He turns and takes a seat again.

"Do you want to know about my family? Do you suppose I have a loving family like yours? What do you know about need? About cruelty? My father lived to be cruel. Should I tell you one of my childhood memories?"

He doesn't wait for my answer.

"I bet you had a birthday party every year, yes?"

I nod.

"Of course you did. Well, I never did. Except when I turned eight. He brought home a dog. A beautiful, fluffy white dog. I was too young to know it was a trick. I took care of that dog—fed it, walked it, cleaned up after it, made sure it was no trouble at all because I knew what he did to anything that caused him trouble. I came home late that day, because my teacher had wanted to see me after class. My father was waiting for me. Had the dog on the leash and was sneering at me and I knew it meant big trouble.

"'You're late, boy,' he said. 'The dog wet in the house.'

"I knew he was lying.

"'You know what that means, dontcha?'

"I ran for the leash, tried to wrest it from his hands, and he laughed. 'You scrawny punk. You think you can take this from me?' He kicked me hard. Then he started kicking the dog.

"My screams filled the air, and the more I screamed, the more he laughed. I covered my ears to drown out the sound of my dog's cries. After an eternity, all was quiet again. I didn't want to look. But he made me.

"'Clean up this mess, boy. Poor dog would still be alive if you hadn't been late.'"

My blood runs cold as my imagination paints the horrific picture. I want to say something, but no words will come.

He arches an eyebrow, leans back in his chair, picks a nonexistent piece of lint from his shirt, and looks at me. "No words of wisdom for me?"

I feel sorry for him despite myself. I look at him, searching for any trace of that eight-year-old boy. Sitting in front of me is a man who appears to be devoid of any vulnerability.

"That's so terrible. I'm—"

"Don't waste your pity on me, I have no need or desire of it. I tell you this so that you may understand my strength, what I have been through to become who I am today. My father paid for his abuse. After my worthless mother died choking on her own vomit, it was just him and me. But I was bigger by then. He couldn't hit me anymore. I towered over him. He could still make my life miserable, but not for long. Everything changed when I went to work for the only man in town worth his salt. He taught me everything that I needed to know, took me in and treated me like I was his son."

"Who was he?" I ask.

"You will meet him soon enough. He's the one who started the Institute. Would you like to see some of the work that's being done here? Work you would have been a part of if you didn't have a greater purpose?"

I can't tell if he's mocking me or not, but anything is better than sitting in this room with nothing to do but think.

I nod.

"Come, then." He stands and beckons for me to follow. Before he opens the door, he stops and turns around.

"Don't think of trying anything stupid. Talk to no one. Just follow me."

I nod.

No one is in the hallway, and I follow him down the empty corridor until we reach a small elevator. He inserts a key, and the door opens. He waits for me to enter and then joins me in the small space, his breath so close that I want to hold mine to avoid breathing any air he has exhaled. Then I remember he has already contaminated me, and my stomach turns.

The elevator doors open, and I follow him again, into a room with a large window looking into a classroom. I realize it is a two-way mirror from which we can watch those in the other room undetected. He sits down without a word, and I take the empty chair next to him.

The children are sitting in rows, both feet on the floor, hands folded, and eyes on the teacher at the front of the room. They are elementary school aged, in maybe third or fourth grade. Their teacher is scowling at a student standing in front of her and holds the bunched-up fabric of his shirt in her hand. I want to go through the glass and pull him away from her. He looks terrified, and his small hands are bunched into fists.

"Can anyone tell me what Matthew has done wrong?" the teacher asks.

No one raises a hand.

She lets go of his shirt, then pushes him, and he falls to the floor. "He gave his answers to someone. That's what. Why is that wrong?"

A little girl holds up her hand. "Because it's cheating?" It comes out as a squeak.

The teacher walks over and puts her face inches from the child's. She mimics her. "Because it's cheating?" She yanks hard on the girl's pigtail. She straightens, then raises her voice. "No! Not because it's cheating. Anyone else?"

A few hands shoot up.

She points. "Malcolm, how about you?"

"Because he got caught?"

"Exactly. Good job." She hands Malcolm a candy bar.

"Only stupid, careless children get caught. Sometimes in life, cheating is necessary. But if you're going to break the rules, you make sure to cover your tracks." She walks back over to Matthew. "Get up. Go back to your seat and don't ever let me catch you again." She turns to the class. "What is the cardinal rule?"

"Don't get caught," they answer in unison.

"Very good. Now it's time for musical chairs. No lunch for the loser."

"What is this? Why is she so horrible to the children?" Outrage has turned my voice shrill, and my face is hot.

He sneers at me. "What you see as horrible, I see as necessary. These children don't need coddling. They are going to be extraordinary leaders one day. They need to learn life's lessons early."

"What lessons? That adults have the right to abuse children? That lying and cheating is good? I would have never agreed to be a part of any of this."

He shakes his head. "This wasn't part of your training. I show you this to give you a complete picture of the empire my child will one day inherit. These children are lucky. Where else would a group of orphans have the opportunity to be educated by the brilliant minds here at the Institute? And what other orphans are being molded into adults who will have impeccable pedigrees and being groomed for positions of untold wealth and power? But first they need discipline and direction."

"Where did they come from?"

He laughs. "They are brought to me. They are throwaways, disposed of by irresponsible garbage not fit to be called parents. Without us, they would be nothing. One day, these children will be judges, politicians, business magnates."

I see where he is going with this. "And you will pull their puppet strings."

"The others coming through here, others like you, we recruit from the top universities. They are all vetted and solidly indoctrinated before they reach this advanced phase of the program. But there is something to be said for getting them while they're young."

He stands. "Just think how much more my own flesh and blood will be capable of."

I cannot speak. Images flood my mind of my child being raised in this hellhole, and I gasp for breath and double over. The prospect is unbearable. I must find a way to escape. Surely even death is preferable to the fate that awaits my child.

CHAPTER TWENTY-ONE

TAYLOR STOOD UP, STEADYING HERSELF BY HOLDING ON TO the sink. Perspiration dotted her forehead. The spotting seemed to have stopped for now, but she was terrified it was a precursor to another miscarriage.

"How can I help?" Jack asked.

"I need to lie down. I think it stopped. For now."

He reached out a hand to help her and they went to the bedroom. "Good. Lie on your left side. Hopefully you're only spotting. We're going to have to lie low for a few days. You should stay off your feet."

She stared at him. "Since when did you go to medical school?"

He looked at the floor. "Dakota started spotting in her third month, but it passed." He cleared his throat. "I'll let you get some rest. I'll be in the next room. Yell if you need anything."

She closed her eyes. Hearing Dakota's name made it all come rushing back. She recalled the day she found out that Jack had betrayed her. Evelyn had been waiting for her at the house when she got home for school break. She'd given Taylor a long hug.

"How was the traffic?" Evelyn asked.

"Easy drive. No problem. Dad home?"

"Not yet. Let's go into the kitchen. I'll make some tea."

She patted Taylor on the shoulder when they got to the kitchen. "Taylor, sit down. I have something to tell you."

"What's wrong? Is Dad okay?"

"Yes, it's something else. Sit." She took a deep breath.

Taylor pulled out the chair and sat down—and waited.

"It's about Jack," Evelyn finally said.

"What about him?" Taylor asked in a shaking voice.

"There's no easy way to say it. He got married."

Taylor shot up from her seat. "What? What are you talking about? What do you mean he got married?" She could barely speak. "I'm going to see him this weekend."

Evelyn answered calmly. "I know it's a terrible shock. His mother is very upset as well. She got the call last night. He met a woman named Dakota Drake last month apparently. They ran off to Las Vegas and eloped. I'm so sorry, Taylor." She reached out to embrace her, but Taylor pulled away. She didn't want comfort from her. Evelyn had been a good friend to her mother before she died, and Taylor had always liked her. But when her father married her less than a year after her mother had died, Taylor began to wonder if Evelyn had ever really been her mother's friend.

She ran past Evelyn and into the bathroom and slammed the door shut. Sinking to her knees, she vomited into the toilet bowl. Sweat broke out on her face, and falling back against the wall, she hugged herself and wailed. Maybe Evelyn was lying. Even as she thought it, she knew it was wishful thinking. Evelyn loved Jack, she was happy for them. *Jack, oh Jack, what did you do?*

Eventually, she found the strength to stand up, and when she did, she ran from the house and got into her car, with no idea of where she was going; she needed to move. In a haze, she drove down Connecticut Avenue, her thoughts racing as she tried to make sense of what she'd heard. This wasn't just some random boyfriend—this was Jack. He knew everything about her and loved her, anyway—or so she had thought. They had nursed each other through all life's bumps, knew all the family skeletons, commiserated over every challenge, every rejection, every hardship. Over the past month he'd been busy on a story—or so he'd told her when she had complained that she could never reach him on the phone. Now she realized he had been avoiding her. How could he do this to her? And who was the woman? His wife! It was impossible. She would go to New York and confront him. He owed her an explanation at least.

She didn't know how fast she drove, but before she knew it, she was in front of his apartment building. As a man walked out of the building, she grabbed the door before it could shut and ran up the stairs. She pounded on the door, her face hot, her heart hammering. The door opened and a creature with flame-red hair and icy-blue eyes stood there, coolly appraising her.

"Can I help you?" Her voice was husky.

"Where's Jack?"

She arched a perfectly shaped brow. "And who are you?"

Taylor pushed her way into the apartment. "I'm his girl-friend. Jack!" she yelled.

The woman's manner was infuriatingly calm. "He can't hear you, Taylor." She drew her name out, mocking her. "My *husband* is in the shower."

Taylor spun around and glared at her. Suddenly, she couldn't breathe, and the room began to spin. She put a hand on the wall to steady herself while the woman continued to stare at her.

"I think you'd better leave."

Taylor ran past her without another word, got in her car, and gunned it. She cried the whole way back to BU.

The rest of the semester was torture. Visions of Jack with Dakota taunted Taylor every waking hour. She imagined them in bed. Her hands everywhere Taylor's should be. His lips on her mouth; their bodies intertwined. It was unbearable. The worst betrayal of all was that he hadn't even told her himself, just discarded her like a broken toy, unwanted and forgotten. It was beyond her comprehension. She tried to throw herself into her studies, but concentration eluded her, and she failed all her courses. When she returned home for summer break, her father was furious. The confrontation took her by surprise. She had never seen him so angry.

He stood in the marble foyer, waiting for her to come inside. In his hands was a letter.

"What were you thinking? Did you even attend one class? Do you realize you've put your entire future in jeopardy?"

She couldn't take her eyes off the vein throbbing in his forehead. Mumbling a quiet, "I'm sorry," she tried to walk past him.

He stepped in front of her, blocking her. "Not so fast, young lady. I'm not finished. Come in to my study. We are going to talk about this."

She walked behind him, with her head down, and slunk into the chair across from his desk.

"Taylor, look at me."

She lifted her head.

"One more semester! One more and you let yourself go from dean's list to this." His voice rose with each word. He threw the paper on the desk.

"I tried, Dad. I did the best I could. All I did was study."

"Thirty thousand dollars! I may as well have thrown it in the trash."

Taylor's eyes filled, and she turned her head.

His tone softened. "Taylor, listen to me. I'm sorry you're hurt, and I wish I could make it all better." His brows knit together in a scowl and he stood up. "Frankly, I'd like to kill him!" He slammed a fist onto the desk, and Taylor jumped. He walked over to her and put a hand on her shoulder, lifting her chin with his other hand so she would meet his eyes. His finger traced the hollow of her cheek.

"You've lost so much weight. My dear, you have to move on. Jack has his own life and you need to make yours, too. I've spoken to the dean and he's willing to call these incompletes and let you come back next semester."

"I don't—"

"Stop. You will go back and by the fall you'll be ready."

"What if I can't do it?" She felt like she'd never be herself again.

He pursed his lips. "You will." He looked up at a noise at the door, and Evelyn came in holding a brochure.

"Here." She pushed it into Taylor's hand. "Your father and I were thinking that a nice trip to Europe would do you a world of good. You can go to Italy, Spain, and then spend a month in Greece, on your mother's island."

At the mention of her mother, a fresh wave of grief enveloped her.

She handed the brochure back to Evelyn. "Thanks, but I don't think a trip to Europe is what I need right now."

The next day Taylor paid a visit to her old parish priest, Father Ted. She hadn't seen him since her mother's funeral, but he greeted her warmly, as if no time had passed.

"So wonderful to see you, Theophaneli." She hadn't been called her given name since her mother died. Her mother had been the only one who'd refused to use her nickname, Taylor.

She swallowed the lump in her throat as they hugged. He motioned for her to sit on the love seat in his office, and he took a seat facing her.

"I guess you're wondering why I'm here after all this time." Suddenly, she felt awkward and second-guessed her decision to come.

He raised his eyebrows and stroked his beard. "Why *are* you here?"

"Because everything's a mess, and I don't know what to do." She began to cry.

"It's okay, *pethi mou*, let it out," he said, handing her a box of tissues.

"It's the only place I could think to come." Her lip trembled. "I miss her so much, Father."

"She would be happy that you came here. She would tell you to turn to God."

She felt the bite of anger rising in her. "Where was God when she was being murdered?"

"Theophaneli, these are questions we wrestle with on this side of heaven. I don't know why she had to suffer that way, but God did not abandon her. He was with her. We aren't puppets. He gave us free will and that is a double-edged sword that the human race has been contending with since the fall of Adam and Eve."

She was only half listening. She had heard it all before. Man's fall. God's grace. Good and evil coexisting in this hell we call earth. She didn't like who she became when she contemplated such things, hated the cynicism that wound its way up from her core until she was thinking and saying things that sounded like someone else. She preferred to keep a lid on those feelings. So what *was* she doing here? She sighed. She was trying to get close to her mother the only way she knew how. Her mother had loved this church, spent countless Sundays worshipping here, and nights and weekends on committees to raise money for the various charities it supported. She had even gotten the priest involved in the shelter her own mother, Taylor's grandmother, had started a few blocks away. Agape House was a shelter for women and children that were victims of domestic abuse, and many of the church members volunteered there.

"Father, I was wondering if the foundation my mother started to support SOS Children's Village has already taken its annual trip to Greece."

The priest shook his head. "Not yet."

She knew what she had to do. "I want to go, too. Is there room?"

He smiled.

"Of course, *pethi mou*. We would love to have you."

Taylor felt movement as Beau nudged her, and she sat up, taking a few long, deep breaths. She would not lose this baby. No matter what Malcolm had done or what was waiting for them when they found Jeremy, she would protect this child.

Beau whined softly and rested his head on Taylor's stomach. She stroked his silky head. He looked up at her adoringly, his luminous brown eyes on her. He was her golden child, and she loved him without reservation. If only he were enough. Beau stretched out on the hardwood floor next to the bed to take up his watch over her and her unborn child. She closed her eyes and waited for the blessed escape of sleep.

CHAPTER TWENTY-TWO

I HAVE LEARNED MORE ABOUT CROSSE'S UPBRINGING, OF THE mother who did nothing to protect him from a father who delighted in tormenting and abusing him. Things changed when he turned fourteen.

He sits expressionless and tells his story. "My father couldn't keep a steady job. He worked odd jobs for the other families until they fired him for showing up drunk and belligerent. So he found a job for me, told me it was time I pulled my own weight. There was a man everyone knew only as 'the cripple in the big house.' He had plenty of live-in help, but he was looking for a companion, someone young to play chess with, to entertain him. The rest of the boys in the town were cretins, too busy drinking beer and driving around in their ridiculous jacked-up pickup trucks. Even though I was worth-less in my father's eyes, he couldn't deny my intelligence. It was his one source of pride. He offered me up to the man as a sacrificial lamb. It was a Saturday.

"My father said, 'Come here, boy. I got you some work.'

"'Where?'

"'Workin' for the cripple up on the hill.'

"'I hear he's a pervert.'

"My father lifted his shirt and scratched his skinny belly.

"Then he said, 'So what if he is? What's he gonna do, chase you? He's in a chair for crying out loud. So if he wants to cop a little feel, let him. What's the difference? You sure as hell ain't getting any action from the girls, ugly as you are.'

"I told him, 'I won't do it.'

"He took a long pull from his cigarette. The next thing I knew, the hot end was on my cheek. I jumped and put my hand up to my stinging flesh. That's when I made up my mind. I would figure out a way to get rid of him forever."

So that's where he got the small scar. His hand goes to his cheek and he unconsciously rubs it. He is on his feet and has a faraway look in his eyes I haven't seen before.

"That is all for today."

"Wait," I whisper.

He looks at me, and the faraway look fades. In its place is hatred, the fierceness of which terrifies me.

I force myself to speak despite the pounding of my heart warning me of my folly. "Your father used his power to control you, and you hated him for it. Don't you see that you're doing the same thing to me?"

He stares at me and says nothing for a full minute. Finally, he speaks. "I am disappointed in you. Did you think such a transparent attempt at pop psychology would work? I won't even dignify that with a response." He shakes his head.

"I'm just saying—"

He puts a hand up to silence me. "You're trying to analyze me. It won't work. I have a purpose, and it won't be thwarted. A shame, really, that your education had to be cut short. You could have been a part of the work here, but at least your contribution will live on. Come, I'll let you have a look at how the training progresses."

We sit in another of his screening rooms. There are ten beds in a row, all with white sheets and wool blankets. Next to each is an IV stand with a liquid-filled bag. My stomach tightens as my mind goes wild imagining what's in those bags. Dr. Strombill walks in, followed by a number of students from my fellowship group, as well as some students I've never seen before. They stand around the perimeter of the room and listen to him as he begins. He holds a stopwatch.

"Are they a new group?" I ask.

"They are recent law graduates, here for a special training program."

I am about to ask him more when Dr. Strombill speaks.

"It is all well and good to watch films and have discussions on the merits of euthanasia." He stops for emphasis. "But it is quite a different thing to experience the agony of disease as well as to make the difficult decision to end a life."

My leg twitches, as if it knows before I do that something terrible is about to happen. He begins to speak again. "In a few moments we will begin the experience. Medical students, please take a paper from the bowl on the left."

I see the student named Brian dip his hand in and pull out a small piece of paper. I wonder what it says. Dr. Strombill moves to the middle of the room and addresses them.

"Find the person who goes with the name on your paper. That will be your patient. Lead him or her to a bed and have them lie down."

He waits until they have all taken their places.

"You can now insert the IVs into your patients."

Brian raises a tentative hand. "May I ask what is in them?"

Dr. Strombill's bushy eyebrows shoot up. "You may indeed. It is diazepam. The students will take the powdered strychnine in those cups." He points. "The diazepam in the IV will counter the effects of the strychnine, so that we won't lose our patients. It will not eliminate the pain or convulsions, but it will keep them alive."

I gasp. In Brian's and the other medical students' faces I see the horror I'm feeling mirrored. It is very likely that they *will* lose some of the patients. I know what the law students do not—strychnine attacks the nervous system, and most people die of asphyxiation, but only after all their muscles spasm and contract into tight balls. The pain will be horrific. I begin to hate Dr. Strombill now, this man whom I have idolized. I turn to Damon.

"How can you allow this? It's inhumane."

"Ah, Maya, you are upset." His voice is soothing, and he puts a hand on my arm. "My dear, sometimes drastic measures are required to pave the way for the greater good. The patients here are the future lawmakers, judges, and politicians. They must experience the agony and pain we subject people to when we refuse to allow a way out of their suffering."

I shake my head and pull my arm from him.

"You're crazy. You don't have to inflict pain on someone for them to have empathy. Not everyone is a cold, nonfeeling monster like you."

"Quiet. You're missing it." He points toward the window.

Dr. Strombill resumes his instructions. "Doctors, you will administer the drug on my cue." He holds up a small cup containing the powder to be swallowed and addresses the "patients." "The onset of pain will be sudden and will continue for the next thirty-six hours, when you will be carefully monitored. There will be no relief for you unless you ask for euthanasia, in which case, you will be given morphine for the pain until the poison is out of your system. If you do not opt for euthanasia, you will be given no pain killer."

One of the law students raises his hand.

"I don't mean to be impertinent, but why would anyone not ask for euthanasia if it's just an experiment and would end the pain sooner?" His southern accent is strong. He smirks and looks around at his fellow students as if he's just solved the riddle of the enigma.

Dr. Strombill purses his full lips. "Because, Mr. Hamilton, five percent of the dosage pumps will give you enough morphine to stop your heart entirely."

They all stare at him.

Dr. Strombill sighs. "In other words, you might actually

be euthanized. We will see who can live with the pain and who cannot. It is time."

Brian hands his patient the cup. The woman's face is ashen, and she has wrapped her arms tightly around herself. Brian looks down at the floor, avoiding meeting her eyes, but I can see the terror in them. He tears open the alcohol patch and rubs it on her arm. He finds a vein and inserts the catheter.

Dr. Strombill clicks the stopwatch. The room is silent, and the air is thick with anticipation. The red hand on the stopwatch dances in circles, ticking off the minutes. A cry stabs through the silence. A second scream, then a third, and soon there is nothing but the agonizing sound of human misery. Then the twitching begins. Arms and legs jerk into the air in a grotesque ballet. I want to shut my eyes and cover my ears to drown it out. I sit helpless, watching as the poison progresses, and I cannot tear my eyes away as the men and women in the beds jackknife into contorted poses of agony.

My face is wet with tears. There is no decency in Damon— his father has killed it. What might he have been in different circumstances? If instead of abusing and torturing the little boy he once was, someone had loved and nurtured him? I think of the baby growing inside me and am filled with an intense agony I have never experienced before. What lies in store for him or her? Will my child become as consumed with evil as Damon? I cannot contemplate the possibility that my child will grow up to be like its father. *Dear God, help me. Help my child*, I pray silently. *Don't abandon us to this insanity.* Does God hear me? Or am I praying into a void?

"Take me back to my room. I can't watch anymore." Bile rises in my throat, and I put my hand up to my mouth reflexively.

He gives me a look of pure disgust. "I'm disappointed in you, Maya. You're not the scientist I thought."

"That's not science," I say.

I shudder to imagine what other experiments are being conducted here. What astounds me is the fact that no one in the room raised an objection. Not one person refused to participate in that horror show he calls science. Surely, I would have been different, would have walked away. Wouldn't I?

He is silent as we walk down the hallway to the elevator. I feel as though I've aged years in an hour. My heart is heavy, and I find it difficult to take a breath. When we reach my room, he doesn't follow me in, and I'm relieved to hear the click of the door behind me. I fall onto my bed and close my eyes, but the images haunt me. I can't erase the picture of those men and women in agony. I clutch a pillow to my chest and let go, my body racked with sobs, until I have no tears left.

Hours later, I refuse the tray of dinner brought to me— the nausea returns when I take one whiff of the beef stew. I think of our conversation about my parents, and I wonder again what Damon meant when he asked if I knew of any treasure from Greece. I try to remember anything, the stories my mother told of those days on the island, but nothing comes to mind. Maybe it's all a misunderstanding. I cannot bear to think of him going near my mama and papa.

I hear footsteps and brace myself. The door opens, and he walks in, carrying my tray.

"You have to eat, Maya. The baby needs the nutrition."

"How do you expect me to eat when everything you do and say makes me sick?"

A flash of anger crosses his face. "This is not open for debate."

I get up from the bed and face him.

"I don't like red meat. I've told you that before. You can force me to stay here, but you cannot force me to eat."

He arches one eyebrow. "The iron is necessary for you and the baby. Maybe I can't force you to eat. But I *can* have you restrained to a bed and hook you up to an IV."

I see red. Before I can stop myself, I rush toward him and rake his face with my nails. I feel something wet and am gratified to see it is his blood. His hand goes to his cheek and he looks at his fingers as he pulls it away again. He grabs both of my wrists and holds them tight while I struggle to free myself. I want to hurt him more.

He speaks, and the calmness of his voice chills me. "It's good to see you have a strong will. I made the right genetic choice for my child."

He still holds my wrists, and they begin to ache. I take a deep breath, trying to calm myself, as reason returns. "Please let go."

He studies me for a moment. "If you ever strike me again, I will have your hands amputated."

It is then that I vomit all over him.

CHAPTER TWENTY-THREE

EVENING HAD FALLEN, AND TAYLOR DOZED ON. JACK'S nerves were frayed—he had to do something. There was no way he would be responsible for another baby dying. He had to get Taylor checked out before they hit the road again. *Think, think.* He flipped open the burner cell and punched in eleven numbers. His contact answered on the first ring.

"Hit it."

"Craig. It's Logan. Thanks for the setup."

"What's up?"

"I need a doc—obstetrician. Can you send someone ASAP?"

There was a brief silence. "Soonest will be tomorrow. I'll see who I can find in the area."

"Thanks." Jack hung up and went into the bedroom to check on Taylor.

Her eyes fluttered open at the sound of his footsteps. "What am I going to do?"

"We're going to get you looked at to make sure everything is okay. I've called a buddy about getting a doctor here. Someone will be here tomorrow. In the meantime, you need to stay off your feet."

"Can you feed Beau and take him out?"

"Of course." He squatted to the dog's level. "Come here, buddy." Beau was so reluctant to leave Taylor's side, she had to coax him to go with Jack.

"It's okay. Go ahead," she said.

The golden retriever ambled over to Jack and looked back at Taylor.

Jack smiled. "Good boy. Let's let your mom get some rest, and you and I will take care of business."

After Beau finished and they were back in the cabin, Jack grabbed a Coors from the refrigerator and sat down. If it weren't for the fact that they were on the run, this could be a nice little slice of domesticity. How great it would be if they were here on a little getaway, if he hadn't screwed everything up.

He downed a couple more beers while sitting and remembering, and finally, when his thoughts started turning maudlin, he switched off the lamp and got up.

"Let's go check on her," he said to Beau and tiptoed into the bedroom. The light from the hallway was bright enough for him to see that she looked like she was sleeping. He was about to turn and go to his room when she spoke.

"What time is it?"

"Almost eleven. Sorry if I woke you."

"You didn't. I've been lying here for a while, just worrying."

He didn't know what to say and finally came up with, "You should probably try to rest."

She flicked on the lamp on the nightstand and sat up, propping a pillow behind her. "Can you sit with me for a little?"

He sat down in the chair by the bed before she could change her mind.

"I've been thinking about this baby, wondering how I'm going to keep it safe. I always thought that was a simple thing, you know, that the hard part was getting here, after all the treatments and disappointments, that once I was pregnant, the hardest part was done."

"It's going to be okay. The baby's going to be fine." A meaningless platitude. He didn't have anything else to offer.

She shook her head. "I'm not even talking about this." She gestured around the room. "I mean, just, in general. I was so busy trying to get pregnant, I never thought about the fact that this little life would be looking to me for all the answers. Poor thing."

"Poor nothing. That baby couldn't have a better mother. I've never known anyone as fiercely loyal to those she loves as you."

She shrugged. "Will it be enough? Will *I* be enough?"

He wanted to tell her that she didn't have to be, that he'd be with her to help her if she let him. Instead, he said simply, "You will be plenty."

She closed her eyes and yawned.

"I'll let you get some sleep," he whispered.

Without opening her eyes, she said, "Would you mind staying until I do?"

He'd do her one better. He'd sit in that chair all night and make sure nothing came near her or her baby.

o o o

When morning finally broke, Jack was still on edge. He hadn't slept well, worried through the night that Taylor might take a turn for the worse. Every time he started to doze off in the chair, he'd hear a sound escape her, and he'd startle awake, afraid she was losing the baby. When she awakened, she had agreed with Jack that she should stay off her feet until the doctor examined her.

Now, he glanced at his watch. A little after noon. *When was the doctor going to arrive?* He decided he should do something productive while he was waiting, so he took a seat at the kitchen table and studied the map Phillips had left for them. A knock at the door made him jump. He was pretty sure it was the doc, but just in case, he grabbed his gun and held it behind his back when he went to the door.

"Who's there?"

"The doctor you ordered."

Jack relaxed, tucked the gun behind the small of his back, between his jeans and shirt, and opened the door. The man had to lower his head to get through the doorway.

Jack gave him a quick once-over: close-cropped hair, ranger boots, hard-muscled arms. Something wasn't right. His blood ran cold when he realized the man didn't carry a doctor's bag.

"Who are you?" Jack asked. The man lunged toward him. Jack realized he'd made a mistake and went for the gun, but the man was quicker. He pulled Jack to him, wrapped his arm around his chest, and pressed a knife against his neck.

"Where is he hiding?" he asked.

"Who?" Jack asked, playing dumb.

The man tightened his grip. "Don't play games with me, Logan. You know damn well who. Where is Jeremy?"

Jack could barely speak with the viselike arm compressing his throat. He had to think. If he gave him nothing, he and Taylor would both be dead. *Think. Who was this and who did he work for?* Had Craig double-crossed him? No way. Jack held his hand out in surrender, and the man let go.

Jack coughed and tried to regain his voice.

"Have an idea. Don't know exactly," he croaked out.

"Tell me what you know," the man demanded.

Jack coughed again, stalling. Then he saw Beau peeking out from the bedroom from the corner of his eye.

"Give me a second. I'll get you what I have." Jack quickly assessed his surroundings, ready to grab the fork from the table when he heard a deep growl. Beau flew from the next room toward the man in a single lunge, sinking his teeth into the man's neck. The intruder toppled over immediately, and the knife fell from his hands to the floor. Jack didn't hesitate. He grabbed the gun from under his shirt and fired. He needed only one shot.

"Good boy!" He hugged the dog with relief.

Taylor rushed in. "What's going on?"

Jack looked from Taylor back to the dead man, splayed on his back just a few feet away.

"That's not the doctor, is it?" she whispered.

THE NETWORK   143

"No. Unfortunately no doctor's coming. Somebody double-crossed my friend. We've got to get out of here."

"What are we going to do with him?" If she was shocked by the sight of a dead man lying there, she didn't show it.

"Leave him. You're in no shape to lift him, and I can't do it alone." Jack had a feeling that his friend Craig would never be coming to the cabin again. He felt sick, worried that by reaching out to Craig to help, he might have put him in danger. But there was no time to think about it now.

"Throw your stuff into a bag and let's go. I'll put Beau in the truck now."

Just a few minutes later, they were driving away down the dirt road, when Taylor turned to Jack, her eyes wide. "Uh-oh."

"What is it?" he asked, his body tensing.

"The lights in the cabin just went on!"

CHAPTER TWENTY-FOUR

THE INSTITUTE, OCTOBER 1975

HAVE JUST FINISHED MY BREAKFAST OF BACON, EGGS, AND toast. I forced myself to eat despite the fact that I feel like my appetite will never return. I am tired all the time, and my breasts are sore.

The door to my room opens, and he comes in.

"It's a beautiful day outside. Why don't we take a walk?"

I jump at the chance to leave these four walls, even if it's with him.

He picks up one of the sweaters that he's provided. "Better bring this along. I don't want you catching a chill."

I bristle at his solicitous comments and the charade of civility he affects. I grab the sweater without a thank-you and follow him down the hallway. I can see from the windows that the sun is shining and for a moment my heart lifts. I've missed being outside, seeing the sky and the feeling of in-finiteness surrounding me, instead of the confinement of my room. We descend in the elevator and emerge on the ground floor. People are coming and going, but no one pays atten-tion to me, and everyone looks away from him deferentially. He opens the iron door, and I walk outside and feel the cool breeze kiss my face. I want to run and never stop. The season is beginning to change, and I pick a fallen maple leaf from the grass. It is bright orange, and it makes me want to cry. Every-thing around me is a symphony of color, and the beauty over-whelms me. My isolation has made me forget what a beautiful world it is.

We walk down a cleared path that leads to a large pond at least two miles in diameter. A paved walking trail encircles it, and I wonder if it's used by the students in phase two. This morning, though, we are the only ones walking.

He begins to speak, and I brace myself for another tale from his childhood.

"The best thing that ever happened to me was meeting Friedrich. He was a genius. He taught me how to play chess, what books to read, how to understand what was important and what was not."

I say nothing and file the information away, in case it can be useful to me later.

"When I was fifteen, we made the plan. It was time for me to go and live with him. Late one night, after my father had finished his bottle of bourbon, I lit the match that would burn that ramshackle hovel to the ground. I barricaded his bedroom door shut. I superglued the windows so he couldn't push them open and let the smoke out. Thanks to his paranoia, he'd had bars put on them years before, so there was no way he could climb out. Then, I stayed outside and listened for his screams. What music they were to my ears. I knocked on the window. He turned and looked at me, wide-eyed and crazed. 'Help me, you worthless punk,' he said, and I raised my middle finger, smiled and watched as the flames licked at his filthy pajamas. He cursed me as the fire engulfed him. Once I knew he was beyond saving, I left. They never connected me to it. The house had burned to nothing, and they assumed it was an accidental fire."

"Wasn't there an investigation? Didn't they look for you?"

He sneers. "We were trash. Dirt-poor, lowest on the rung in a Podunk town with crooked cops and small-minded people."

"Didn't anyone see you living in the house on the hill?"

He waves his hand dismissively. "Are you being deliberately obtuse? The point of the story has nothing to do with how I escaped. But I'll satisfy your curiosity. We moved."

I shiver in spite of myself and avert my eyes. I can't deny that I am glad he escaped from his father, but it shocks me that I'm not more horrified that he did this. He has drawn me into his past, and I feel myself rooting for his escape, angry at this abusive monster that has so warped him. But even as the thought crosses my mind, it occurs to me that he will never escape his father. And then I shudder when I consider the fact that he was able to stand, watching and unmoved to mercy knowing his father was inside burning. What hope do I dare have if he was capable of such an act when he was still a child?

His father has turned him into a sadistic murderer. Could he have been saved if Friedrich had been different?

We walk in silence for the rest of the time, and I am surprised by how tired I am. When we return to my room, I thank him, but only because I hope that we will do this again.

He turns to leave when I ask, "Why was Friedrich in a wheelchair?"

He turns back and answers. "He was diagnosed with Parkinson's disease after the war, when he was in his sixties. Only a few years before I met him, but by then it had progressed aggressively."

"Did they try Levodopa?"

"Yes, of course. It worked for a while, then stopped. They classified him as a nonresponder."

"Is he still alive?"

His lips part in a smile. "Why don't you see for yourself?" He looks above my head, to somewhere on the wall, and nods. I follow his line of sight and squint. It is then that I see it—a small hole. My face is hot, and I glare at him.

"You've been spying on me all this time?" The fact that someone has been watching while I take my clothes off, sleep, talk to myself—it's unthinkable. "Have you enjoyed seeing me naked, you pervert?" I ask him.

He laughs again. "I'm no pervert, Maya. No one cares about seeing your body, especially as it grows fat. We're just making sure you don't try to hurt yourself or the baby."

The blood rushes to my head, and I turn away from him and walk to the window so he can't see the tears running down my face.

Ten minutes later, the door opens, and I turn around. Steel-blue eyes lock onto mine. The white hair is receding and reveals a still-smooth forehead for a man who looks like someone's grandfather. His features are unremarkable; in fact, his face looks rather benign. His thin lips are set in a straight line, and he looks at me as if he knows me. When he crosses the threshold, I see he holds a cane in his left hand. It is a struggle for him to walk.

Damon runs to him, placing a hand on his back and helping him to a chair.

"Father, can I get you some water?"

He waves him off, impatient with the fussing, and lands with a thud in the chair.

"Dr. Papakalos, it is a pleasure to finally make your acquaintance."

The German accent is thick. "You're Friedrich?" I ask.

A look of disdain appears, and he looks up at Damon, shaking his head.

"The youth today—no respect." His eyes settle on me. "You must call me Dr. Dunst."

He spits the words at me, and I recoil. I see it now in his eyes—the same predatory look that Damon has. They may not be related by blood, but they are the same. He looks at me, expectantly, and I say nothing, watching the fury build in his eyes.

Dunst leans back in the chair, pulls a silver case from his suit pocket, and extracts a cigarette. His hand shakes as he fumbles trying to ignite his lighter. After several failed attempts, it spits out a flame. He takes a long pull and blows smoke rings. I cannot stop looking at his mouth making the small *o*'s. As he holds the cigarette in the air, my eyes are drawn to a purplish discoloration on his skin.

"I have met your parents," he says finally.

My heart skips a beat. "When?"

He arches a white eyebrow. "Before you were born, back when I was stationed on their island."

"During the war?" I ask.

"When else?"

It dawns on me with sickening certainty that this man before me must be a Nazi. Can this very ordinary, frail old man be one of the legion of fiends responsible for the anguish and slaughter of millions?

"You are a Nazi?" I whisper.

He looks at me as if I were a cockroach under his foot. "I am an American citizen, a respected scientist. Your country says so." He laughs.

"But you were part of the Nazi regime that occupied my parents' island?" I know it must be true, but I need to hear it from his lips.

He shrugs. "I was not there on holiday." He pulls a bottle of eye drops from his pocket, leans his head back, and squirts two drops into each eye. A thought occurs to me, and I continue to watch him.

Damon moves a chair next to his and sits.

"Did your mother talk about bringing something of value with her to America? Of hiding a treasure?" Dunst asks.

Again, I search my mind for any memory, but I still come up blank. I shake my head.

"She never talked about some coins, silver pieces?" he persists.

They are both staring at me with an intensity that makes my skin crawl.

"My mother doesn't like to talk about those days. The occupation was hard on them. The Germans"—I give Dunst a pointed look—"were cruel. They took whatever they wanted with no regard to anyone or their feelings. All the islanders were starving while they ate like pigs and—"

"Quiet." Damon's command slices through the air, and I feel the anger emanating from him. Dunst seems unaffected by my outburst. I suppose he is used to the hatred of others.

Dunst sneers at Damon. "Don't waste your energy. Her opinion matters not." Then he leans forward and enunciates very slowly. "Think hard, Maya. Try to remember where your mother might have put them."

"How do you expect me to tell you anything if I don't know what they are?" This provokes a reaction. I am lying, though. I have no knowledge of anything at all related to treasures or silver from Greece. But I want to know what they are so desperate to find.

They exchange another look, and Dunst nods his head so slightly I wouldn't have seen it if I hadn't been looking.

Damon turns to me and says, "The thirty silver pieces Judas received for betraying Jesus."

CHAPTER TWENTY-FIVE

Taylor grabbed Jack's arm. "Someone's back at the cabin!"

Jack swore. He had to gather his thoughts.

"He must have had a partner. This is bad. They'll use that man's death to their advantage."

"What do you mean?"

Jack looked at her.

"My fingerprints are all over that cabin and so are yours. Since we got away, they'll make it look like I'm a murderer and a kidnapper." He hit his hand hard on the steering wheel. "I don't understand how they found us. It's my friend Craig's cabin, and he's the only person who should have known we were there. I just tried calling him again before we left, but there was no answer. If he was alive, he would have answered my call."

"If Malcolm knew about the cabin, maybe whoever killed him did, too," Taylor said.

Jack bit his lip. "Maybe. The guy said he was the doctor I'd asked for. So somehow he knew about the conversation I had with Craig."

"Could Craig's phone have been tapped?"

"Doubtful. It's a burner. And no one should have been able to trace the call—we didn't talk long enough."

He had a sinking feeling he knew what had happened. "Someone must have tapped into my conversation with Craig. His house may have been wired without his knowledge. Whoever we're up against must have one massive intelligence network. If they've investigated my background, they'd know Craig and I worked together in Colombia. After they heard the details, they could have gotten to him before he had a chance to call a real doctor."

"This is unreal. Who are these people?"

"I wish I knew. Damn it! I know in my gut that they killed him. He would never betray me. We can't reach out to anyone, Taylor. Not your dad. None of my friends. I won't be responsible for putting anyone else in harm's way."

They had even less time now. By tomorrow morning Jack's face would be all over every news station, every paper, every media outlet. He might even make the FBI top ten. If they arrested him, Taylor would be on her own—an easy target. His thoughts turned back to Taylor.

"How are you feeling? Any more spotting?" he asked, worry suddenly flooding him.

She shook her head. "No, not since yesterday morning. I'm hoping it was a fluke."

"I wish I could take you to the doctor, but we can't take a chance right now of being found."

He felt so impotent. He'd promised Malcolm he would keep her safe. How was he supposed to do that when he couldn't even make sure she received proper medical care?

"Jack?"

"Yeah?"

She cleared her throat. "What happened with the baby?"

He felt the color rise to his cheeks, and he tightened his grip on the wheel.

She pressed on. "I read about it and followed the trial. Did you have any idea she was capable of something like that?"

He sighed. "Things were bad for a long time. I tried to help her, but she didn't want any help. All she wanted was an audience for her suffering. I was ready to leave her when she told me she was pregnant, and then I couldn't bear the thought of leaving a child alone in her care. She was five months along by the time she told me. She was so thin I couldn't even tell."

"Did you tell her how you felt?"

"She didn't care how anyone else felt. I don't think she even wanted kids. It was just another way for her to manipulate me."

"What do you mean?"

He didn't want to rehash it all, but she was looking at him with that expression, the one that said *you can tell me anything*.

"She refused to take her prenatal vitamins. Once I came home and found her doing a line of coke."

"What? That's horrible. I can't imagine. Couldn't you talk some sense into her?"

"I tried. It backfired. She held that baby hostage, and I had no choice but to go along."

"Tell me the rest," Taylor whispered.

Jack shook his head. "I can't talk about it, Taylor. Please." Jack was sorry for what he'd put Taylor through, but it was a long time ago. She had no right to go dredging up memories that he wanted to keep buried.

CHAPTER TWENTY-SIX

THE INSTITUTE, OCTOBER 1975

M Y MOUTH DROPS OPEN.

"You're serious?"

"This is a waste of time. The girl knows nothing." Dunst leans on his cane and struggles to a standing position. As he stands, his eyes roll back in his head, and he faints. Damon catches him just before he hits the floor.

"How long has that been happening?"

Damon lays him on my bed and pushes the button next to it to call for help.

He narrows his eyes at me. "Why do you care?"

"I think he's been misdiagnosed."

"What are you talking about?" He whips around and looks at me.

Before I can answer, the door opens, and a large man pushes a wheelchair in. Dunst has started to rouse and is mumbling. Damon helps him to a sitting position, where he falls back one more time until, finally, he begins to stabilize. They settle him into the chair and wheel him out. He looks straight ahead, completely ignoring my presence, embarrassed, I assume, by his show of weakness.

Damon escorts him to the hallway and I hear the murmur of conversation. A few minutes later he returns.

"What do you mean you think he was misdiagnosed?"

I see hope in his eyes, an expectation perhaps of good news. What I have to tell him is not good—not for him or Dunst—but I feel no sympathy for either of them.

"The dry eyes, the skin discoloration, fainting upon sitting up or standing—they are symptoms of something more. I believe he has multiple system atrophy, MSA. It mimics Parkinson's but is much more aggressive and debilitating."

He rushes toward me, his hands poised to strike me, and I shrink back.

"You're wrong." He pulls back suddenly and appraises me as if seeing me for the first time. His voice is calmer now. "Why didn't his neurologist figure it out?"

"When was he diagnosed?"

"Nineteen fifty-seven."

"MSA wasn't fully understood until 1969. And it looks much the same as Parkinson's in the beginning. The fact that he stopped responding to Levodopa is a red flag. Did he continue to see his neurologist?"

Damon shakes his head, looking at the floor.

"When the medicine stopped working, he went a few more times, but there was nothing else they could do. He said it was a waste of time."

"One thing I don't understand, though, is how he's walking. If he's had the disease for almost twenty years, he should be completely bedridden by now."

"It has to do with the coins," he says.

"What?"

"During the war, Friedrich was part of a unit that specialized in religious relics. He was Himmler's second-in-command and was responsible for finding artifacts and relics for the cause, and he came across the set of coins."

I shudder. The fact that Dunst worked directly for Himmler chills me to the bone. "What does that have to do with his health?"

"The coins have . . . special properties." He walks over to the table and pours a glass of water for himself. "Friedrich has been trying to find them for over thirty years. In the hands of someone who knows how to use them, they are powerful indeed. Friedrich dispatched a team to search for them after the war. He found ten, and that was enough to heal him. For a while."

The manner in which he conveys this information is shockingly banal, as if the story is commonplace. "How could *coins* heal him?"

He ignores my question, sits down, and crosses his leg, leaning back into the leather chair and clasping his hands together.

"I will get to that. He found out about them through his work with the Ahnenerbe."

"The Ahnenerbe?"

"The Ancestral Heritage Research and Teaching Society. It's a group Himmler started. Friedrich led the charge in searching for relics in Romania and Greece. Before that, he had worked in their top-secret section, the Institute for Scientific Research for Military Purposes, doing scientific experimentation. But he found the occult more compelling. When he learned about the coins, he knew he had to have them."

"Why are the coins so important?" I ask.

"Judas ended up regretting his actions after he betrayed Jesus. When he saw that they were going to put Jesus to death, he went back to the chief priests, returned the thirty silver pieces, and confessed his sins, but it was too late. So he hanged himself." He shrugs. "The chief priests decided they couldn't keep the money in the treasury, as it was blood money. Instead, they used them to buy the potter's field—a burial place for strangers—called the Field of Blood to this day."

"So the man who sold the field to them took possession of the coins. What happened to them after that?"

"According to legend, he didn't want to keep the coins, so he threw them into a fountain in Solomon's temple. They were taken from there and paid to the guards stationed at Jesus's tomb. When Mary Magdalene came to the tomb to tend to Jesus's body, they were in such shock that he was gone that they gave the coins to her. Mary then handed them over to Peter, who kept ten and gave ten to Matthew and ten to John."

"The same Saint John who wrote the Gospel?"

He nods. "Yes. But then that John gave them to John of Patmos, the author of Revelation. During the war, when Friedrich was stationed on the island, he searched the cave where Saint John had lived and ordered an archaeological dig of the area around it, but they couldn't find the coins. He found the ten that Peter hid while he was in Ephesus, but nothing on Patmos. Their healing power got Friedrich out of his wheelchair, but he knew it wouldn't last forever. He suspected that someone on the island was hiding them. He went from house to house with the soldiers, but his search was interrupted by the end of the war."

"Where are the other ten?" I ask. "The ones Peter gave to Matthew." It feels surreal to be sitting here talking about the saints from the Bible as though they are people I know.

His face clouds over. "They are supposed to be in Jerusalem. We are still searching, and we *will* find them. But he needs more time. We know your parents have ten. That will be enough to help him for now."

"How can you know that my parents have them?" This seems utterly preposterous to me.

"I went back on Friedrich's behalf, when I was eighteen. Took a tour of the monastery and visited the site where Friedrich believed one of the islanders may have buried them after the war was over. It was obvious that it had been disturbed, that someone took them. I talked to the locals, got a list of all the families who had left. I've spent the past ten years interviewing them. I found out something very interesting at the last stop."

He doesn't wait for me to say anything.

"I found out that your mother was the sister of one of the monks at Saint John's monastery, and that your uncle had been entrusted with guarding the coins. I am told he gave them to her to take to America."

It can't be true, I think. *My parents are just regular people.*

"I have been watching them, and so I was delighted when you decided to pursue the fellowship we offered you."

"You lured me here because of this connection?" I sputter. "I know nothing of these coins. They have nothing to do with me."

"On the contrary, Maya. You have history in your blood. You are related to one of the monks in service of Saint John. My child will have even more power when he comes of age and holds those silver pieces. He will rule the new order."

"I hope you never get your hands on any of them. And just so you know, Friedrich's decline will be swift and brutal. He won't have the ability to rule anything, not even his own body."

He lunges toward me, his hand coming so fast that I feel the slap before I see it. The sting is so sharp; I feel my cheek vibrating. But I don't regret speaking up. The look of anguish my words have caused him was worth it.

He is on his feet within seconds, striding to the door. "What a pity for the world that your keen diagnostic talents will die along with you," he throws over his shoulder as he leaves.

CHAPTER TWENTY-SEVEN

Brody Hamilton held a chair for Rita Avery. Even though Rita knew him well, and there was no need for beating around the bush, he wanted to have a little fun. He smiled at her.

"Well, my dear. What have you got for me today? What new deceit awaits the good people of this country?"

"Now, Senator, that's not fair. I'm just trying to make sure my clients stay solvent so that we can continue to enjoy the fruits of their labor." She paused and pulled a plastic container from her purse, took out a pill, and swallowed it. "Case in point— without these antibiotics, I'd be home in bed right now."

He raised an eyebrow.

She continued. "We would like to remove the contraindications handed out with medicine. It's a huge waste of money—no one reads them anyway. Not to mention that it's ecologically irresponsible, having to kill all those trees for every prescription in the country. Instead we want to put a web address on the bottle's label where customers can look them up."

It started as a chuckle, but within seconds, he was doubled over laughing. "Ecologically irresponsible? Oh, my dear. You have hit a new low."

She waited for him to finish.

"Ah." He sighed. "I needed that laugh." He became serious again as he spoke. "Well, I'm just a small-town country boy, but I have to wonder, what about folks who don't have a computer? You know, the majority of your market, those over seventy-five?"

Her shiny, glossed lips parted in a fawning smile. "There will also be the option to request the literature from the pharmacist."

Sipping his Johnnie Walker Blue, he rubbed his chin with his free hand. "Just a suggestion, but maybe you ought to lead with that. Tone down the altruism. Ain't nobody gonna believe the drug pushers give a whit about the planet. That dog won't hunt. Make it about efficiency. Cost savings passed down to the customers. Have it to me by the end of the week."

She nodded in agreement. "Thank you, Senator."

He fidgeted with his fountain pen after she left. It would be easy to get this one through. She was right: no one did read the inserts. This bill was only the beginning. The framing for what was to come later. One step at a time, as his grandma used to say. Everything that happens starts one step at a time.

CHAPTER TWENTY-EIGHT

S THEY DROVE IN THE DARKNESS, MORE MEMORIES RUSHED back to Taylor, moments she hadn't let herself relive in ages. Jack was inextricably entwined with her past. Some of her most cherished memories of childhood included him. Of course, it wasn't all good. There were the times Jack had come running to her house, the pain fresh in his eyes, after a shouting match with his father when he'd forgotten a chore or hadn't completed it to his dad's standards. She'd wanted to make it all better for him, make him feel loved. When they were still little, she'd grab his hand and pull him outside; then they'd jump on their bikes and race to the park, pedaling as fast as they could. That always got his mind off things. When they were finished, her mother would make them chocolate milkshakes, and they'd drink them and giggle, as if nothing were wrong.

As he got older, the stakes increased. No matter what he did, it was never enough for his father. Jack had to go out for the varsity football team, make the honor roll, and hustle to get more lawns mowed or driveways shoveled than anyone. But the thing that had infuriated Jack the most was his father's insistence on Jack being an altar boy and pushing him toward the priesthood. As the only son of a large Catholic family of five girls and him, his parents pinned all their hopes on Jack becoming a man of the cloth. What they didn't realize was that he'd given up on the church long before he'd graduated from high school. He confessed to Taylor that he'd lost faith in a religion that spat out rules with no regard to how they affected its members. He'd watched his mother battle depression his entire life and refuse to get any help. Her friends and her priest told her to pray more, to give her problems to God. It wasn't until years later that Taylor realized it was postpartum depression made worse by her almost constant state of pregnancy.

When he'd gotten an acceptance letter from Columbia University, his sisters and Taylor had been the only ones cheering for him. If it hadn't been for the football scholarship, she doubted he would have been able to go, despite the fact that his father's grocery store chain had grown to include chains in ten states, and they could easily have afforded it.

She remembered that his father had made a spur-of-the-moment trip to Jack's apartment in New York the weekend before he died. But they hadn't talked about it at the funeral— she'd known better than to press him. She'd meant to draw it out gradually, over the months following, but never got the chance. He'd met Dakota soon after.

"Jack?"

"Hmm?"

"That weekend when your father visited you in New York . . . I've always wondered, did you resolve things with him?"

He gave her a quick glance, then his eyes went back to the road. "It's strange. But I think maybe he knew, somehow, that he was on borrowed time. You know, he never once came to see me at school, except for graduation of course. Then out of the blue he calls and says he wants to come see my apartment."

Taylor waited for him to go on.

He sighed. "I asked if he wanted to see the sights. But no, he said, he just wanted to spend some time with me. We went to McSorley's and threw back some beers. He told me he was proud of me." He cleared his throat. "That's the first time I ever heard him say that."

"That must have made you happy."

Jack shook his head. "It pissed me off. Why did he have to wait twenty-four years to tell me? All my life, I was never good enough, and then suddenly he's proud of me? We spent the rest of the night talking sports."

She was sorry to hear it, but she supposed it was unrealistic to expect one weekend to undo years of strife. "He loved you, Jack. In his own way. He did the best he could."

"Sure." He paused. "There *was* something else."

"What?"

"He told me that I'd made the right choice with you. That you were the real deal and to never let you go."

She felt like all the air had been sucked out of her lungs. "He—"

Jack tapped the steering wheel. "Guess it's a good thing he didn't live long enough to see that I'd disappointed him once again."

CHAPTER TWENTY-NINE

THE INSTITUTE, OCTOBER 1975

I AM READING WHEN THE DOOR OPENS AND CROSSE WALKS in. He gets right to the point.

"Any message you'd like me to take to your parents?"

I feel my blood turn to ice. "No" is all I can manage. He can't go near them. Please let him only be taunting me.

"Since you don't have any useful information, I have no choice but to go to the source."

I scramble to come up with a solution.

"Let me talk to them. They'll tell me. I can get the coins for you and then you can let me go."

He laughs at me. "You have no bargaining chips, Maya. Once they know I have you here, they'll hand the coins over, I'm quite sure."

My parents were expecting me home a month ago. I wonder if they believe the lies they have been told by Damon's
people. That I failed out of the fellowship and took off to parts
unknown. They may believe that I was ashamed enough not
to return to them. It's a feasible cover story, considering how
I've always defined myself by my accomplishments. They must
be so hurt. But my sister will know better. She knows I would
never do that to her. I know with certainty that she is searching for me.

I think back to the last Sunday we were all together.
Mama always made a big dinner, and I joined them whenever
I could. As soon as she and Papa would return from church,
my mother would cook—homemade meals full of calories and
love. Over dinner she would tell me about the priest's sermon.
She was always trying to talk me into going back to church
with them, but I refused. How many times did my mother
look at me, tilt her head, and cluck her tongue? *Maya, my girl,
God loves you. Don't you know he loves you?* After dinner, we'd
linger, sipping our coffee and sampling the assortment of pas-
tries sitting in the middle of the table on a large platter. I close
my eyes and will myself there, to that table I took for granted,
where my papa's smiles warmed me, and my mama's hand fed
me. What I would give for one more dinner.

"I suppose you think your parents are wonderful, don't
you?" His voice brings me crashing back to the present.

I don't know whether he expects an answer or not.

"Well, Maya? Are they? Are they wonderful?"

"They're good parents," I stammer. "We never wanted for
anything. They did their best to provide good futures for us."

I become emboldened. "They sacrificed to pay for medical school for me and my sister." I sit up straighter. "Yes, they're great parents."

He laughs. A soft, mirthless laugh. "You are a fool if you believe that. Sacrificed? Nonsense. You fed their egos, fulfilled *their* purpose in your life. Two doctors in the family. How admirable. What good parents. They didn't do it out of love for you. No, they did it purely for bragging rights."

I shake my head, lift my hands, and cover my ears. He's wrong. My parents love me with all their hearts, and I love them. But I may never get to tell them that again. I will not allow him to steal my past. To pervert my memories, as well as trying to claim my future. I haven't given up on getting out of here, though. I've been studying everyone who comes in and out of my room. Striking up small talk, trying to identify if there's anyone I can convince to help me escape. There doesn't seem to be a way, yet there must be. I only have a few months to figure it out. Once my baby comes, I am certain he will kill me.

He stands up. "Cover your ears all you like. The fact remains: no one loves anyone but themselves. The sooner you accept that fact, the sooner you'll learn not to be taken advantage of."

"Not taken advantage of?" I explode. "I'm a prisoner. I've lost everything. My freedom—even the right to my own body. You dare to lecture me on how to live? What choices are left to me now?"

He advances until he is towering over me. I recoil and slide back.

"Why are you complaining? You always wanted to be the best. You beat out all your fellow female students for the privilege of bearing my heir. You should pat yourself on the back that you were selected. But remember, pride goes before destruction and a haughty spirit before a fall." He laughs again. "Imagine that: *me*, quoting from the Bible."

CHAPTER THIRTY

J ACK PULLED THE CAR INTO THE PARKING LOT OF A SMALL highway motel and turned the ignition off. Taylor glanced at Jack's hand as he pulled out the keys and remembered his touch. He had strong hands. They were nice hands, she thought, not too big but still masculine. They were hands you could depend on. Or they were once. *Forget about his hands.* What was wrong with her? She sighed.

He put on dark sunglasses and went to the front office. Minutes later he returned with a room key, and she looked up as he got back in the car.

"Any problems?"

"Nope. The guy hardly looked at me. I gave him an extra twenty to let us bring in Beau."

"Good thinking."

In the room, Taylor threw her bag on the bed and sorted the dishes and food they had picked up for the dog.

"Tomorrow we'll go to the library and find the address. This time tomorrow night we could be talking to Jeremy," Jack said.

Taylor nodded at him absentmindedly while she fed Beau.

"Any luck on tracking down the pharma company involved with the vaccine?" he asked.

"No, but I did some digging on Brody Hamilton and he *has* sponsored a number of bills relating to a company called Alpha Pharmaceuticals, mostly lessening of regulations, like labeling and side effect warnings," Taylor answered. She pursed her lips. "Wouldn't surprise me if they're the ones developing the vaccine."

"Could you find any connection between them and the latest bill? Or the vaccine?"

She shook her. "Not yet."

"Hopefully Jeremy can shed some light on it," he said.

"We'll know soon enough."

She went into the bathroom to get ready for bed.

"Taylor! Come here!"

She ran out. "What's wrong?"

He pointed to the television screen. "Guess who's on the news again."

She listened, horrified, as the anchor spoke.

"Police are still looking for Senator Phillips's widow, Taylor Phillips, who went missing the same day her husband was found dead on an overseas diving trip last week. It's now been confirmed that she's been kidnapped by Jack Logan, an investigative reporter who spent some time as a mercenary. A motive is unknown at this point. He's believed to be armed and dangerous." Jack's picture flashed on the screen.

"Mercenary? What is she talking about?" Taylor asked.

He swore. "They're making it up. I was a bodyguard. This is bullshit!"

"Why would they say that, then?"

He sighed. "Taylor, come on. If I was a mercenary, would I be writing articles about civil liberties and living in a tiny apartment in New York? I went there after Dakota . . . did what she did. I was protecting people, not killing them."

Taylor had to admit, she didn't see him as a killer, but she couldn't think straight anymore.

"I'm beat. Why don't we get some sleep?" she said, climbing into the bed closest to the wall.

Beau hopped up and nestled by her side. Her mind was racing. A part of her wanted to call out to Jack, to feel his arms around her and relax in his comforting embrace. It would be so nice to just pretend everything was good between them. She shifted again, restless. *Stop thinking ridiculous thoughts.* She felt disloyal to Malcolm, then a quick surge of anger coursed through her when she remembered she didn't owe him anything. She didn't even know who he really was. She still didn't understand how she could have been so easily deceived.

Watching as Jack bolted the door and pushed a chair against it for good measure, she noticed how the T-shirt he was wearing showed off his muscled back and trim waist. The stirrings of desire fluttered as she remembered the feel of those strong arms. She flipped over to face the wall, her back to him, and pulled the covers up to her chin.

When he got into the other bed and turned the light off, she closed her eyes, but sleep wouldn't come. She kicked her leg out from under the sheet, trying to find a comfortable position.

"You still awake?" Jack whispered.

"Yeah."

"Did you ever have any idea about Malcolm? Any suspicions that something was off?"

"Of course not. Some journalist, huh?"

"It's not your fault. People aren't always what they seem, and we want to see the best in those we care about."

They had both married frauds, she realized. But surely, there had to have been more to her marriage than Malcolm's deception. She couldn't believe that everything between them had been a lie. No one could be that good an actor. Lying there in the dark, it felt comforting, unburdening, to talk about it.

"I met him the night I returned from a trip to Greece. My father had invited him to dinner."

"Were they friends?"

"My father supported his campaign for Senate. I'd heard about him, but it was the first time I'd ever met him. At first, I wasn't interested, thought he was too much older than me. When you're in your twenties, a ten-year age difference seems like a lot. And you know how I've always felt about those Washington-power types. With Dad's position at the paper there was always some blowhard politician or another over for dinner. But Malcolm was different. When he told me that he'd lost both his parents when he was a teenager, it made me feel close to him."

"I can see that. What you went through, losing your mom—not many people get what that does to you."

She thought back to the days following her mother's funeral, after everyone had gone back to normal and expected her to do the same. Everyone except Jack. He'd been by her side, not asking anything of her, instead offering a steady and consistent comfort.

"I'll never forget how you helped me through it. Looking back, I don't know how you stood it."

"What do you mean?"

"All those nights when I snuck next door to your house and crawled in your room, and you held me while I sobbed. That went on for months. It had to get old."

She heard him shift in his bed. "It never got old. But it broke my heart."

The raw pain of that memory took her by surprise, and she brushed a tear from her cheek. All of a sudden, she didn't want to talk anymore. "Good night."

"Taylor . . . Good night."

She tried to empty her mind and fall asleep, but memories bombarded her, playing like a video reel. Images of Jack faded and were replaced by Malcolm. After Jack, it had felt impossible for her to trust again. The hard shell she'd built around her heart had served her well. She had gotten her career on track, she was doing work she loved, and she was happy. When she finally opened her heart again, she'd believed she had found someone who would never hurt her. The bond she and Malcolm had shared over the tragedies they had suffered, and then their ardent desire to create their own family, had eradicated any remaining reservations she'd had about opening herself up again. Malcolm's betrayal wasn't just hurtful, though—it had caused her to lose faith in herself. If both times she'd fallen in love she'd been deceived, what did that say about her? Maybe there was some part of her that sought men who were incapable of true intimacy. Masks. Everyone wore one. She was done being a fool. She would take nothing and no one at face value ever again.

CHAPTER THIRTY-ONE

THE INSTITUTE, NOVEMBER 1975

H E HASN'T COME FOR THREE DAYS NOW. I AM GOING CRAZY with worry, imagining all sorts of scenarios involving my parents. Desperation has driven me to prayer. If there's any chance that someone up there can hear me, I have to try. I hope with all my heart that they give him what he wants, and he doesn't hurt them. But I don't really believe that's possible. I think of a story my mother used to tell me when I was a little girl. It was about three men in Babylon who refused to worship a gold image made by the king because they would worship only their god. They were thrown into a fiery furnace so hot that it burned even the soldiers who threw them in. The next morning, the men were all still alive, not a hair on their heads singed. The king was astounded, promoted them to better jobs, and ordered everyone in the land to worship their god. I remember asking my mother why they didn't just pretend to worship the image, just say something to save themselves. She told me that true faith requires sacrifice, and that to love our lives more than we love God is not serving him but ourselves. So I asked if God would always step in and rescue his people like that. She hugged me, put her hand on my face, and said that, no, not always in this life, but yes, always in the next.

My door opens, and it's him. I hold my breath, dreading what he has to say. His eyes are stormy, and his face looks tense. He slams the door behind him and stares at me.

I stand and put one hand on the table behind me, steeling myself for whatever he is going to say. He just looks at me, until finally I can't stand it anymore.

"What happened? Did you see my parents? What did you do?"

"Yes, I saw them. You look like your mother."

"Please!" I shout. "Just tell me. Are they alive?"

"They were when I left them."

"What do you mean?"

He sits.

"Patience, Maya. I was waiting for them when they returned from church. They're very polite. When I mentioned I knew you, they let me right in. Gave me coffee and some delicious Greek pastry." He taps his index finger against his chin. "Thiples, I think they're called?"

I want to scream. I tap my foot and wait for him to get on with it.

"I told them I'd worked with you here. They're quite heartbroken that they haven't heard from you."

"Stop toying with me." I can't stop the tears now.

"Indeed. Well, I got around to the real purpose of my visit. When I asked about the silver pieces, it was obvious by their reactions that they knew exactly what I was talking about."

I hold my breath, waiting for him to continue.

"Your father was the first to figure out that I wasn't just someone who knew you. He demanded that I return you to them. He's a brave man."

"You're loathsome."

His eyes narrow. "Do you want to hear the rest or not?"

"Go on."

"I promised I would let you go if they told me where they hid the coins. Even told them they have a grandchild on the way. That garnered a mixed reaction." He looks at me with a triumphant expression. "You should have believed me when I told you they didn't really love you." He pauses for effect. "They said no."

All the breath whooshes from me.

"They said no?" I whisper.

"Oh, they blabbered on, said how much they loved you, but they had a sacred trust in guarding the coins. They couldn't betray it or betray God. The fools."

I sit up straighter. "They are not fools. They knew you wouldn't let me go. You're the fool if you think you can trick them so easily." I want to wound his pride, to say anything to wipe that smirk off his face.

He arches an eyebrow. "It doesn't matter. We'll get it out of them. They could have done it the easy way."

"What are you planning to do?"

He stands. "It's done. Friedrich's men are interrogating them. They're extremely skilled in getting information."

I clutch my chest as a knifelike pain sears me. "You're torturing them?"

He tilts his head. "Well, *I'm* not."

"You monster!" I pick up the glass pitcher from the table and throw it at him, narrowly missing his head. It crashes to the floor.

He shakes his head, steps over the broken pieces, and opens the door.

"I'll send someone in to clean this up." And he leaves.

I walk over to the mess and begin to attend to it myself. Making sure my back is to the camera, I take the largest jagged piece and slide it into my pants pocket.

CHAPTER THIRTY-TWO

DAKOTA SAT IN THE COMMON ROOM OF BELLEVUE STARING straight ahead, missing nothing. The chaos surrounding her made her want to scream, but she swallowed her rage and remained silent. To her right, a woman carried on an animated conversation with no one, gesticulating, grimacing, and flailing her arms about. Dakota wanted to slap her, tell her to shut up, but she kept her expression neutral. Across the room, a man pinched his own arm every few seconds then yelled, "Ow, stop!" No one paid any attention.

A young man in his early twenties was screaming as a nurse chased him around the room.

"No needles, beetles, stop, lop, mop. No!"

Dakota sprang up from her seat and ran to his side. "Nathan, eyes!" She got between him and the nurse.

He looked at Dakota with terror in his eyes. She spoke

calmly. "The nurse is not giving you a needle. It's just your medicine. I promise." She turned around to the nurse who was new to the floor. "You have to show him the pill, be careful how you approach him."

The nurse held her hand out, showing Nathan the cup holding several pills. "See, Nathan? It's okay."

His breathing became less ragged, and he took the pills and water from the nurse and swallowed them. Dakota led him over to a sofa and sat next to him, whispering in his ear. "I'll come back and get you out of here, I promise. Just be good until then. Okay?"

He looked at her with adoration. "You promise?"

"Cross my heart."

"Okay, dokey, lokey."

"Good. Now just relax and watch the TV. I have an appointment with Dr. Clary."

She had been here over two years—after the court decided her mental state deemed her not criminally responsible for what she had done. She had to make Jack understand how miserable she was at being forced to accommodate the intruder that was taking over her body. In the beginning, when she still looked pretty and thin, she had liked the attention. Everyone was congratulating her and smiling, making her feel so special. But then things began to change. Her breasts were sore, and her legs turned lumpy with ugly blue veins. She had to pee constantly, and she was always exhausted. She was sick of being told what to do. No drinking, eat right, take your bloody vitamins. And Jack, always looking at her as though she was doing it all wrong, like he didn't trust her with his precious child. She knew what he had planned, could see the disdain in his eyes when he looked at her. He was biding his time until she had the baby and then he would leave her. Take the wretched thing and start a life without her. Well, she wouldn't let him. The baby was in her body and he would never get his hands on it. She chose the day knowing he would be working late. She intentionally started a fight with him so that when he came home and found her he would blame himself. The last words he said to her—that she made him say to her—would haunt him forever. She recalled the conversation with satisfaction. Her vitamins had been sitting on the table, unopened.

"Haven't you been taking these?"

"They make me sick."

Jack exhaled slowly. "It's important for you and the baby."

She stuck out her tongue. "All you care about is the stupid baby."

Jack gave her a withering look. "Stupid?"

She put her face inches from his and sneered. "Stupid. Just like its father. Stupid, stupid, stupid."

He grabbed her by the shoulders. "What's the matter with you? How can you talk about our child like that?"

"Because, Jack, as you've pointed out, I don't have a maternal bone in my body."

He was speechless.

She goaded him. "Say it."

"Say what?"

"Say you're not cut out to be a mother."

He turned his back on her and walked toward the door. "I'll say no such thing."

She ran up to him and grabbed his arm. "Be honest for once in your pathetic life. Maybe then we can start to change things. Say it!"

He spun around, defeat in his eyes. "You win, Dakota. You're not cut out to be a mother."

"Ha." She was triumphant. "I knew you felt that way. Get out of here."

When he got home that night she was nearly unconscious, but she was determined to hang on until he appeared, so that she could whisper the condemning words to him: "I guess I'm not cut out to be a mother."

The lawyers advised her to plead insanity, and the court-appointed shrink had diagnosed her with bipolar disorder. Her attorney argued that the pregnancy hormones had sent her over the edge. She was more than happy to go along with them. She knew how to play the game. So here she was, waiting like a good little girl to see the useless doctor and continue to feed him the lies that would get her released. She had studied hard for her role as the improving patient and had no doubt her brainless doctor would soon let her out.

He opened his office door and called her in.

She bestowed her most enchanting smile on him. It was so easy. It bored her to death. She spoke her well-rehearsed lines, cried when appropriate, made her voice catch in the right places. He was nodding at her now, his facial expression one of earnest empathy.

She was a great actress. Her stint with Jack had been her longest-running role. Oh, the long seasons of depression left her bored, but the one thing that kept her going was her amusement at his clumsy attempts to cheer her up. He was pathetic, and his codependent behavior sickened her. When she was tired of being "depressed," she would miraculously recover and become the Dakota he loved once again. What delight she took in the knowledge that his happiness was short-lived and at the complete whim of her moods. She threw herself into their lovemaking with one goal—to enslave him. She reveled in the sexual power she held over him. She broke him down, built him up, and broke him down again, all the while mocking him in her mind. She was sorry when the role came to an end, having grown fond of the game and crushing his spirit. She got her parting shot in, though—cutting the baby out of her stomach had been her idea—her masterpiece. She wanted to destroy him, make sure he would be no good for anyone else. She did so knowing she would have to pay for it, but it was worth it. The session was almost over.

She dabbed at her eyes with a balled-up tissue and looked at the therapist. Her lip trembled.

He stood. "Dakota, I'm so pleased with the progress you've made. I do think you're ready to take the next step."

She feigned grateful surprise. "Really, are you sure, Doctor?"

He smiled at her. "Yes, quite sure. You are ready. I'll make my recommendations at your hearing."

Dakota thought he looked pleased with himself. Soon she would be free of this place and back where she belonged. She had played her hand well and was ready, finally, to claim her reward. She couldn't wait to be with him again. The only man she considered her equal and worthy of her devotion. Damon Crosse.

CHAPTER THIRTY-THREE

CROSBY HIT THE PLAY BUTTON ON THE VIDEO STREAMING on his computer. The latest episode of *Teenage Wasted* had been shot and edited, and he was taking one last look before it aired. These were college kids—eighteen and nineteen years old.

Two girls are sitting in a dorm room, talking.

"It's easy, Mindy. And when you graduate, you have no debt."

"I don't know." The other girl looks at her fingernails. "I don't think I could do it."

The first girl stands, brushing her long blond hair from her shoulder with a manicured hand. She walks to her dresser, opens it, pulls out a wad of cash and fans it in front of Mindy's face. "Fine. I'm going shopping with my little tip here. You can let that cheapskate of a boyfriend touch you for free. I'm doing exactly what you are, but instead of being paid with dinner or a movie, I'm getting what I deserve."

Mindy looks up at her friend. "How did you even find out about it, Lucy?"

Lucy smiles and sits back down. "That's the great thing. It's super easy and organized. It's run by a girl just like us, and she vets all the guys. You can even pick from a picture and get a cute one. They're older, but, you know, handsome. Just rich older guys bored with their wives. It's fun really. They have these clubs on every campus."

Crosby stopped the video. It was just enough to titillate and get people thinking. What they were doing was illegal everywhere in the US—everywhere, that is, except for where it was filmed, in Nevada. He had no doubt that men of a certain age and resources would begin googling to find willing college girls. Cash-strapped girls would do the same. He sent an email to his YouTube contingent and closed the laptop. It was so easy to manipulate people, especially with the public appetite for reality television shows. If anyone bothered to read the disclaimer, they would see that it was a scripted reality series and mostly fabricated, but it didn't matter. As long as other people were doing it, it legitimized it for the masses. It wasn't even difficult to get sponsors any longer. The public outcry was easily drowned out by the advocates of whatever outrageous idea they put on film. Set the right context and people bought into anything. After the show aired, there would be a plethora of videos of good-looking young women singing the praises of such a service. They would be actors, of course, but no one would realize that. Students would begin prostituting themselves, convinced that it was no big deal. They had no idea of the permanent damage it would do to their self-esteem. That would be something they wouldn't realize until they were in the thick of it. And by then, it would be too late for many of them. Once they'd serviced their first client, they'd feel so bad about themselves they wouldn't have the emotional reserves to stop.

Of course, there wasn't really such an escort service on every college campus. Yet.

CHAPTER THIRTY-FOUR

TAYLOR WAS AWAKE BEFORE DAWN. THEY COULDN'T LEAVE for the library until it opened at nine. But she was going stir-crazy. She fed Beau, then went to the bathroom and got dressed. When she came out, Jack was awake.

"Everything all right? You're up awfully early."

"Of course everything is not all right. My husband's dead, our lives are in danger, and I don't even know what we're doing. What if this is just a huge wild-goose chase? And when it's all over, then what? I thought I had a good life with Malcolm. Turns out he was a liar, too."

Too? Jack thought. Was that how she saw him? A liar? "Come on, Taylor. I know you're grieving for Malcolm, but time will heal."

Anger flashed in her eyes. "Is that what you think, Jack?

Time will heal? Let me tell you something—it doesn't heal. It only numbs the pain tearing your heart apart until you can't feel anything anymore. It wasn't supposed to be like this." She glared at him. "You and I were supposed to be together. But you went off and married that psycho!" She ran back into the bathroom, slamming the door.

Jack sat shamefaced, Taylor's words ringing in his ears.

Maybe it was a good thing that Taylor had gotten angry. It was time they cleared the air. He wanted to explain about Dakota, but how? He barely understood it himself, and he had no excuses for what he had done. He couldn't blame her for hating him. Despite their roller-coaster relationship, it didn't occur to him to leave Dakota in the beginning. No matter how low she sank, how nasty she became, he stood by her and opened his heart again when the loving Dakota returned. He held no grudges, never threw her heartless words back at her. For her part, she seemed to have amnesia regarding her black spells. There were never any apologies, no pleas for forgiveness. She accepted it as her due that he would be there, on the other side of her depression, waiting for her return to him. His friends told him he was crazy, that he should leave. It was out of the question. Was he happy, they wanted to know? Happy? Had he ever been happy? In those rare moments of self-reflection, he would admit that yes, he had been happy—when he had been with Taylor. She'd been the only bright spot in a childhood marred by many seasons of melancholy and moroseness.

How had he failed to see it? He'd replicated his childhood when he'd married Dakota—it was the same wretched, unpredictable, insanity-filled life. Each pregnancy his beautiful Irish Catholic mother—with a poet's soul and a mournful heart—had endured had plunged her deeper into depression, her emergence from the depths more arduous with each subsequent baby. Jack was her second. For as far back as he could remember, she had always been pregnant. When he left home at eighteen, he had five sisters and a mother barely functioning. He'd begged his father to do something. Get her help. Stop knocking her up. They were Catholics, his father reminded him. Birth control was a sin. His father rebuked him for interfering with their "personal business" and insisted there was nothing wrong with his wife that a little time wouldn't cure. Taylor had been Jack's only mooring. How different both of their lives would have been if he'd kept his word to her. God knows he had paid the price for his mistakes—was still paying it every day. But that did nothing to alleviate Taylor's pain or to absolve him for causing it. Taylor came out of the bathroom.

"I'm sorry, Jack. I don't know what got into me."

He shook his head. "Don't apologize. You were right. I should have never married her. To say I'm sorry doesn't even begin to cover it, and I don't know what I could ever say to make up for what I did."

She ran her hands through her hair.

"It's water under the bridge. Long time ago," she said quietly. "The stress of all this, it's making me a little nuts."

"No, it's not. Taylor, can we please talk about it? I can't stand to have this huge thing between us. I know what I did was unforgivable. I'd like to at least try to explain."

"I don't think I really want to rehash it all. I know things didn't turn out well for you, and I'm sorry." She looked down.

He didn't mince words.

"Are you talking about the baby?"

She looked up. "Yes." She ran her thumb back and forth over her fingernail. "How could she? I'll never understand it." She shook her head.

Clearing his throat several times he finally answered. "She blamed it on me."

"What?"

"She hated being pregnant, gaining weight. She used to berate me daily about what I'd done to her."

Taylor said nothing.

"The day it happened, we'd had a fight. She kept egging me on, trying to get me to say that I thought she'd be a terrible mother. I finally did. I've never seen a look of triumph like the one on her face that day. When I came home, I found her in the tub. The water was so red from all the blood. And the baby . . . Right before she passed out she told me it was all my fault."

Taylor was horrified.

"Jack, don't you see that she'd planned it all along? No woman is going to cut a child out of her stomach just because of a few words her husband says. No sane woman."

He put his head in his hands. "I know that intellectually. But I still feel responsible. She killed my child just to spite me. That's how much she despised me. How could I fall for a person like that?"

Taylor pursed her lips. "How did you?" It came out as a whisper.

He was anguished. "I wish I knew. It was the worst mistake of my life. Will you ever be able to forgive me?"

She closed her eyes and finally answered, "I don't know if I can."

CHAPTER THIRTY-FIVE

THE INSTITUTE, DECEMBER 1975

M Y BABY IS GROWING. I AM INFORMED AT MY WEEKLY EX-
ams that all is going perfectly. The heartbeat is strong, and
I'm gaining just the right amount of weight. How could I
not, with my diet so carefully controlled? I am visibly pregnant
now. The months are dwindling down to my delivery, and I've
still found no way to even attempt an escape. Instead, I sit and
rub my belly and talk to my baby. Despite the fact that this
nightmare is something I could never have imagined, I feel a
love for this child growing inside me. I allow myself to imagine a
different life. One in which I have a loving husband eager for the
child's arrival. A life in which I will get to watch my child grow
up. I glance down at my stomach and at the gray cotton shirt
and black stretch pants Crosse has provided. A drab uniform

of solid colors and practicality. Dreams of beautiful maternity clothes, a loving husband, and joyous expectation will all go unfulfilled.

It has been a week since he told me about going to my parents. I haven't seen him since, have been left on my own to do nothing but worry. Even though I tried not to show it, when he first told me that my mother refused to turn over the coins, I *was* wounded. How could she not do anything in her power to save me? All because of a legend about some pieces of metal? Because that's what it must be. Legend. An inanimate object has no power. Right? But now I wonder. Dunst is a renowned scientist. That's what got him his entry into this country. And he believes in the power of the coins, that they healed him. I wish I could do some research, find out more about the coins and their history, but all I have to go on is what they tell me. And if my mother and father, who I know with certainty *do* love me, wouldn't give them up, then maybe, just maybe, they do contain the power he claims. It's hard enough to sacrifice your *own* life for your faith—but the life of your child? The only way that is possible is to have an unshakable belief that to betray your faith would have monumental repercussions and that the stakes are truly of eternal significance. Now that I am to become a mother, I already feel an overpowering love for my baby. I would lay down my life for this child without a second thought.

So are my parents fools? Is their faith misplaced? I am beginning to think *I* am the fool. When did I give up on my faith? I search my memory and try to remember what it was that turned me away. Did something happen to shatter my belief? Some terrible trauma that made me realize there was no God? I can think of nothing. The reality is, I just drifted away. There was no defining moment, no reason other than it was easy to walk away. I gave my allegiance to myself and to science. I didn't think I needed God or anybody else. Is it too late for me to turn back now? I kneel by my bed, the way I did as a little girl, and clasp my hands together.

"Dear God, I don't know if you can hear me, but I hope you can. If there was ever a time I needed to know if you are there, it's now. Please give me a sign, anything, that you exist, that you love me, that I'm not doomed to die in this place with no hope of a life after." I stay that way for a long while, my head bowed, my spirit still. Then I feel my baby move. It is nothing more than a flutter at first, so subtle, I'm not sure if I imagine it or not. But then, another movement—this time stronger—and a kick. I look up and whisper, "Thank you."

o o o

I pray every day now. Last night, I felt a peace wash over me, covering me like a warm blanket. It was comforting and strangely tangible, emanating from a source outside of myself. My hand goes to my neck, and I grasp the christening cross that I've worn each day of my life since I was thirteen. Until now it had ceased to hold any significance, other than nostalgic. But now, it is my most precious possession, my only real possession, and merely feeling it against my skin fills me with hope. I think of all it symbolizes and make myself meditate on its meaning. It was taken from me when we first arrived but was with my belongings when I was moved to this prison. I wonder why he has allowed me to keep it, but I don't dare ask for fear he will take it.

With every fiber of my being, I rebel against the lies he tries to instill in me. That I carry within me the continuation of evil. I won't accept it. I hold fiercely to the belief that I am connected and forever bound to the God of the universe. Damon may hold my body captive, but he will never touch my soul. How ironic that I owe my salvation to the man who imprisons me. Would I have turned back to God if I'd been allowed to continue on my chosen path? Education was my god. Medicine was my god. And yes, I even made myself into a god. What a terrible thing pride is. If it were only my life to be lost, I could almost be grateful, for in losing it I have found it. What grieves me with unrelenting desolation is the knowledge that I am leaving my precious child, alone and unprotected, helpless to resist the evil that will encapsulate him. I will pray for this child until my dying breath.

I am talking to my baby, telling him how much I love him—I feel I'm having a boy. I tell him stories of his family. The yia yia and papou who would spoil him, the aunt who would adore him.

I don't know how long Crosse has been standing outside my door, only that he has overheard some of it. He opens the door, stares at me, and then begins to laugh.

"Love! My child will have no need of this emotion full of fallacies. They say God is love. My child will have nothing to do with either. Don't waste your time, Maya. You are merely the vessel. You will have no influence on what my child thinks, feels, or believes. He is going to be powerful. More powerful than you can ever imagine. I would have thought that would have been enough for you. Your ego should love that, no? You, the mother of the most powerful man in the world?"

"You are insane!"

"Insane? Far from it."

"What has happened to my parents?" I demand.

He gives me a contemptuous look, and his lips form a scowl. "No matter what we did, they wouldn't give up the hiding place. They admitted they brought them from Greece, but they refused to say where they are hidden." He shakes his head. "I don't understand it. They were unshakable."

"What did you do to them?" I choke the words out. I don't want to know, but I have to suffer, too, must know what they went through.

He makes a dismissive gesture with his hands. "It doesn't matter. They are gone now. Your sister will believe that they had an ordinary automobile accident. Nothing to arouse suspicions. And we will keep watch on her. Surely there will be something in the will or in their papers that she will find and lead us to the coins. We will wait for as long as it takes."

My grief is intermingled with relief. They won't kill my sister. She is useful to them. For now at least. And maybe I'll be able to get to her somehow. I can only hope and pray that my parents took the secret of the coins with them to their graves.

He stands and paces. "What would make someone so stubborn? Their faith could not be broken, no matter how hard we tried." He brings a fist down on the table so hard that the glass on it tips over and water runs off.

My parents didn't die in vain. Now I understand the faith

my mother told me about—the one that sent those three men into the fire. I sit up straighter and stare into his eyes.

"My child *will* return to God one day."

He looks at me with such murderous rage that I shrink back, afraid he will strike me. He comes close to me, until he is just inches from my face, and I can feel his breath on my cheek.

"My child will never worship your god. He will rule nations and be responsible for turning others *away* from your god. Know this, Maya: your prayers are impotent. His destiny is sealed."

I bite my lip and take a deep breath. Then a thought occurs to me, and I move my face even closer to his, in our own twisted version of chicken.

"We shall see about that, *Damon*. We both know how the story ends. I assume you have read Revelation, the book written by Saint John on Patmos. The Battle of Armageddon will see your master thrown into the pit forever. Christ will be victorious. The battle is already won."

His eyes narrow to slits, and he flies from the room, and the lock clicks behind him. My heart is still pounding, and I breathe deeply to regain my equilibrium. I begin to wonder if I've gone too far. When dinnertime comes, there is nothing but beef stew. He knows I hate red meat. By morning, I am ravenous but it's a bloody steak this time. So he will have the last word after all.

CHAPTER THIRTY-SIX

S IR," JONAS SAID AFTER ENTERING DAMON'S PRIVATE chambers. "Your guest has arrived."

"Bring her in," Damon instructed him.

Once Jonas had withdrawn, Dakota knelt before Damon and bowed her head.

"Master. Thank you for calling me home. I am ready."

He placed a hand on her head. "You have served me well. Rise. There is still much to do."

She stood. "It is my greatest honor."

He nodded and pointed to the door.

"Your room is ready. They are waiting to examine and prepare you."

She hesitated for a moment, and he took a deep breath. She was loyal but needy. He forced himself to smile at her and say the words he knew she was waiting for. "I am well pleased with you."

After she left, Damon opened the connecting door that led to his bedroom and called out to Peritas. He had to keep the dog separate from Dakota. Even though Peritas was obedient, he couldn't be calmed if Dakota was anywhere near him. He growled and barked ceaselessly whenever he saw her.

"Come here, my boy."

Peritas sniffed furiously and growled low in his throat. "It's all right. She's gone. We only need her for a little longer."

An hour later, Jonas came in to tell him the procedure was finished. He left the room and went to check on her. Dakota looked like she was still groggy from the anesthesia, so he sat and waited until her eyes opened.

"How many did they get?" she asked.

Damon looked pleased.

"Eight. You're a very fertile young woman."

She laughed. "Good to know. How many are they going to fertilize?"

He cocked an eyebrow. "What does it matter to you?"

"They are my eggs, so I think it is my concern. Who is the surrogate?"

He had no intention of sharing that information with her. After her self-inflicted abortion, her uterus was no longer viable. He didn't trust her not to be jealous that someone else would carry his future heirs. The only reason he wanted her eggs was that she was brilliant and ruthless. She had the characteristics that would assure him that this time his heirs wouldn't have an attack of conscience and betray him. He rose. "Don't concern yourself with the details. You are being spared the indignity of another pregnancy. That's all you need to know."

"Shouldn't I have some say in who hosts my babies?"

He gave her a sardonic look. He knew the only thing she was worried about was her position with him. "I'm well aware of your maternal instincts. These children will be kept far from you."

He left the room without another word. He went to his library and sat down at his desk. There was a knock on the door.

"Yes?"

Jonas poked his head in. "Dr. Whitmore would like a word with you, sir."

"Send him in."

The doctor came in and stood until Damon invited him to sit. This was a man he had known for over thirty years, yet their relationship was still as formal as it had been on the day they'd first met. The doctor looked at the floor, then at his fingernails, and finally at the folder on his lap—anywhere but at Damon.

Damon cleared his throat and the doctor reluctantly met his eyes. "Well?"

He blinked repeatedly, then pushed his wire-rimmed glasses up to the bridge of his nose.

"I'm running out of patience," Damon warned.

"It seems that, ahem, your sperm count is quite low."

Several seconds of silence ensued before Damon spoke. "How low?"

The doctor looked down at his feet. "Nonexistent actually. I'm afraid that even intracytoplasmic sperm injection won't work. I see no viable options here."

Damon nodded. He would not react. "That is all."

The doctor rose and hurried out of the room.

How could this be? It had never occurred to him that he

had anything to worry about. If the idea of producing a specimen wasn't so disgusting, perhaps he would have made provisions earlier. It had taken him weeks to provide the sample for Jeremy. He wasn't wired with a single sexual urge. He was horrified at the messiness of it, the loss of control. It was something he would never understand. The irony. How many men had lost kingdoms, untold wealth, all they held dear, because of sex? He was not susceptible to such yearnings and for that he had always been grateful, but now it had the power to be his undoing. Never one to wallow in regrets, he stood and began mentally preparing for his next steps. He was filled with renewed resolve as he pondered his good fortune in concocting a contingency plan so long ago. He went to his bedchamber and packed his suitcase. He rang for Jonas, his thoughts racing while he waited.

"Yes, sir?" Jonas came into the room.

"I'll be gone for a few days. Please see that everything runs smoothly in my absence. What time is the new group scheduled to arrive?"

"Five o'clock, sir."

"I presume everything is prepared?"

Jonas nodded. "Of course, sir."

Damon sank down onto the soft cushion of his silk chaise, suddenly tired. He felt all of his seventy years. In the space of an hour, he had gone from a vital thriving man to a withered shell. No. He raised his head. He was Damon Crosse. He was never out of options. He knew where he must now focus his efforts. In the end, all that mattered was that he had a suitable heir. Perhaps this was better after all.

CHAPTER THIRTY-SEVEN

THE INSTITUTE, DECEMBER 1975

Every time he comes to visit with me he tells me more. His revelations leave me breathless and heartsick. Is there no one who can stop him? He interrupts my desperate prayers.

"A futile effort, Maya." He laughs derisively. "Don't count on any help from your god. He has abandoned you just as you will abandon your child." He sneers at me as he lifts his coffee cup to his mouth.

"But don't worry. Your child will have a crucial role in my plan for society. By the time he's grown and ready to take his place beside me, so much will have already been accomplished. The important work being done here will assure that."

I can keep quiet no longer. "Important work? Like torturing unsuspecting students? You're a sadist. Pure and simple."

He shakes his head. "You disappoint me, Maya. I'm building a better world," he says, laughing again. "Or at least that's what I tell those in my employ. And my best is still to come. One day, it will be virtually impossible to give birth to anything but a physically perfect child."

"I don't understand."

"Genetic testing. We will use it on pregnant women, and if the child has a birth defect, we will mandate abortion."

"You're crazy! A law like that will never pass."

"That's what they said about abortion. It will happen, and when it does, it will make the abortion rates skyrocket." He was gleeful.

"What does increasing the abortion rate do for your cause?" I ask.

His eyes look upward. "There's nothing more precious in the eyes of God than new life. Anything I can do to destroy those lives, I'll do. If I can prevent the birth of just one true believer who might shape the world in a better direction, I'll have done well."

I am without words. The more I am forced to endure his lectures, the more tainted and soul sick I feel. I say the only thing I can think of to make him angry.

"You won't prevail. No matter how important you think you are, there will always be many more good men and women who will fight you."

"Good men and women? There are no *good* people. They

are all self-interested, easily manipulated little pawns. I'll show you."

I shake my head.

"I don't want to see any more of your work."

He grabs my arm. "It's not a request."

Still, I refuse to move. "Why do you care what I think? What difference does it make if you show me these things?"

"You will accompany me to this meeting, but you will say nothing. Do you understand? Or should I have your sister brought here?"

"I understand." I stand and follow him from the room. He has taken my parents from me, and I can't let him take her, too. Despite all he is capable of, I cling to the hope that he will leave her alone. Do I believe she is truly out of danger? As long as she is his only connection to the coins, I think she is. But I can't take any chances.

He opens a door to a boardroom and sits at the head of the table. He points to a chair on his right, and I take a seat. There are three people sitting at the long, chrome table. No one asks who I am; they only glance quickly in my direction.

"Good day, Doctors. I trust you have found it easy to work together and come up with a program with which you all agree? Let us hear from the psychiatrist first."

A man who looks to be in his mid-forties, balding, with round-rimmed spectacles answers, "It has been most interesting to hear the opinions of my esteemed colleagues. I now have a better understanding of neuroscience, as well as sexual medicine. We have put together a protocol that we believe will please you." He hands Damon a folder.

Damon opens it and makes a face. He looks disgusted. I get a glimpse of a naked woman being restrained. I can't see the rest of the photo, but my imagination fills in the blanks.

Damon puts the picture back in the folder and throws it down. "How does it work?"

The psychiatrist looks at the woman next to him and then back at Damon. "I will let Dr. Droskin, our neuroscientist, answer that."

Droskin speaks. "We will combine video, magazines, books, and auditory measures to stimulate the subjects and to measure which has the greatest and most immediate effect. Video will leverage the mirror neuron tendencies by zooming in and making the subject feel he is experiencing what is happening on the screen. We will measure response to stimuli and whether or not we can change the sexual appetite by repeated exposure to negative stimuli if it follows positive stimuli closely enough."

Damon is nodding. He turns his attention to the last man in the room. "Let's hear from our sexual medicine specialist."

"In a nutshell, we show them something that turns them on. Right after, we show one of the scenarios they find abhorrent—rape, torture, bondage. We see if repeated exposure to the negative, closely after erotic stimulation, eventually pairs the two scenarios until the subject is aroused by all the scenarios. It is our theory that sexual predators are made, not born. If we can understand the process behind it, we have great hopes of curing them."

The psychiatrist picks up the thread. "Most of these criminals have been exposed to this behavior from their male caregivers. They have been subjected to torture and abuse themselves, then forced to participate in these crimes until their sexual appetites are perverted. We will attempt to replicate this to see if our theories are indeed correct. We will also inundate them through their auditory channel, with the sounds of women pleading, anguished cries, and so on, until they become desensitized to them. It is a protocol that we've—"

Damon interrupts him. "So you believe you can find the key to how rapists and sadists develop?"

"That is our hypothesis. We can begin tomorrow."

Crosse stands. "I look forward to your updates." He turns to me. "Let's go."

As we walk down the hall I can't help but see how pleased with himself he looks.

"They think they're working on a cure, but you're going to use it to make sexual predators."

He smiles at me. "Ah, Maya. You're catching on."

"If they're looking for a cure, why wouldn't they take existing deviants and try to do the opposite, to make their appetites normal?"

"It's too late by then. Those men are too damaged. We need to reach people earlier. The research wouldn't bear it out, and I couldn't find anyone to agree to experiment on children. This way, if it works, they can reverse the methods to be used on younger subjects that are pulled from such circumstances."

I shake my head. "It's a specious argument. Your scientists are charlatans."

"They are not your traditional doctors. If, at first, they worried about turning normal men into rapists and sadists, their egos allowed them to believe the lie—that they could turn them back. They are lured by the promise of becoming pioneers, of discovering a cure for what is currently incurable. To turn a predatory sexual deviant into a contributing member of society is the head shrinker's holy grail." He arches an eyebrow. "See? Self-interest at work once again."

"And how are you going to implement this in society? Are you going to kidnap young men and brainwash them?"

"Of course not. I will implement another training program at the Institute and rewire the brains of our future leaders. I'll be judicious, but done to the right men, the consequences will be far-reaching. You'd be amazed at what men will do to satisfy their deviant urges. Only a little tweak here and there to a select few—I can't risk turning out an army of sociopaths, after all, I need to keep control."

I hate him with every fiber of my being. I want to crush him. I want to watch him bleed and die. I now understand how someone can murder. I know we are supposed to love our enemies, but this man standing before me is not worthy of love. There isn't a shred of humanity in him. If I didn't know better, I would believe he was the devil incarnate. I can't allow him to raise my child. I must figure out a way to prevent this child from being born alive. I will find a way and hope that God will forgive me.

CHAPTER THIRTY-EIGHT

D AMON CROSSE SIGHED IN ANNOYANCE AT THE PERSISTENT ringing. He hated being interrupted.

"What?" he barked into the receiver.

"We've located them."

His hold on the phone tightened. "Where are they?"

"A motel in New Hampshire. We just got a call from one of our men inside Jeremy's organization. They checked in last night."

"And I'm only being informed now?"

The voice on the other end grew quiet.

"Well?"

"My phone died. I forgot the car charger. I just picked up the message."

He clenched his jaw, swallowed, then spoke evenly. "Have you dispatched someone to intercept them?"

"Yes, sir. They're on their way now. They'll arrive within the hour."

"Contact your people and tell them to call me once they have them."

"I can take care of it, sir. I—"

"Have them contact me directly." He terminated the call and pressed the button on his desk.

Jonas entered in under a minute, and Damon handed him a piece of paper. "Give this to Dakota. Tell her she can indulge herself with this one."

"Yes, sir."

"Tell her to make sure there is no mistaking her work. I want it to serve as a warning to the others that we take carelessness very seriously."

"Very well, sir."

When the door had closed behind Jonas, Damon picked up the crystal goblet and threw it across the room. It smashed against the brick wall, and Peritas jumped up, startled.

"Come here, my boy." Damon pushed his chair back from the desk to allow room for the dog.

Peritas put his head on Damon's leg and wagged his tail while his head was rubbed.

Damon closed his eyes and continued to stroke the lush fur. It would do no good to lose control, he reminded himself. They would be in his possession and then Taylor would play her part in leading him to Jeremy—all in good time. In the meantime, he *must* keep a cool head.

CHAPTER THIRTY-NINE

THE INSTITUTE, DECEMBER 1975

I RETRIEVE THE SHARD OF GLASS FROM MY HIDING PLACE and slip it into my pocket. I don't dare to try anything in my room or my bathroom—he has cameras everywhere. But today he is taking me to the screening room. He wants to show me the television programming of the future. I plan to ask to use the bathroom in the middle of it, and then I will do what needs to be done.

"Would you like to see an example of one of these shows?"

Not really, I want to say, but I know he'll show me anyway. I merely nod.

"This first one will be what we'll call a 'true-life show.'"

"A what?"

"A show where the characters are real people, not actors.

Cameras will follow them, and we'll get a glimpse into their actual lives. This is the model for one of these shows."

The room goes dark and the screen lights up. Red letters appear one at a time until the title is displayed: AFFAIRS OF THE STREET. It looks like a normal neighborhood backyard barbecue. There are five couples sitting around a fire pit, drinking alcohol, laughing and talking. One of the women stands up and walks over to a hot tub.

"Anyone want to join me?" She takes off her top and her pants and climbs into the steaming water in nothing but her bra and underwear.

A few more people follow suit until there are just two people left sitting on the patio.

The woman who is left behind goes into the house, and the others are drinking and laughing, seemingly oblivious.

A short while later, the man she was sitting with goes inside.

The camera cuts to the interior of the house, to a bathroom, where the couple is kissing and peeling off each other's clothes.

The woman throws her head back and laughs. "I wondered if you'd follow me in."

He looks at her. "I've been wanting to do this to you all night."

The next scene shows them getting into the hot tub five minutes apart. She sits down next to her husband as if nothing has happened.

Damon gets up and turns the light on.

"You get the idea."

"What's entertaining about that? Why would anyone watch that garbage?"

"I've only shown you the highlights. We'll make them care about the people. By the time a scene like that airs, the audience will already be invested in their stories. We'll make them sympathetic to the couple having the affair, make it seem justified. But there's more. That's just the beginning."

I sit riveted over the next several hours watching all kinds of shows that promote promiscuity, the occult, perversion, abortion, prostitution, criminal lifestyles, and more. The villains are the heroes, and I can see how people might root for them. He's right. Commercials are as bad as the shows: ads for condoms, sex aids, and pornographic materials abound.

Then he tells me about a drama—his favorite idea—one about demons. He calls it *Sympathy for the Devil*. It's about a cadre of demons exiled from hell due to an act of kindness. They are sent back to earth to prove that they are worthy of their roles in the dark kingdom. The twist is that these demons have a compassionate side they can't seem to shake. In each assignment, they start off doing what is expected of them, but somewhere along the way, they meet a human who sparks a seed of sympathy or empathy, thus beginning the cycle all over again. He says he'll make sure they cast actors with boyish good looks and rakish charm, whose transformation into demons will be mildly appealing.

"You see, Maya, after a few episodes, the fact that these are *demons* will recede to the background of people's consciousness. Some people will even like it. In the next few decades, less and less will be offensive. In fact, the only thing that will be offensive is intolerance to these things."

I glare at him. "You won't rest until you strip society of every shred of decency."

"There is no decency in humanity. All I'm doing is stripping away the facade."

At first, I find it utterly impossible to believe that people will ever accept this type of thing. Deep in my heart, however, I fear that he's right. Over time, and with the right framing, I think he will accomplish his goals. I shudder when I imagine this bleak future, beset with darkness and iniquity. *My beloved child, I am more convinced than ever that I must release you from this dark destiny.*

"I need to use the bathroom. I feel nauseated."

"Can't it wait until we return to your room?"

I pretend to gag. "No!"

He makes a face and leads me out to the hallway to the lavatory.

"I'll wait here."

I go in. There are four stalls. I turn the water on, hoping the noise will be enough to keep him from hearing my screams until it is too late. I choose the stall farthest from the door.

"Forgive me, God."

One deep swipe is all it will take. Nick the jugular, and I'll bleed out before he can do anything. I pull out the long shard of glass and take a deep breath. I hold my hand in front of my neck, bracing myself. As I am about to do it, I feel a kick. An overwhelming anguish overtakes me. How can I do this? But how can I not? I position myself again and tell myself to get it over with. It's the only thing I can do to save my child. Another move inside my belly causes me to pause, and I hear my mother's voice inside my head. *Life is sacred. God has a purpose for each of us.* Can he really have a purpose for my child? The battle wages in my heart as I wrestle with myself. My shirt is damp with perspiration, and I am dizzy. What should I do? *God, what should I do?* A small, quiet voice stops me. If I am to embrace my faith, I must embrace it all. I have to believe that God is stronger—stronger than Damon and Dunst and the evil one they serve. I throw the glass into the toilet and flush it down. I stand and watch as it swirls away, disappearing—along with my last hope of saving my child.

CHAPTER FORTY

I T'S ALMOST DAWN. WHY DON'T YOU TAKE HIM OUT, AND then we'll hit the road before the sun comes up?" Jack said.

With his face plastered all over the news, Jack was keeping the lowest profile possible.

"Come on, buddy." She put the leash on Beau and stepped out into the bracing air.

Jack frowned. "Be careful."

Taylor walked Beau to the back of the motel and gave him enough leash to find a satisfactory place to relieve himself. Why were dogs so particular about that? It seemed to her that one blade of grass was as good as another. She hopped from one foot to the other trying to keep warm. The temperature had dropped suddenly and sharply. Now she wished she had some gloves. She shoved her free hand in her coat pocket and tugged on the lead. Enough was enough. "Come on, boy. Go!"

He finally obliged and trotted back to her with a contented expression as they walked toward the front of the motel. Then, he growled, a deep, suspicious snarl from the back of his throat.

"What is it?" she whispered.

He was still growling, and she stood still, paralyzed by indecision.

She pulled on the leash and tried to coax Beau slowly forward, but he refused, seemingly rooted to the ground.

Then she saw them. Two figures in black skulking in the shadows, moving in the direction of their motel room. What should she do? She had to warn Jack, but how?

As if reading her mind, Beau bolted upright, tore away from her, and went bounding at the two men at full speed.

He leaped and sunk his teeth into the first man's arm. The man screamed as he tried to shake loose of the determined canine.

"What the hell?" he screamed.

The man next to him lifted the hand holding a gun and pointed it at Beau.

"No!" Taylor yelled, and instinctively ran toward them.

The motel door flew open, and Jack rushed out, flinging himself at the man with the gun. They both toppled to the ground wrestling for it. Taylor reached into her coat pocket for the can of Mace and ran toward them. Just as Taylor collided with Beau and fell onto the pavement, the gun went off.

CHAPTER FORTY-ONE

THE INSTITUTE, JANUARY 1976

I SPENT NEW YEAR'S DAY THINKING OF RESOLUTIONS, AND OF years past, when I had my entire life in front of me. This New Year will be my last. I think of how different things could be if I were free. My precious son would have an entire family to love him. It is too unbearable to ponder. I try to relish the little time I have left and use it for some good. When my thoughts become too torturous, I pray.

My stomach lurches as I hear the familiar clicking on the cold, marble floors.

His boasting begins as soon as he enters the room.

"Maya, how is it possible that you are still so naive? Do you imagine the throngs will resist me? I have Madison Avenue in my back pocket. The fools believe whatever we tell them to. Slowly, very slowly, we have been shifting society's values. Small steps, moving the line ever so slightly until they don't even realize the gigantic leaps we have taken. Just a few years ago we couldn't show a married couple sleeping in the same bed. Soon, they'll be watching strangers having sex, during the so-called family hour, and no one will blink an eye. By the time we're through, morality will be a distant memory and the very few that try to hold on to it will be classified radical fanatics."

His arrogance is infuriating. "What's in it for you?" I blurt out.

He looks right through me. "I am serving my master. He desires the ruination of souls. It is my pleasure to assist him in that quest."

"Enjoy it while you can. I can assure you, eternity is not going to be fun for you."

"Don't preach to me, Maya. You have no idea what you're talking about. Too bad you won't be around to see your son serve the master."

He knows exactly what to say to shut me up.

CHAPTER FORTY-TWO

TAYLOR LIFTED HER HEAD UP FROM THE COLD CONCRETE when she heard a rapid succession of popping noises. Everything had happened so fast, and she looked around in confusion. The man Jack had been fighting with was lying on the ground, blood pooled around his middle, eyes closed. Was he dead? Jack held his gun to the head of the other man, at whom Beau was growling, ready to pounce again. There was a different man, shorter and bald, standing across from Jack with a gun in his hand aimed at Jack. Where had he come from? Taylor winced as she put her weight on her arm and pushed herself up and stood.

"Who are you?" Jack was glaring at the man whose gun was trained on him.

"Name's Paul. Jeremy sent us."

"How do I know you're really with Jeremy?"

"Saint Christopher is on your side."

"I'll be a son of a—"

"Come on, we've got to move before someone sees us," Paul said.

"Give me a hand with this guy," Jack answered. They walked the man he was holding on to over to a black van with its back doors open and engine running. Three men jumped out. One cuffed Jack's prisoner, while the other two retrieved the dead body. It was all cleaned up within a matter of minutes.

"How did you find us?" Jack asked.

"There's a tracking device in the St. Christopher medal. We've been keeping tabs on you. Jeremy got inside intel that we've been compromised. We found the traitor, but not before he alerted the Institute," Paul explained.

"The what?" Taylor asked.

"No time to explain. Jeremy will tell you everything when you get to him. We've got to get going," Paul answered.

"Can you take us to Jeremy?"

The man shook his head. "Don't know where he is. We were dispatched for this only. No one has his location. It's safer for him that way."

Jack felt inside his jacket pocket for the medal and handed it to the man. "Take it back. I don't want to throw it out, but I'm not keeping it on me in case you're compromised again."

The man took it, ran back to the van, and they drove away.

"What was he talking about? What's all this with the Saint Christopher medal?" Taylor asked.

"It was a code. I didn't realize when she said it, until I heard him repeat it."

"What do you mean, a code?" she asked.

"I'll tell you in the car. Are you okay?"

She nodded. "Yeah, hurt my arm a little, but I'm fine."

"What were you thinking diving in front of Beau like that?"

She shrugged. "I guess I wasn't."

Jack looked down at Beau. "Come on, furball. You deserve a big treat." He opened the back door, and Beau jumped in.

Taylor put on her seat belt, still trying to catch her breath and steady her shaking hands. She looked out of the back window as they drove away.

"So are you going to tell me what that was all about?"

"A nice old lady gave me a Saint Christopher medal the other day when I helped her to her car. The last thing she said was 'Saint Christopher is on your side.'"

He continued to surprise her. "When did you help an old lady?"

"When I went to the drugstore for supplies, she was in front of me in line and fell. I walked her to her car."

"Still the Boy Scout," she said wryly. His stint in the Boy Scouts had lasted exactly one meeting. She remembered him telling her that it was a little too gung ho for him.

"Hardly," he said.

She leaned back against the seat and closed her eyes. The image of the man lying on the ground filled her mind and she sat up.

"Jack? Was that man dead?"

He ran his fingers over his lips then nodded.

She shivered. "It's strange. I know they were there to kill us, just like the man at the cabin." She swallowed. "But I still feel bad. I mean—they were people. Two days ago, all I could think about was getting ready for my baby. Now we're being chased by killers. How can that be?" She turned and pressed her forehead against the cold window. Her eyes fixated on the yellow line on the road stretching out forever, toward nowhere. Her future unrolled before her like a foreign scroll, inscrutable and indecipherable.

CHAPTER FORTY-THREE

WHAT DO YOU MEAN, THEY GOT AWAY?" DAMON CROSSE barked into the phone.

"We didn't know the girl and the dog were outside. They snuck up and attacked us."

Damon shook his head in disgust. "A dog and a pregnant woman *attacked* you?"

"They had help. Four men showed up out of nowhere. Lucky for me, they threw me out of the van instead of killing me."

"Too bad they didn't. They would have spared me the trouble." They must have been Jeremy's men. No one else would be stupid and soft enough not to finish the job. Threw him out of the van. How disappointing. Jeremy was weak. How did he think he could ever win when he couldn't handle the simple matter of disposing of an enemy properly?

"If they're in New Hampshire, Jeremy's facility must be close. I want aerial surveillance over the whole state and the surrounding ones. Find them." Crosse hung up.

CHAPTER FORTY-FOUR

WHEN THEY PULLED INTO THE PARKING LOT OF THE Claremont Library and Taylor opened the car door, Beau jumped up from his position in the back seat.

"You're hanging here with me, buddy," Jack said as he ruffled the fur on his head.

Taylor got out and walked to the entrance of the small brown brick building. Once inside, she scanned the signs on the shelves, looking for the fiction section. It didn't take her long to locate the *M* shelf.

She found the book immediately and blew the dust from the top of it. She held it close to her, suddenly irrationally fearful of it being snatched away. Sitting down at the empty table, she opened it and began to slowly turn the pages. There it was. A plain white slip of paper with one word written on

it. She crumpled the paper, sticking it into her pocket, returned the book to the shelf, and left.

She got back into the passenger seat. "Do you see a road
called Clayton?"

"Yeah, here it is." He pointed to it on the map.

"Then we are off to number thirty-seven."

"Great going, T." He held her gaze and smiled broadly.

"Well, what are you waiting for? Let's go!"

o   o   o

An hour later, Jack and Taylor pulled onto Clayton Drive. It
was another long and dusty road that seemed to go on forever.
There were a few small farms and a random house or two,
but it was a mostly deserted stretch of road. Just when they
thought they had hit another dead end, they pulled in front of
a small Cape Cod that backed into woods. There were no other
houses around. Jack turned to Taylor and raised his eyebrows.

"Not what I expected, but here goes nothing."

She unlatched her seat belt, but he put a hand over hers.

"Wait here until I assess the situation. I don't know what
we might be walking into. Get in the driver's seat—that way
you can take off if you have to."

"Seriously? We're in this together. I can take care of myself."

"Okay . . . sorry."

They approached the front door, which opened before they
had a chance to knock. Standing before them was an older man
with white hair and black-framed glasses. He smiled warmly.

"We've been expecting you. Certainly took your time getting here." He chuckled at their shocked expressions.

Jack held out his hand. "I'm Jack—"

The man interrupted him. "I know who you are." He turned his attention to Taylor. "You, child, must be Taylor. Come in, come in."

Taylor gave Jack a bemused look as they walked into the foyer. Now that they were inside the house, she saw that it was actually quite large—she could see into a long, eat-in kitchen and beyond it another large rectangular room. Before the door was shut, Beau began to bark from the back seat.

"Well, well. Who is that?"

"My dog," Taylor replied.

"Go get him. Poor thing must be going crazy all cooped up."

Taylor smiled gratefully and went immediately to retrieve him.

Beau ran into the house whimpering and licked the man's hand, his tail swishing in a frenzy.

"Are you all going to stand in the hallway all day or come in the kitchen and have something to eat?" a voice called from the other end of the house.

The man smiled. "That's Gilly. Come on, she's eager to meet you."

They were greeted by a sweet-looking older woman who was bustling around the kitchen and setting out a variety of scrumptious-looking desserts. She held out her arms and insisted on giving each of them a warm hug.

They sat at the round, wooden kitchen table. Jack cleared

his throat, ready to start asking questions, but the man spoke again.

"Guess you'll be wanting some explanations. I'm Professor Carl Rittenhouse and this is my lovely wife, Gilly. I taught at Harvard for the past thirty years. Retired a few years ago, so I could devote myself full-time to my research and writing." He leaned back in his chair.

"Jeremy was one of my students many years ago. One of the brightest but also the most troubled. He hated my class, didn't think it applied to him, even sought to get it removed as a program requirement."

Taylor looked at him with interest. "What do you teach?"

He smiled. "Glad you asked, my dear. I teach medical ethics. I have my PhD in bioethics, but I'm not your typical bioethicist. You see, most in the field are working to push the limits, see how far they can go to optimize care, allocate limited resources by building a hierarchy of who deserves what. I'm what they consider a fringe lunatic. Pro-life, anti-euthanasia, anti–embryonic stem cell research, and anti–assisted suicide."

Beau ambled over after drinking from the bowl Gilly had set on the floor for him and sat at Carl's feet. Carl stroked his head while he continued.

"Jeremy was not aligned with my views—many of my students weren't—but he harbored a hatred I'd not come across very often. Only way I can put it—he had an evil aura about him."

Jack couldn't keep the skeptical expression from appearing. Carl seemed to notice.

"I don't use that word lightly, Jack."

Gilly set a plate of coffee cake on the table and joined them.

"I knew the only thing I could do was pray for the boy. Nothing I could say or do on my own was going to influence him, although I tried. An angrier atheist I have never met. When he graduated, I thought I had seen the last of him."

Gilly patted her husband's hand. "You'd have to know my husband to understand. He lives his faith more than anyone I know. Over the years, there have been some complaints about him professing his faith, but it's never stopped him. Did you know that Harvard was named after a Christian minister?"

Jack and Taylor both shook their heads.

Carl continued. "It's my belief that as long as we still have the power of free speech, no one should have the ability to stop us from sharing our convictions. My belief in God is so intricately wound up in my philosophy, my view of medicine, that to leave it behind would mean leaving all that behind as well. Of course, I didn't preach to the class, but I would not skirt any questions on the issues of faith and how they affected my beliefs. It worked for everyone, except for the occasional rabble-rouser who felt the right to his or her own beliefs supplanted my own. But I digress. Jeremy. The Lord let me know that I needed to keep on praying for him. So I did. A few years ago, he showed up on campus. I took one look at him and knew something had happened to change him."

Jack and Taylor were enthralled as Carl continued his story.

"Jeremy had discovered the truth about his father, Damon Crosse, who he really was and the extent to which he had sunk to attain his goals. The only affirmation he ever received from Crosse was for his academic achievement. Friendships were discouraged. He was groomed for one purpose. To one day take over the Institute."

"What's the Institute?" Jack asked.

"A training facility. And so much more."

Taylor shook her head. "I don't understand. What does this have to do with Malcolm and his vote? With the people trying to kill us?"

Jack put his hand on her arm. "I'm fairly sure Damon Crosse is who Malcolm worked for." He looked back at Carl. "What truth?"

"It's a very long story, and it's Jeremy's to tell. He came to me after this happened. Instead of Crosse's revelations bonding him to his son, they alienated him."

"Where is Jeremy now?"

"I don't know exactly. All of us have limited information, just what we need to help you reach the next waypoint."

Jack stood up, pacing. "Hold on. Doesn't Jeremy trust you?"

"Of course, but if Damon found us . . . well, he would stop at nothing to get his hands on Jeremy." He arched a brow. "No one is immune to torture."

Taylor's eyes widened. "The more I learn, the more incredible this all is."

"It's true. Once you get to Jeremy, you'll get the answers you seek." He stood. "I'll go and get your instructions."

Gilly got up and cleared the table. She looked at Taylor with warm eyes. "How are you feeling, my dear?"

"I'm doing okay."

"How about a quick cup of tea before you get going?"

"No thanks, I'm fine." Taylor felt strangely grateful for these small kindnesses and swallowed the lump in her throat. She wanted to sit in this kitchen all day and pretend that this sweet woman was someone who loved her, an aunt or a grandmother. Why was she being so silly? She had just met her.

"Gilly, do you and Carl know anything about my husband? About his role in all this?"

The older woman stared at her for a long moment. "I think it's best if you wait to ask Jeremy."

Taylor looked up as Carl came back into the kitchen.

Jack cleared his throat. "It's time to get moving. We've still got a couple hours to go."

She nodded and pushed back in the chair. "All right." She looked at Gilly. "Will I see you again?" She was reluctant to leave her.

Gilly smiled warmly. "You bet. Our home is always open to you. We'll talk again after you've seen Jeremy. We're here to help."

Carl looked at Taylor. "I think it would be best if you left Beau here while you visit with Jeremy."

Taylor began to object, but Carl put a hand on her shoulder. "I promise we'll treat him like he's our own, and he'll be here waiting for you when you return."

Taylor nodded reluctantly. It *would* be better for him here. Safer. "If anything happens to me, you will take care of him?" Her voice caught.

Carl's eyes were kind. "Nothing is going to happen to you." He put his hand on Beau's back. "We'll take good care of him no matter what."

"Thank you." Taylor bent down and embraced her beloved dog. Tears spilled from her eyes as she stroked him and whispered, "I love you, boy. I'll be back for you—don't worry." She laid her head on his and then turned away. It was unbearable.

"Here's your next set of instructions," Carl said as he handed the paper to Jack. "Godspeed, son." He gave Jack's shoulder a squeeze.

Outside, they walked to the car. Taylor glanced back for one more look at Beau. He was watching her from the door, a somber expression in his wise eyes. She blinked back tears and tried to push away the feeling that she would never see him again.

CHAPTER FORTY-FIVE

THE INSTITUTE, MARCH 1976

THE BABY IS COMING. I WAKE UP IN A COLD SWEAT, AND with a jolt, I feel another contraction. A moan escapes my lips, and I roll to my side and grip the edge of the bed. *It hurts, it hurts.* I didn't know it would hurt so much. I scream and try to bring my knees to my chest, but my belly is too big. I remember what I learned about the Lamaze method in medical school, and I rock and breathe, rock and breathe. It helps a little. The contraction passes, and I push my sweat-drenched hair back from my forehead. I look at the clock on the table to time my contractions. I sit up, trying to work out the dull ache in my back. In ten minutes, another one starts. The pain snakes its way from my toes, up my legs, and to my belly until it feels like there's a vise inside me smashing all my organs.

I push on my stomach. It is rock hard. I feel like my bowels are going to explode. I need to bear down, push, but I know it's too soon. *Breathe.* It will be over in a minute. I clutch the sheets and bite my cheek. It stops again. Eight minutes this time. A spasm in my back makes me jerk forward, and another scream flies from my mouth. Sweat stings my eyes, and I swipe at my face with my sleeve. I start to shake and the whole bed seems to move with me. Why am I so cold now? Another convulsion and I'm racked again. Only four minutes. *No. You're coming too fast.*

I cry out as another wave of pain overtakes me and fall back on the bed. My knuckles are white as I squeeze the pillow. The contractions are faster now, each one leaving me more breathless than before. Something is wrong. A searing pain rips through me and a wetness spreads down my legs. Blood, there is too much blood. Someone needs to come.

"Help. Something's wrong." I push the call button over and over.

The door bursts open, and I'm thrown onto a gurney. He is there, panic written all over his face.

Time is running out. *Once you are born, I will die.* He'll kill me as swiftly and as easily as he did his own father—as he did my parents. But I don't fear death—not anymore. I know my Savior awaits me and that he will shepherd me from this hellish existence into paradise. *But leaving you?* This is a pain so deep, an anguish so terrible it slices through me like a knife. *I love you, my child.* There is nothing more to say.

They rush me to the elevator and down to the first level. I'm wheeled into a cold room with shiny steel tables and counters and bright lights. He has his own operating room. The pain is excruciating now. I can't stop the screams. My eyes are clouding, and all I can hear is the clang of instruments and the voices shouting all around me. From the corner of my eye, I see Dunst. He is sitting, directing them.

A nurse hooks an IV up to my arm, and I beg for some relief. I know it's too late for an epidural and I don't want to be knocked out—I want to see my baby if only for a second—but I need something for the pain.

"Please, give me something for the pain," I gasp.

She looks in the direction of Dunst.

"Dr. Dunst?"

He doesn't hesitate. "No. She can get through it. Medicine is not good for the baby. Give her nothing."

The doctor is yelling. "There's no time. The placenta is abrupting. We have to deliver now!"

My God! They can't really be going to cut into me with no anesthesia. They don't even bother to put up a drape, so I see everything unfold. Betadine is thrown on my stomach; the scalpel is out, and the pain is white-hot the second the knife touches my skin. I howl, and the nurse clamps her hand down hard over my mouth. I feel my organs being jostled and almost pass out from the pain. I'm trying to hold on for a glimpse of my baby—just one look. I am being torn in two. The agony is indescribable, and I yearn for the release of death. Everything begins to fade, and I know I'm bleeding out. It won't be long now. A cry pierces the air, and I see him lifted from me. I try to raise my arms, but they don't move. I long to hold him—to kiss him.

"Please, let . . . see." I can hardly speak.

The doctor hands my child to Damon. He is walking away, then stops, turns around, and holds him in front of me, close enough to touch if I had the strength. He is beautiful. So beautiful. *I love you*, I want to say, but nothing comes out.

And then it doesn't hurt anymore. The pain is gone and a warmth washes over me. Arms of love embrace me, and there is no more fear. I'm lifted, beckoned from this dim and fading room to another place that shines so bright, like going from darkest night to brightest morning. I'm free! I turn back for one last look, and the last thing I see before I leave is my son's beautiful, beautiful face.

CHAPTER FORTY-SIX

MELANCHOLY ENVELOPED TAYLOR. SHE STARED OUT THE window and took in the bleak surroundings as they drove down what seemed to be a never-ending road. She felt like the trees—stripped of their leaves, bare and vulnerable, their insides exposed for the world to see. When she thought of her baby, she was overwhelmed with a sense of helplessness. A week ago everything made sense. Now, her very survival depended on her partnership with the one man who had broken her heart—the man she swore she would never trust again.

"Jack?"

"Hmm?"

"Did the two of you discuss me?"

He exhaled slowly. "No, Taylor. Never."

"I met her once. Did you know that?"

"What? When?"

She exhaled. "When I found out you'd gotten married, I drove up from Maryland. She answered the door. You were in the shower. She knew my name, mocked me."

"She never told me. She knew who you were, but I didn't talk about you. I swear."

She didn't know whether she believed him or not, but plunged in anyway. "Why did you let her take you from me?"

He looked at her. "Are you sure you want to hear this?"

"No. But I can't stand having it between us anymore. We can't keep pretending everything is okay. You broke my heart, Jack." Her voice caught, and she turned away.

"I know."

A heavy silence filled the car for a long while. And, then, finally, he spoke.

"You can't imagine how often I've gone over it in my mind—back to when I first met her—changed the scenario. Walked away. Never gone to her show. I wish to God I could go back in time and undo it."

"You still haven't answered my question."

"I don't know how! God knows I've spent years regretting it. She took me by surprise, knew exactly what to say and how to get under my skin. She was an addiction. One that nearly destroyed me."

"I know what she did to you. But you were supposed to be committed to me. How could you turn your back on us so easily? How could you sleep with her in the first place?" Now she was sorry she had started the conversation. Far from breaking down any walls, she felt new resentments and hurts arise.

He shook his head. "It wasn't about the sex. There was something else—"

"Stop." Of course it was about the sex. How many times had she imagined the two of them together? "I don't want to hear any more. I guess I'm not ready to discuss it after all."

He tried again. "I really wish I could make you understand—"

"So do I," she responded sharply. She looked down at the map then at the handheld directions.

"Turn up there." She pointed to the left.

Jack slammed on the brakes and made the sharp left-hand turn down the narrow dirt road.

"Wait. Take note of the odometer. We have to go exactly one point seven miles and then take another left. There's no road."

A few minutes later, Jack parked in a small, round dirt enclosure. He took the paper from Taylor.

"We have to follow this trail and there will be a four-by-four waiting," she said.

"Here, put these on." He handed her the hat and gloves Carl had given him before they'd left.

Taylor slipped them on, and they got out of the car.

Jack reached out to take her arm. "It's a little slippery here. Hold on to me."

They walked arm in arm into the woods.

"Feels a little like Hansel and Gretel," he joked.

She smiled in spite of herself. "Let's hope our story has a happy ending, too." Taylor pointed. "According to Carl's map, the truck should be up ahead about a hundred feet."

The trees seemed to close in upon them, the brush growing

L. C. SHAW

denser with every step they took. It was impossible to see anything but the branches around them.

"I have an idea. Give me the keys," Taylor said. "You think it matters if we make a little noise?"

He shook his head. "The only people around here are Jeremy's folks. I think we're fine."

She depressed the panic button and immediately a loud blaring filled the air.

They followed the noise, got in the vehicle, and began the descent down the mountain toward Jeremy's hideout. Taylor held tightly to the handle hanging above her door as they bounced down the hill.

Jack looked at her apologetically. "Going as slow as I can."

She grimaced. "I know."

They finally reached the bottom of the steep hill and got out of the truck.

"This is getting a bit tedious," Jack mumbled as Taylor read Carl's instructions aloud.

They counted to the prescribed number of steps and came to a hill. They reached a tall tree with a birdhouse hanging from a low branch.

"That's it."

Jack put his hand in the box and retrieved a key. They walked another hundred feet and came to a small cabin. Using the key, they entered, and Jack turned on the flashlight and looked around the small one-room building.

"What's that?" Taylor asked, pointing to an envelope taped to the wall.

Jack snatched it down and tore it open. It was another set of directions and a compass. They went back outside.

"We need to go east twelve hundred feet and we'll be there. Are you okay? It's a lot of walking."

She arched an eyebrow. "I may be pregnant, but I'm not out of shape."

He held his hands up in surrender. "Sorry."

They reached the entrance to what looked like a cave, the opening large enough to accommodate one person. There was a wall blocking it made of a smooth plaster. Jack pulled the phone Carl had given him from his pocket.

He dialed the number on the sheet of paper. A male voice answered.

Jack spoke the words as instructed: "This is the day that the Lord has made."

A whirring filled the air, and the door slowly opened as it slid into the wall.

"After you." Jack moved aside for Taylor.

As soon as they were both inside, the door closed behind them.

Taylor looked around at the bright and cheerful surroundings. She didn't know what she had expected, maybe something more ominous and akin to the underground hideouts she'd seen in James Bond movies. Instead, the narrow entranceway was painted a light yellow, and the shiny hardwood floors were covered with vibrant oriental rugs. There was no one waiting to greet them, so they began to walk in the only direction they could—straight ahead. When they reached the end of the hallway, they came to an elevator and pushed the button. Immediately, the door slid open.

"What floor?"

Taylor exhaled a deep breath, suddenly very nervous. "I don't know. Pick one."

He depressed the top button, and they ascended.

When the doors opened, a man was waiting. He was tall and trim, with light brown hair worn on the longish side, and looked to be only a few years older than Taylor. He gave them a wide smile that transformed his face from merely nice-looking to handsome.

"I thank God that you made it! I'm Jeremy."

So this was the mysterious Jeremy. He looked at her like he already knew her, and Taylor didn't know what she was feeling. When he got closer, she realized that he reminded her of someone, but she couldn't put her finger on who.

She held out her hand, and he grasped it in both of his.

"I'm Taylor."

They followed him to a living room, where an assortment of snacks and drinks awaited them. "Would you like to freshen up?"

She didn't want to wait another minute to find out what he had to say. "We're fine," she answered for both of them.

"Let's sit down then," Jeremy said.

They had made it! She should have felt a tremendous sense of relief, but she still felt suspended in anticipation. Jeremy seemed so normal, though, and a warmth emanated from him that made her feel immediately comfortable with him. She took a seat in the plush chair closest to the fireplace so that she could see the fire and also enjoy the view of the outside from the floor-to-ceiling windows. There was nothing but tall evergreens and mountains in the distance. Looking out made her feel far away from danger, hidden away and safe from the faceless enemies they were running from.

"Thanks for the help back at the motel," Jack said. "But one question that's been nagging at me—Paul said that the St. Christopher medal was how you were tracking us. How did the woman at Walgreens even know I'd be there so she could give it to me?"

Jeremy nodded. "I knew Malcolm was going to you for help, so I've been having you followed ever since he was killed."

"Well, I guess that answers that," Taylor said to Jack then turned to Jeremy. She was feeling impatient suddenly to understand what this whole quest was really about. "Who was my husband?" That's what it all boiled down to after all—why they were here in the mountains of Vermont with a stranger.

Jeremy took a seat across from her, his expression neutral.

"That's a complicated question. We'll get to it, I promise, but I think it may make more sense if I tell you who I am."

"We know you're Damon Crosse's son," Jack said.

Jeremy nodded. "Yes, he is my father. He runs a research and training facility but it's a front for much more. In private circles, it's called the Institute, and its graduates are placed in positions of power in all spheres of influence."

Taylor leaned forward. "So Malcolm was one of the graduates of the Institute?"

"He was. Groomed for his position and firmly in Damon's pocket."

She was still having a hard time wrapping her head around it. "Was Malcolm even his real name?"

Jeremy stood up and paced. "I don't know what his real name was." He stopped and put a hand on Taylor's shoulder. "I don't think he did either. He was an orphan, raised at the Institute."

"What? How old was he when he was orphaned?" She thought of the parents he'd told her he'd lost to an accident when he was fifteen, the way they'd shared their grief at experiencing a sudden and devastating loss. That was his way into her heart—and it was all one big lie. She thought of the picture they'd kept on the mantel of "his parents." Another fabrication apparently.

"According to his file, he was brought to the Institute by nuns when he was a small child."

"How was he able to keep that a secret with such a public life?" Taylor asked.

"Because all his documents were legitimate. His birth certificate, school records, et cetera. My father has connections everywhere. It's not hard to give someone a new identity. Think of all the spies that stay undetected for years."

"Liar," she whispered as she clenched and unclenched her fists.

She caught Jeremy and Jack exchanging a look.

"For what it's worth, Taylor, he did love you," Jeremy said.

"How could you possibly know that?" It was ludicrous to think that this stranger knew more about her own husband than she did.

"It's why he did what he did—to protect you and your child.

Let me explain. The only thing my father ever cared about was my accomplishments. He pushed me to excel at everything at the expense of all else. In my desire to please him, I worked hard. After I graduated from high school, I entered Harvard, where I earned my undergraduate degree in biology. I continued through their doctoral program and attained my PhD."

He went on. "During my visits home, my father began my indoctrination into the dark world of magic. He taught me the spells and incantations that he knew, the secret books that he referenced. I had been raised with no religion and had always assumed he was an atheist. But he was suddenly showing me an unseen spiritual realm and teaching me of its power. He made me do things and say things that I will never be able to forget. He wanted me to believe that I could never turn back, that I was beyond redemption. I helped him blackmail people, made them commit crimes. When I finished my studies, I returned home to begin my work full-time. I'd fallen in love for the first time. I will never forget the look on his face when I told him about her. The combination of indignation and outrage took me completely by surprise. *No* was all he said. I asked him why, but he wouldn't answer. He got up from the table and left. The very next day, when I went to the lab, she was gone. No one would give me any answers. I went to her apartment, and it was empty. There was no trace of her anywhere. I searched for her for months, and finally gave up."

She felt her earlier anger at him evaporate. "I'm so sorry, Jeremy. What did you do then?" Taylor asked.

"I went to his study and demanded that he tell me what he had done. He looked at me with derision, asked if I was still so naive as to think I could lead a normal life. He told me there would be no wife, no family, in the cards for me. I was to be the heir to something far greater. 'You have a role to play in the shaping of humanity,' he said. 'You will be instrumental in undoing the unselfish sacrifice of the one who thinks he has won. You were chosen for a specific purpose.'

"Then he showed me a video of my mother." Jeremy grew quiet and looked off into the distance. "He explained how he had lured her to the Institute with the pretense of a medical fellowship, then impregnated her and locked her up. She begged him to let her live. He told her that I didn't need a mother, that her role in my life would end the moment I was born. The look of despair in her eyes will haunt me forever. He thought I would see the weak, disposable tool that he did. Instead of binding me closer to him, the video turned me against him. The last thing he said was how she couldn't even give birth without making a mess. Apparently, something happened during the delivery, and she bled to death."

Taylor gasped.

Jeremy was whispering the story to himself as much as to them. "He did nothing to help her, nothing to ease her pain. I hated him then with every fiber of my being—for what he had done to her, and what he had made me into. I left then, driving aimlessly, and before I'd realized it, I was back at Harvard, outside the office of my ethics professor."

"Dr. Rittenhouse," Jack said.

Jeremy nodded. "Yes. He didn't even look surprised to see me. It was like he had been waiting for me to come. I told him everything. I don't know how long I was with him. He listened without judgment. When I was finished, he asked me why I had come. He was the only person I knew from the university who had no shame in publicly declaring his faith. I wanted to know if his god could forgive me."

Both Jack and Taylor were leaning forward in their seats.

Jeremy smiled. "He told me that, yes, he could. That his god was a loving and graceful god who had sent his son to die for me. For *me*. What about everything I had done, I asked him. Could God overlook blackmail? Could he overlook my involvement in the occult? Carl told me that God would forgive all of it—all I had to do was ask from a sincere heart. Carl and I worked together to devise a plan to bring my father down. I had to go back, to pretend that I was still on board. Then, I slowly began to amass my information, to make lists, target those who didn't want to be under his influence but were forced to and those he had tried to win over but didn't. I had to know who I could and couldn't trust."

"How could you go back there? Couldn't he tell that you had changed?" Taylor asked.

Jeremy tented his hands. "He sees what he wants. I went back and told him that I hated what he had done to my mother, but that I knew I had to live up to my purpose. I convinced him to let me spend most of my time in the lab, working on one of his pet projects. That way, I didn't have to do any more of his dirty work. He was eager for the breakthrough I promised him, and I made sure, over that time, to come close but never complete it."

"What kind of project?" Jack asked.

"Genetics. He had me testing delivery vehicles for germ-line therapy."

"Germ line?" Taylor asked, confused.

"Sorry," Jeremy said. "It's a form of genetic modification that changes DNA down to future generations."

"I've read about gene therapy. It's wonderful. Diseases are being cured, people helped. How can that be a bad thing?" Taylor asked.

"Because he wants to use it for his own purposes."

"Like what?" Jack asked. "Is Crosse planning on doing the opposite? Causing diseases?"

Jeremy shook his head. "I'm not sure. He's too paranoid to trust anyone with the whole picture—not even me before he knew I'd changed my loyalty. All I know is whatever he has planned, it won't be to help people. He wanted to test something in a vaccine."

Something suddenly dawned on Taylor. "Hold on." She pulled her notebook from her purse and flipped through it. "Alpha Pharmaceuticals is a company I mentioned before to Jack. The one Brody Hamilton sponsored bills on. Is that your father's company?"

"Yes. Alpha Pharma is a blind trust, but he's the owner. I was working alongside their vaccine researchers, trying to figure out a way to incorporate germ-line genetic material into a vaccine."

"So is Alpha Pharma the one developing a TB vaccine with the TB Vaccine Initiative?" she asked.

Jeremy nodded.

Jack jumped up. "Crosse is behind the bill to mandate the TB vaccine?"

"Yes. I believe he wanted to test his research with the new vaccine."

"Why would the scientists at Alpha go along with adding something secret to a vaccine? Are they all unethical, too?" Jack asked.

Jeremy shook his head. "Not at all. They think they're doing vital work that has the potential to help thousands."

"Carl said you were a scientist. Did you have any hand in the research before you left?" Taylor asked.

Jeremy put his back to them and stared into the fire. Taking a deep breath, he turned around to face them. "My research was focused on perfecting the delivery system for the germ-line changes. He has others working on the genetic material. I was close to getting to the truth when he found out I'd betrayed him." Jeremy shook his head. "He's brilliant and dangerous. His scientists think they're working on gene therapy breakthroughs. But a handful of former Nazi scientists know what he's really doing and that all takes place far from the main institute, in a secret facility."

"Sounds very vague and like a lot of supposition on your part," Jack said.

Jeremy shrugged. "You can't possibly understand the depth of depravity that is Damon Crosse. I don't have to know the details to know that whatever he's doing in that lab is not for the common good. But that's only a part of his work. The Institute has been working for over forty years to corrupt society. He has thousands of people working for him, and they're everywhere. His assault on morality began before I was born, and he's still using every means at his disposal to continue it."

"I don't understand. How can one man launch an attack on all our morals?" Jack asked.

"He's got lobbyists, politicians, advertising people. Take a look around—at television, at the direction our laws are moving in. He's like a maestro, orchestrating it all from his fortress in the woods."

"I don't have a problem with our laws, Jeremy. You're starting to sound a little paranoid to me."

"Jack." Taylor gave him a look.

"Well, seriously, come on. People aren't sheep. One man cannot be manipulating an entire nation."

"You'd be surprised at how easily people are influenced, Jack," Jeremy answered. "The decline in church attendance is something he's gleeful about."

That raised Jack's hackles. "If you're trying to tell me that church is the answer to society's problems, don't waste your breath. In my opinion, organized religion is the cause of most of society's ills."

Jeremy looked at him for a long moment before speaking. "I won't argue with you, Jack. Church attendance is merely a symptom of a greater problem. I'm talking about the loss of faith, the elevation of self, and the move in society away from good."

"We can debate this later. Let's get back to the issue at hand—stopping Crosse. He admitted to watching your mother die without lifting a finger to help her. You said he even recorded it. Do you know where he keeps the tape of your mother? Can you use that against him?" Jack asked.

Jeremy nodded. "I'm sure it's still at the Institute. I tried to find it before I left. I'm thinking it's in his private chambers. He has too much pride to destroy it, and he likes his trophies."

"We need to get our hands on that tape," Taylor said.

Jeremy shook his head. "Impossible. We can't go there. We'd never make it out alive. The only reason I have been able to stay in hiding all this time is because of the generosity of my benefactor. He helped me to find and finance this place."

"Who is it?" Jack asked.

"The man who has been the CEO of Damon's pharma company for the past twenty years. When I told him—his name is Sinclair Devlin—the truth about Damon's work at the Institute, he agreed to help me."

"Is he still heading up the company?" Jack asked.

"Yes. Damon has no idea that Devlin is helping me. He's keeping a close watch on the TB initiative and the work on genetic therapy."

"That makes me feel a little better," Taylor said.

Jeremy looked at them. "I have something to show you. The quality is very poor. I did my best to enhance it, but it was converted from tape that is over thirty years old."

The television screen came to life and the image of a young woman, visibly pregnant, filled the screen. She was sitting in a plush velvet chair with a stained-glass window behind her.

"You'll never get away with this."

A melodious voice answered her.

"Don't you see I already have? Your parents are gone. Your sister thinks you've abandoned her. We've sent her a letter from you saying that you never want to speak to her again, that you've made a new life in Europe."

She shot up from the chair. "She'll never believe that!"

He laughed. "She'll forget about you."

"Never."

"Trust me, Maya. She'll find a new family. Now that you and your parents are dead, she'll move on."

The man rose and walked toward her, his back to the camera. He put his hands on her shoulders and spoke slowly and deliberately to her. "She thinks you've run off with someone you met from here. She's very hurt that you missed her wedding."

She hung her head.

"Eva got married?"

The screen went blank, and Jeremy got up and turned off the television.

Taylor looked at Jeremy. "Eva?"

Jeremy hesitated. "Your mother."

Jack looked back and forth between the two of them, bewildered.

"My mother and your mother were sisters," he said.

Taylor looked up, trying to remember. "My mother told me that her parents died in a car crash a few years before she got married, but she never mentioned having a sister. Why would she keep it a secret?"

Jeremy shook his head. "I don't know. Maybe it was too hard for her."

"We can use that tape to prove he kidnapped her," Jack said.

"It's not enough. It'd be impossible to authenticate. He could say it was fake. Plus, you never see his face," Jeremy answered.

He handed a piece of paper to Taylor. "This is a letter she wrote to your mother. I guess she knew it would never get mailed, but she wrote it anyway. I found it when I was searching my father's office before I left."

Taylor took the paper from Jeremy with a shaking hand and read aloud.

February 11, 1976

My darling Eva,

He has shown it all to me. It is appalling how easily he has managed to manipulate the people who work for him. They are zealots who actually believe in the philosophical rhetoric he uses to blind them. There are already dozens of his graduates placed in key positions—politicians, judges, doctors, captains of industry, media executives. They are everywhere. There are files on all of them, evidence of his empire and all those who have done his bidding to build it. Brainwashing, torture, even murder—there is no method that is beneath him. He took great pride in sharing his collection of memoirs with me.

His favorite topic these days is how, through his efforts, it will one day be legal to decide who should live or die based on their worth to society. Life will

have no intrinsic value. The so-called bioethicists,
a term he uses with malicious irony, will succeed
in convincing otherwise intelligent people that the
greater good is served by weeding out the weak. Those
with incurable illnesses and diminished mental and
physical capacity are better off being released from
this world, so resources can be better used for the
healthy and firm.

My time is coming to an end. I have so many re-
grets. I never got to say good-bye to you and to Mama
and Papa. I wish I could tell them that I returned
to my faith—and that I love them. How difficult it
can be for a person of intellect to accept the things of
God. If it couldn't be scientifically proven, I had no
use for it. Now I see how small we are in relation to
God, yet how interested he is in us personally. The
magnitude of his grace is beyond my comprehension.
I am grateful that this temporary detour to hell has
brought me to my senses. I know, beyond a shadow of
a doubt, that when my usefulness to Damon is gone
and he kills me, I will be sent into the arms of Jesus.
And I will be at peace at last.

All my love always and forever,
Maya

"I'm so sorry. So very . . ." Her voice broke and the tears fell. She took a deep breath and put her hand on Jeremy's. "They're together now."

"Your mother was a believer?"

Taylor smiled. "Yes. Her faith defined her." She gave Jeremy a long look. "So our mothers were sisters? We're first cousins?"

Jeremy didn't answer.

She leaned over and embraced him. "I thought I felt a connection when I met you." She laughed. "Not to mention that we have the same green eyes."

Jeremy looked at her somberly.

"I have something else to show you." He opened up a drawer in the table next to her and pulled out a photograph. "This is my father, Damon Crosse."

Staring back at her was a man with emerald-green eyes—eyes the exact color of hers.

CHAPTER FORTY-SEVEN

NATHAN TRIED TO IGNORE THE TWITCHING IN HIS EYE. *Count to ten*, he reminded himself. *Shut up. Shut up. They're looking at you. One, two, three four, five, six seven. Breathe, breathe, look normal!*

She'd come for him a few days after she got out, just like she'd promised. The first thing he did was what she'd told him. Go to the Beans and Leaves coffee shop in Woodstock, New York. He was in line, getting ready to give them his order. Regular coffee, no sugar, light on the cream. Regular coffee, no sugar, light on the cream. It was his turn.

"Regular coffee, sugar, no cream," he stammered. "No! Wait! No sugar, light cream." Phew. He'd almost messed up. *Think right, think bright, light, sight, might. STOP IT! One, two, three, four, five, six, seven, eight. Breathe, breathe.* "Thank you."

He looked around suspiciously. There were lots of them everywhere. He could tell. They thought they were so smart, that they could fool him. Ha! He knew better. He narrowed his eyes at a particularly tricky one. She was masquerading as an innocent old lady, but he saw through her. He thought about smacking her right in the head, but he had been warned not to make a scene.

He found a seat at one of the tables in the back, just like she told him. He tapped his foot while he waited, his eyes darting around the room, surveying everyone in the crowded café. Where was she? *Wouldn't wait forever. Couldn't wait for never. Thought she was so clever. Someone's head to sever. STOP! One, two, three, four, five, six. Breathe, breathe, breathe.*

"Hello, Nathan."

His head jerked around. She had come! He grinned, and a relieved laugh escaped his lips.

She sat down across from him. "Good boy. You did exactly as I asked. I'm very proud of you."

He beamed.

"Did you bring it?"

He nodded his head excitedly. "Yes, wanna see it now?"

"Not here!" she snapped.

He tensed, and a scowl replaced his smile.

She patted his hand with hers. "What I mean, my dear, is it's not safe here. I wouldn't want you to get in trouble."

He relaxed, and his shoulders fell back into their usual slump. "Okey dokey, smokey. Where should we go?"

"Come with me and I'll show you."

They walked outside into the bracing air. Nathan had

no coat and shivered as the cold wind nestled under his thin shirt.

He began to sing. "Freezing, wheezing, cold, old, sold, fold."

She stopped at a black Jaguar. "Here we are."

He backed away from the car as if it were alive.

"No black. I don't like black. It's black, it's black, attack."

She grabbed his arm hard.

"Ow," he yelled.

"Stop it now. Count. Do you hear me? Count. It's fine. Get in."

He gave her a terrified look but obeyed. She was being mean. He would ignore her. That would teach her not to be mean. They drove in silence for the next twenty minutes. She stopped the car at a warehouse.

There was a big car sitting out in front of it. "What's that?"

"That," she said, "is your gateway to freedom."

"I don't understand."

"I'm taking you to a place where the doctors can help you."

He screamed. "No doctors! No needles! Needles! Beetles! No more!"

She turned to look at him. "Eyes."

He looked at her.

"Have I ever hurt you?"

He shook his head.

"These doctors are different. They're going to help you think clearly. No medicine. No machines. No needles."

The door to the large car opened and the driver emerged.

"Mr. Crosse would like to know the reason for the delay. He is eager to be on his way," the man said. He talked funny.

Dakota gave the man a fast nod, got out of the car, and walked around to open the passenger door. "Come."

He looked around. She was moving toward the car without him. He didn't want to be left alone.

"Wait." He hurried to catch up and followed her into the big car.

CHAPTER FORTY-EIGHT

TAYLOR WENT COLD. "ARE YOU TRYING TO TELL ME THAT Damon Crosse is my father? How can that be?"

"He is nothing if not thorough. He had his people spy on Maya's family—your mother, your grandparents. He arranged for your grandparents' death. When your mother married Warwick Parks, he made sure they were watched—and that people who worked for him befriended them, even worked for Warwick at the paper. When your mother couldn't get pregnant, their family doctor steered them to a fertility clinic in England that performed the IVF treatments. It was one of Damon's clinics. Instead of your father's sperm, they used Damon's," Jeremy said.

Taylor's hand flew to her mouth. "How do you know this?"

"He bragged about it to me. He said Maya would be horrified that he was the father of her sister's child, too."

"But why? Why did he want my mother to have his child? He's never been in my life."

"He talked about some sort of power in your family's blood."

"What are you talking about?"

Jeremy cleared his throat. "Taylor, do you know anything about some silver coins that have been held by your family?"

"What?"

"My father is obsessed with them. It's the reason he chose my mother in the first place. He wanted to know what her family had done with them. Damon has been searching for thirty pieces of silver that Judas received for betraying Jesus for many years. He believed some of them were hidden by Saint John on that island."

"I've never heard anything about them," Taylor said.

"Okay, so why was he looking for these pieces of silver?" Jack asked.

"My adoptive grandfather, Fred Crosse, was a German scientist. He'd been on Patmos during the war and told my father about them. By the time I was old enough to know him, he was completely bedridden. He had MSA-P, multiple system atrophy, a debilitating illness resembling Parkinson's. I used to visit with him when I'd come home from school on breaks. He talked about the old country sometimes, and made mention of the war, but nothing coherent. I found out later that he came after the war and worked for the government for a while before he got sick. He was convinced that my mother's family had them, that they'd brought them to America when they left Greece. He'd been in Greece at the same time. Before he died he started referring to himself as Friedrich, not Fred, though my father would get angry and tell him his name was Fred."

Taylor's heart began to pound. The thoughts were coming too fast now. She took a deep breath. "What year did this Friedrich come to the United States?" Taylor asked.

"Some time in the 1940s, I think."

"What kind of scientist was he?" she pressed.

"A geneticist."

Taylor's heart raced. It was all making sense now. "Have you ever heard of Operation Paperclip?"

Jeremy had a blank expression on his face. "Operation what?"

"Paperclip. It was a covert operation where the United States smuggled in Nazi war criminals, whitewashed their histories, and made them citizens."

"Why would they do that?"

"Because they were more afraid of Russia at the time and wanted to get the best scientists and spies before the Soviets did. I'm wondering if Friedrich was one of those scientists," Taylor said.

"Are there any photos? I think I'd recognize him as a younger man. Besides, how many geneticists named Friedrich could have come over?"

Jack walked over to the corner of the room where their belongings were huddled in a corner and got his laptop.

"Can we narrow it down through a search?" he asked Taylor. "Look for geneticists and see the names?"

"Maybe, but there were over sixteen hundred scientists and doctors, and I don't know that we'd find them easily using

Google. But I do have all the names from a piece I did years ago for Karen Printz's show. I save all my research." She deflated. "Of course, it's all at home, filed. I did that story almost ten years ago."

Jack's fingers were tapping the keys. "Let me see what I come up with."

"Do you remember anything odd about Friedrich? Anything he had that could be tied to the Nazis?" Taylor asked.

Jeremy jumped up. "He had a ring. I remember because it fascinated me as a kid. He told me I'd have it one day. But when he died and I asked my father about it, he said it belonged to him now. He wears it all the time. I got so used to it, I almost forgot."

"What did it look like?"

"Silver. Like a large signet ring with a symbol in the middle, a sort of stick with a line wrapped around it and it had two German words, one on each side."

"Were the words *Ahnenerbe* and *Deutsches*?" Taylor asked.

"That sounds right! How did you know?"

"That's the ring given to members of the Ahnenerbe, a Nazi occult group. He must have indoctrinated Damon into the occult. If we can prove that the Institute was founded by a Nazi, that will bring it under scrutiny, shine a light on what's been going on there," Taylor said.

"The Ahnenerbe? Isn't that the Nazi group that hunted down religious relics in *Indiana Jones*?" Jack asked. "Why did they want the coins so badly?"

"They believed the coins would give them power. The lore surrounding these religious relics is very potent. It says

the coins represent evil triumphing over good and that whoever possesses them has the power to accomplish whatever
they desire."

"According to this, the coins were hidden in the temple of
Solomon." Jack slid the laptop over to Jeremy and Taylor, and
they leaned in to look at the web page.

Taylor read aloud. "*Medieval apocrypha.* What is that?"

"A Greek term for secret teachings that could not be shared
publicly," Jeremy answered.

Taylor continued to read, fascinated. "According to this,
the coins originated with Abraham. Abraham's father made
them, and Abraham gave them to his son Isaac to purchase a
village. From there the coins were given to the pharaoh who
sent them to Solomon for the temple he was building. Solomon placed them around the door of the altar."

Jeremy broke in. "That's where they stayed until Nebuchad-
nezzar took over and enslaved the Israelites. He took the coins
with him to Babylon where he gave them to some Persians who
gave them to their fathers. When Christ was born, they took
the coins with them to give as gifts with the frankincense and
myrrh, but fell asleep and left the pieces there without realizing
it. Some merchants found them and used them to purchase a
beautiful garment to give to King Abgar. When the king ques-
tioned how they had come upon such a beautiful garment, they
told him they had found the money. He sent for the shepherds
who now had the pieces and took the silver from them and gave
both the garment and coins to Christ, who kept the garment,
but gave the coins to the Jewish treasury because he knew they
would be used to secure his betrayal."

Jack gave a low whistle. "So the coins that Judas received to betray Christ can be traced back to Abraham, the father of the faith? That's some history."

"Yes, many powerful hands have touched them. But what makes them capable of evil is that Satan entered Judas and when Judas held them, Satan's power was conveyed to the coins."

Taylor was staring at Jeremy. "You seem very familiar with this story," she said.

"I've heard it all my life from Damon. He has ten of the coins, but he's determined to find the rest of them, and he believes our family is the key."

Jack's expression grew worried. "He's not going to rest until he finds Taylor and those coins. Do you think her family knew about them?"

"He told me that he interrogated and tortured our grandparents," Jeremy said gravely. "They admitted that they had brought them over from Greece and hidden them, but they wouldn't tell him where."

Taylor turned white. "He *tortured* our grandparents?"

"What exactly does he believe he'll be able to do once he finds them?" Jack asked.

With all seriousness, Jeremy replied, "Unleash the power of hell."

CHAPTER FORTY-NINE

NATHAN'S NOSTRILS WERE BURNING. THE SMELL OF THE leather interior of the car nauseated him and he felt as if he were drowning. *Stop, stop, drop. Stop, drop, and roll. One, two, three, four, five, six, seven, eight, nine.* "Smell!"

Dakota was giving him a mean look. Why was she looking at him that way? He breathed in the way the nurse had taught him—in through the nose, out through the mouth. In and out. In and out. The car stopped in front of a gigantic house. It looked scary. The big gates opened, and Nathan put his hands over his eyes.

"Huge, huge, huge. Where are we?" His voice rose, and he felt a firm hand come down on his arm. He looked at Dakota. Her mouth was a straight line. He didn't like that. He was scared. *Laired. Faired. Mared.* They kept driving down the long driveway until finally the car stopped. Dakota opened the door and came to fetch him.

"We're here. Come with me."

"This place is too huge. Too huge. Like a luge. Deluge. One, two, three, four, five." He tapped the side of his head with his hand.

"NATHAN!"

His bottom lip trembled, and he looked up at her from the corner of his eye.

She lowered her voice. "Focus. I'm right here. We are home now. Everything is going to be okay."

This wasn't home. "Don't want to."

Dakota smiled and took his hand. "Have I ever lied to you?"

He shook his head.

"Come on now. It's all going to be fine. No one will hurt you."

She was being nice now. He followed her to the front door.

They were greeted by another stranger who led them into the tremendous marble foyer.

Within seconds a big, bearded man appeared and nodded at Dakota. He looked like a grizzly bear. Nathan didn't like bears. He backed away as quietly as he could.

"I will take it from here," the bear said in a funny accent.

Dakota let go of Nathan's hand.

What was she doing? He looked at her in shock and began to stammer.

The bear stuck him with a big, long needle.

Before he passed out Nathan's eyes widened, and he gave Dakota a pitiful look.

"You promised no needles!"

"I lied."

CHAPTER FIFTY

THAT SOUNDS COMPLETELY INSANE. THE POWER OF HELL? What exactly is Crosse's endgame?" Jack asked.

"Control. Manipulation. Corruption. He serves a dark master, and his mission is nothing short of the obliteration of all that is good. He wants to destroy the family, the individual, and, most importantly, all connections to God," Jeremy told him.

"You're joking, right?" Jack said.

"I've never been more serious."

"You're telling me he's doing all this just to get rid of morality? That he has a bunch of satanists working for him?"

Jeremy stood up and began to pace.

"No. There are many different motivations he exploits. Some of them have venal motives." He cleared his throat. "And some of them have what they consider to be altruistic ones. He uses people's beliefs, or greed, or vulnerabilities—whatever is the most expedient to gain allegiance. He has true believers in a certain philosophy—those that fight for end-of-life choices, euthanasia, women's rights, freedom—and they serve him out of allegiance to their cause. Others are simply power hungry or greedy and work for their own advancement." He took a seat again and leaned forward, looking Jack in the eye. "He has all the money he could ever want. He's behind the scenes pulling political strings, influencing the media and advertising we see. He does it all for one purpose."

There was no mistaking the look of skepticism in Jack's eyes.

Taylor furrowed her brow, starting to wonder about Jeremy's hold on reality. "Are you saying he's the Antichrist?"

Jeremy shook his head. "No. But he is heavily involved in the occult. He considers himself a prophet—not for the benefit of mankind, but for its destruction. He believes that man deserves to be destroyed and the way to do it is to eradicate a clear sense of right and wrong. His machinations have been behind the legislature responsible for legalizing drugs, mandating pregnancy screening and forced abortions, euthanasia, assisted suicide, legalized prostitution, relaxing of the ratings system—all of it his. He revels in it."

"How did he get started? Where did he get the money to do all this?" Taylor asked.

"From Fred, or Friedrich, whichever is his real name. He was the richest man in my father's small town. I wonder now if it was spoils from the war. My father wanted to carry on his legacy and I was supposed to carry on for both of them."

"If you are not going to continue his work, who is?" Jack asked.

Jeremy's eyes went to her belly.

As the realization dawned on Taylor, she stood up and began to back away. This couldn't be happening.

"Oh no! No. No! What am I going to do?"

Jack put his arms around her. "Nobody is going to take that baby from you."

Jeremy walked over to them and put his hand on Taylor's shoulder. "I don't mean to alarm you, but your baby is in great danger. Damon has a long reach. I believe he is trying to engineer a way to get your child, with no one ever finding out."

"Then what are we going to do?"

"I have the proof now. The file—the one he had bragged about, his people file—it has the name of everyone under his control, what they have done for him, and what he has on them. It's taken me almost a year to find a way to get it. I finally have a connection inside the Institute. He got the file a few weeks ago."

"What kind of people are in the file?" Taylor asked.

"I haven't been able to decrypt it, but it should have the names of judges, politicians, business magnates—people in all areas of influence."

"Okay, so why not take it to the FBI?" Jack asked.

"Because he has his people everywhere. I can't be sure who to trust, he has connections everywhere, and they're not all in his file." He looked at Taylor. "We need your father's help."

They both looked at him. "What are you thinking?" Taylor asked.

"You need to stay here in hiding. Jack can take the information I've gathered to your father. He's the only one in the press we can trust, and he has the resources to investigate the names on the flash drive, put together the evidence linking them to Damon, and show that they've taken bribes and committed crimes."

"What if Damon's people have infiltrated his paper as well?" Taylor asked.

Jeremy shook his head. "It's a chance we're going to have to take." He looked at Jack. "You're going to have to impress upon him the need for his greatest discretion, that he needs to use as few resources as he can, and only ones he feels certain he can trust."

Jack rubbed the back of his neck and looked at the floor. "Is there enough on that file to really get any evidence that will stick?"

"I believe so. It should have proof of bribes. The problem is that the file is encrypted, and it has a digital timer that measures how long it's been opened, and I don't know what he set it for. We'll be able to validate it quickly, but we'll have to let Warwick read it because it'll expire if we keep it open too long. That's where the two of you come in."

Taylor looked at him quizzically.

He explained. "I've run all sorts of computer programs to break the encryption, but nothing has worked. My source has just gotten information on the password and how to get into it."

"How?" Taylor and Jack both asked in unison.

"It's our DNA. That's the key."

"Huh?" Taylor had no clue what he was talking about.

"He has a sick sense of humor," Jeremy said. "He, the man with no paternal allegiance whatsoever, has used our

DNA sequence as the code breaker. I have it on good authority that he has combined the letters of the codon from each of our DNA sequences."

"Hold on. DNA fingerprinting wasn't discovered until the eighties. You were born in 1976," Jack pointed out.

"Yes, but it would have been easy for him to get a sample from me when I was a kid without my knowing it."

"How would he have gotten mine?" Taylor asked.

"Most likely kept a blood sample, a hair, something from your birth. He likely monitored your mother's pregnancy and had contacts at the hospital where you were born. As I said, he likes his trophies."

Taylor was nauseated at the thought.

"How are we going to get our DNA sequence?"

"My lab will run the test. I can take the samples now." He pulled out a kit containing gloves, cotton swabs, and envelopes. "Just swab your cheek. We'll have it in a few hours. Once we have the information from the flash drive, we can move forward with the plan."

"And what about the Institute?"

"Once he is out of the way, I will fight to take over as his legal heir."

Taylor's head was spinning. She thought of something. "Did Crosse orchestrate my meeting Malcolm?"

Jeremy uncrossed his legs then crossed them again.

"This is not easy to tell you—either of you." He sighed. "You and Jack were deliberately kept apart. But it wasn't just Malcolm." He turned and looked Jack in the eye. "Dakota was a setup as well. You were her mission. She knew all about your background, your mother, and she played her part to bewitch you. She—"

Jack jumped up from the sofa and grabbed Jeremy by the shoulders. "Are you insane? What are you talking about?"

Taylor sprang up and pulled Jack off Jeremy.

"Jack! Stop it. It's not Jeremy's fault. Sit down."

Jack shook his head, then put his hands over his eyes. "I'm sorry. Sorry." He sat next to Taylor, and she grabbed his hand.

Jeremy gave him a sympathetic look. "I understand. He had to get you out of the way, so that Taylor could marry Malcolm."

Taylor gulped for air. The room began to spin, and then there was nothing but darkness.

○ ○ ○

When Taylor came to, she was in a bed. Standing next to her was a woman in a white coat.

Jeremy walked over to her and picked up her hand.

"Taylor, this is Dr. Haller. I'd like for her to examine you, if that's okay. Jack told me about the spotting from a few days ago."

Relief filled her. "Yes, thank you."

"When's the last time you ate?" the doctor asked.

Taylor thought. "Breakfast."

"Well, if you don't want to faint again, I'd suggest you eat more regularly. Let's do a quick finger prick and make sure your sugar's not out of whack." She took Taylor's finger and stuck it with the glucose meter. "Looks okay, but I'll run a blood panel to rule out any other issues."

"I'm fine. I just forgot to eat."

"Even so, I want to be thorough."

Taylor sighed and stretched her arm out to let the doctor draw her blood.

The doctor pulled a portable sonogram machine next to the bed, and Jack and Jeremy left to give her some privacy.

When she had finished with the exam, she called them back in.

"I'm happy to report that the baby is doing fine. There's a strong heartbeat. Taylor is eight weeks along, and everything looks good. Spotting in early pregnancy is more common than you may think and is not always cause for alarm. Her blood pressure is fine; we'll have the blood results in a little while."

A grin broke across Jack's face. "Whew! That is a huge relief."

"Thank God," Taylor whispered.

Jeremy walked over to the bed. "You'll be well looked after here. We have our own medical facility and staff."

"It's like its own little city."

Jeremy pulled a chair up next to the bed. "I think it's time I told you the rest of the story." He looked at Jack. "Get comfortable, this will take a while. Let me start where I left—"

"I'm not going to lie here like an invalid," Taylor interrupted.

They both turned to look at her.

"You heard the doctor. I'm fine. Now get out of here so I can get dressed, and let's go somewhere else to have this conversation."

Jack looked at Jeremy. "You heard her." Then, turning again to Taylor, he said, "Good to have you back."

CHAPTER FIFTY-ONE

SHE KNEW NATHAN WAS FURIOUS WITH HER. AFTER LYING to him, Dakota had to earn his trust back. She smoothed the tight skirt and admired her shapely legs in the mirror. Pleased with her appearance, she descended to the chamber where he was being kept.

He looked up from his breakfast, then back at his plate, making a point of ignoring her.

"I know you're mad at me," she said.

"Liar, liar pants on fire. Lied, tried, fried, died. One, two, three, four." It took everything she had not to roll her eyes. *Friggin' counting. Enough already.* She took a seat across from him. She wanted to look nervous, so she bit her lip and made her eyes wide.

"He made me do it." Her voice cracked.

Nathan looked up.

"I'm his prisoner. I needed your help, and I didn't know what to do." Tears fell from her blue eyes.

"Who made you do it?"

"The man with the big, black car. He won't let me leave here unless I do what he asks. I'm afraid."

Nathan puffed out his chest.

The rube was falling for it.

"What does he want you to do?"

She cleared her throat. "I don't know if I should tell you."

"Tell me, sell me. I want to know."

"There are people. These people are hurting babies. He wants me to stop them."

His eyes grew huge. "Hurting babies is bad. Bad, bad, sad, mad."

She nodded. "Yes, but I'm afraid they'll hurt me, too, if I try to stop them. I'm not brave enough."

"I'm brave."

"Yes, you are, Nathan. That's why I thought you could help me, but now I'm not so sure."

"Why not? Don't you think I'm brave?"

She covered his hand with her own. "Of course, I think you're brave. You're the bravest person I know. But I don't want to be unfair to you."

"I want to help. What do you want me to do?"

She smiled.

"You will be driven to the place where they hurt babies. You will need to leave a package there. And you'll leave a note saying you did it to save the babies."

"That doesn't sound hard. Easy, peasy, leasy."

"That's because you are a brave, brave man."

He leaned toward her.

"Then he will let you go, and we can be together?"

She licked her lips. Like taking candy from a baby. "If you do a good job."

He sat up straighter. "I will. Good. Hood. Should."

CHAPTER FIFTY-TWO

THEY GATHERED TOGETHER IN THE STUDY WHERE JEREMY had had some sandwiches brought in.

Jack rose from his seat. "Jeremy, you said earlier that Dakota was a plant. I need to know more."

Jeremy nodded. "You and Taylor were together, but Crosse had someone else in mind for his daughter."

"Please don't call me that," Taylor cut in. She would never be his daughter.

"I'm sorry. Dakota works for Crosse. They arranged for her to meet you. She was the third one they tried. Apparently, you resisted the other two women they sent your way."

"I don't know what you're talking about. What other two women?"

"Your senior year of college, a girl in your study group made a pass at you. She was one."

Jack's mouth dropped open. "You really know how to make a guy feel like a loser. So much for thinking I had charm."

"The point is, you said no. Then there was a colleague when you first started at the Associated Press."

Jack shook his head. "I remember. Nancy. I thought she'd never leave me alone."

"You have to understand that when they want something, nothing gets in their way. They do deep background checks, psychological evaluations, and they make sure that the health professionals in your life are in their pockets. They knew what kind of environment you grew up in, Jack, the depressions and mood swings your mother experienced. They use profilers to help them when they have a delicate mission."

"Why not just kill me?" Jack asked.

"Because they wanted to break Taylor, to drive her into Malcolm's arms. What better way to induce her to fall for an older, stable man than to have you betray her? It was easy for Malcolm to insinuate himself into Taylor's affections."

"But why did he care if I married Malcolm?" Taylor interjected.

"Because Malcolm reported to him, and through him Damon stayed privy to your life without your knowing it. Damon thought Malcolm wouldn't stand in the way when Damon was ready to execute his plan for you, but obviously he underestimated Malcolm's feelings for you."

Taylor ran a hand through her hair. She felt like she was going to explode. "I want to kill that monster."

"It's like we're all a bunch of lab rats," Jack said bitterly.

"He may have manipulated parts of your lives, but not

anymore. You've both gotten free, and you're going to help me take him down." He walked over to Taylor and spoke gently. "I only found out that you existed after Damon and I had our fight when I wanted to get married. You weren't pregnant then, but he knew you were trying. He called you his contingency plan. He thought it would save me having to provide an heir since he didn't want me distracted by a wife."

"Are you telling me that he has been watching and waiting for me to breed? That all along, he was waiting to take my child?"

"It's not that simple. If I hadn't betrayed him, he probably would have just watched the child from afar. Nurtured him through others and, when the time was right, brought him into the fold. Eventually, he would be told of his true identity."

"Did Malcolm know that I was Crosse's daughter?" she asked.

"No. And when I went to Malcolm and told him everything, he agreed to help me. He did it to save you and your child. He wasn't an evil man, Taylor. He never really had a chance."

Taylor felt her anger rise again. She was tired of people making excuses for their bad behavior. Malcolm was a liar and a fraud and nothing anyone said would ever make her change her mind.

CHAPTER FIFTY-THREE

Dakota was driving them to their mission. Nathan was going to be a hero. She told him so. He couldn't wait to make her proud.

"Now remember, you walk in, go to the waiting room, and sit down for ten minutes."

He remembered. They had gone last week, and she showed him where to sit.

"After exactly ten minutes, you go to the bathroom and leave the package in the trash can. Okay?"

"Okey dokey, lokey, smokey."

"Nathan!" Her voice was too loud.

"Don't yell! Tell. Bell."

"Tell me again, exactly, what you're going to do. No rhymes!"

He folded his arms across his chest and jutted out his chin. He didn't like it when she talked mean.

She sighed and reached out to put a hand on his arm. "I'm sorry. I'm just nervous. Please, dear, tell me again." Her voice was nice now.

"Go to the waiting room. Sit. Ten minutes. Bathroom. Trash can. Man. Stan. Lan." He couldn't help it.

"Okay. When you leave the bathroom, you wait for me outside to pick you up. Wait for the policeman and then give him this note." She handed him an envelope.

"Policemen are scary. Very. Merry."

"It's okay. You are very brave. It's important that you give him the note. I can't pick you up until you do. You just wait until he comes, and then you'll see me."

She dropped Nathan off a block away from the clinic. He knew where to go; they had practiced.

"I'll see you soon."

He walked the block quickly, staring straight ahead. The briefcase was heavy, and he shifted it to the other shoulder. What was he supposed to do with the briefcase after he dropped the package in the can? *Man, shan, lan, tan. One, two, three, four, five, six, seven. Stop! Think!* Did he keep it or leave it, too? He didn't want Dakota to be mad at him. What had she told him? Keep it. That's it. Put the box in the trash and keep the briefcase.

He arrived at the clinic and opened the door. A woman was coming out and smiled at him. He squinted his eyes at her. She couldn't fool him. She was another snarkie. He pushed past her and walked over to the seat closest to the bathroom. Someone was sitting there. *No, lo, mo, bo, so. Stop! One, two, three, four, five, six, seven.* Deep breath. In and out. What to do? He gave her a mean look. Maybe she would get up.

"What are you looking at, weirdo?"

A lady came over and whispered something to her. The stupid girl got up and followed her. Good. Now he could sit.

The lady turned back around. "May I help you, sir?"

He spat out the line he had rehearsed. "I'm waiting for my girlfriend."

She smiled and turned back around again.

He checked his watch: 10:24. Time to get up! He walked over to the bathroom door and stood, watch in hand, and waited. When the numbers changed again, he pushed the door open and walked in. Unzipping the briefcase, he pulled out the heavy box and pushed it in the trash can. It didn't go in all the way. There was too much paper in there. He shoved with all his might. The top closed. Good. He picked up the briefcase and went outside to wait.

He didn't see a policeman. He hoped they would come soon. He wanted Dakota to pick him up. After a while, he looked at his watch again: 10:31. He was trying to decide whether to walk down the street and look for her when he heard a loud boom. He crouched down and covered his ears. Why were all these people screaming? And the building was on fire. It was so loud. *Smoke. Smoke. Evoke. Provoke.* All he had done was put a package down. Why was everything on fire?

Nathan was scared. Where was she? When was he going to get to go home? People were running past him, and he looked for the policeman. Where was the policeman? Now there were lots of them, running up the steps.

"Stop!" He jumped in front of one of the policemen. "Take this." He shoved the envelope at him and the policeman grabbed it and gave him a funny look. He opened it and read it. Then he put a silver bracelet on Nathan. "Where are you taking me?" he wailed.

The policeman pushed him hard toward the car. He put his hand on Nathan's head and pushed him hard again. Nathan landed with a thump on the seat. The policeman stuck his head in the car and gave Nathan an angry look.

"To jail, where I hope you rot forever," he said.

Nathan looked at him bewildered. "No! I have to leave. Cleave. Retrieve. Where is she? She said I was helping babies." His voice rose with each syllable until he was bellowing like an injured animal.

"Shut up!" a second policeman yelled.

Nathan started to cry. He looked out the window as the car pulled away. He didn't want to go back to the hospital, especially now that she wasn't there. She would come for him. She had promised.

CHAPTER FIFTY-FOUR

THE DOCTOR HAD CLEARED TAYLOR, TELLING HER ALL HER bloodwork looked good. She was relieved and almost able to believe that this pregnancy might turn out differently than the others. They had all just finished breakfast and had turned on the news while they waited for the DNA results. Taylor looked up when she saw the commotion being covered.

"Can you turn that up?" She pointed to the remote next to Jack.

"This is Sally Mason reporting for *Newsline*. Late this afternoon, a family clinic in Kingston, New York, was bombed," the anchorwoman said. "So far, there are nine confirmed deaths and numerous injuries. The alleged bomber has been arrested but not yet identified. All police are able to tell us is that he handed them a note from the group claiming responsibility for the bombing. They are called the Voice of the Victims and claim to be Christians bringing God's wrath down on those who, and I quote, 'are responsible for the massacre of God's children.'"

Smoke and screams filled the screen as cameras captured the horror of the attack. First responders were shown coming out of the ruins carrying stretchers. There was a close-up of a stretcher carrying a body covered by a white sheet. A woman with blood running down her face stumbled from the front door and fell into the street. A crowd had gathered outside the clinic, and the horrified onlookers watched as more victims were brought outside.

The male anchor shook his head. "I'll never understand what would drive anyone to do something like this."

Sally Mason cast a steely look at the camera. "We'll bring you more news as soon as we have it."

"What the . . . how do these people expect their cause to be taken seriously when they do horrible things like this?" Jack felt the fury fill him. "It's disgusting."

"It may not be what you think," Jeremy said.

Jack jumped up from his chair, his face red. "What are you talking about? Please don't tell me you've turned into some religious nut who thinks these kinds of tactics are acceptable." He'd met enough of those freaks to last a lifetime.

Jeremy didn't appear rattled. Without raising his voice, he said, "Of course not. What I'm saying is that the perpetrators might not be who you think they are. My father hires people to commit atrocities and then blames them on groups whose reputations he wants to damage."

"What?" both he and Taylor said at the same time.

Jack was aghast. "Please explain. Because I know for sure

that there have been plenty of occasions when these insane groups *have* done things like this. I've done stories on them."

Jeremy nodded. "Yes, that's true. I'm not saying they're all fakes. I'm just telling you that I've seen him frame groups for things they haven't done. Anything he can do to give Christians a bad name, he does. Do you remember the story a few years back about the prostitution ring being run out of a local church?"

"Of course," Taylor said. "It made national news."

"That was Crosse's doing."

Jack was skeptical. "Come on, Jeremy. There were lots of girls involved. Are you telling me they all lied? You can't do something like that without someone leaking it."

"There was no way for that pastor to prove he hadn't done something, because they were using the facility, but he didn't know anything about it. People are falsely accused every day," Jeremy said.

"And," Taylor said, "once the story's out, if someone comes back later and recants, no one really notices."

"We need to see what's in that file," Jack answered.

o o o

Jeremy walked in with a printout of their DNA results. Now they had to try to break the code in order to open the file.

Jack was hunched over, staring at the computer screen. Taylor's hand shook as she held the paper with their DNA fingerprints. Now they just had to figure out in what order to input everything to open the file.

"Ready?"

"Go."

"Should I read yours or mine first?" Taylor asked Jeremy.

"Mine. I'm older. He's a stickler for order."

She read the letters aloud as Jack typed.

"Didn't work. Maybe he only used a part of it."

"The strand is cut into four pieces. The possibilities are endless," Taylor commented.

They tried combination after combination for the next three hours with no break.

Jeremy rubbed his eyes. "He would have chosen something meaningful to him, something ironic. Let me think. Try every sixth letter in each one."

"Still nothing," Jack said.

"Try only three for each—from the first eighteen letters, and pick the sixth, twelfth, and eighteenth letter. It would represent 666 to him."

Password successful: Do you wish to proceed?

"Bingo," Jack said.

Jeremy leaned back in the chair, looked up, and gave Taylor a wide smile. "We did it."

"Well, let's see it," Jack said.

Jeremy shook his head and typed *Later.* "Let's not run the clock out. We have to let Taylor's father open it. It can't be printed. All Damon's files have an automatic self-destruct function if they're printed anywhere but the main computer. Warwick will have to take screenshots with his phone."

"Can't we do that?" Taylor asked.

"Sure, but do you really think your father's going to go to

print on a story based on some fuzzy screenshots? Better for him to see for himself."

"What if there's nothing on it?" Jack asked.

"There will be. It's the right file. You just have to trust me. There'll be names and dates, and I'm sure those dates will correspond with bank deposits. When it goes public, the FBI can investigate. But it's more important now that your father has a chance to look at it so he'll believe it. Better close it now."

Taylor shook her head. "I hope there's enough information for my father to authenticate it."

Jeremy sighed. "They'll be enough information to convince him. He's kept records on Senate votes, inside information he couldn't make up. We also have the tape he kept of my mother; it could be enough to get a warrant to search the Institute. Just need the papers to make enough stink so whoever he does have in law enforcement can't cover it up."

Jack raised an eyebrow. "We really need to get into that institute and get our hands on his real files. Do you think he has printouts anywhere?"

Jeremy nodded. "I'm sure he does. He always has a backup. But this is what we have to work with for now."

"I still think I should go with you," Taylor said to Jack. She couldn't stand waiting around like a damsel in distress.

"Once Jack has delivered the file and it goes public, we can leave, but we can't risk Crosse finding you. It's better for you to stay here for now."

Jack exhaled. "I'll make your father believe me." He looked at Jeremy. "You take care of your sister until we're together again."

Taylor saw a wistfulness come into Jeremy's eyes, and the full realization of his emotionally barren life broke her heart. Here was this lovely man who had suffered such atrocities, yet he hadn't allowed them to destroy him. He had found a way to salvage his humanity.

She took his hand in her own. "You are my family, Jeremy. Nothing is ever going to keep us apart ever again. I promise."

He looked back at her with a solemn expression. "And I will never let anything hurt you or your baby."

CHAPTER FIFTY-FIVE

JACK ENJOYED THE HOT WATER BEATING ON HIS BACK while he soaped his body. He scrubbed hard, imagining that he was washing away all the mistakes he had made. He would leave and meet Taylor's father, and soon everything would be brought into the open. This was the story of a lifetime—but he couldn't care less about that. All that mattered was that he was going to bring down Crosse, the man who had manipulated all their lives. He got out of the shower and quickly dressed. If he drove straight through the night, he would be in DC by morning.

He wanted to say good-bye to Taylor before taking off. He knocked on her door.

She opened it and smiled at him.

"Well, this is it. I'm heading out."

Their eyes met.

"Jack, I never thanked you for dropping everything to help me."

He shrugged. "You don't owe me any thanks, T. I should've been there all along."

She placed a hand on his cheek. "Oh, Jack." Her voice broke. "It's not fair. Both of us, manipulated like puppets. It wasn't supposed to be like this."

He took her hand in his. "Our lives aren't over. We've got a chance to set things right." They moved closer toward each other at the same time and their lips met. Jack's insides melted. He wanted to stand there forever and keep kissing her. He tore himself away and took her face in his hands.

"I'll fix it, Taylor. I promise. This isn't the end."

She wiped a tear from her cheek and squared her shoulders. "I can," she said.

"Can what?"

"Forgive you. I can forgive you."

Those were the words he'd been waiting to hear for years now. "Thank you," he said, his voice choked with emotion. He pulled her to him for another embrace and kissed her again. "See you soon." He winked and left.

Jeremy was waiting for him in the downstairs hallway.

"Ready?" Jeremy asked.

"Ready as I'll ever be," Jack said. He tapped the pocket of his jeans where he'd put the flash drive.

Jeremy put his hand on Jack's shoulder. "Remember, that file is all we've got. Tell him to guard it with everything he's got. Remind him that none of it can be copied or printed out. Once he's run the story, he can take the file to the FBI and their people can figure out how to secure it."

"Who would've thought a little flash drive could bring down an entire empire?" He grinned at Jeremy, then grew serious. "You'll take good care of her?"

Jeremy nodded. "Of course." His eyes met Jack's. "I love her, too, you know."

o o o

Jack borrowed a late '90s Ford Escort from Jeremy, and a few hours into his drive, he saw a convenience store and pulled in at the last second. Walking to the counter, he nodded to the cashier.

"Pack of Lucky Strikes," he was surprised to hear himself blurt out. *What the hell*, he thought. If being hunted by killers wasn't reason enough to fall off the wagon, he didn't know what was. He took the cigarettes, got back behind the wheel, and lit one up. He took a drag and inhaled deeply. Man. It still felt good. He smoked it fast and leaned his head back to steady the dizziness that washed over him. He crushed the pack in his hand and threw it on the seat next to him. Maybe it hadn't been the best idea after all.

He got back on the highway, thoughts racing as fast as the car, and planned his next move. He'd been given an untraceable smartphone. He would text Taylor's father when he got into town—no sooner, in case his phones had been tapped—and ask him to meet him at East Potomac Park, a special place for Taylor and her father when she was growing up. Taylor had come up with the message.

"Text—Taylor *enai endaxi*. Then *m'les tipota*. *Ellas sto topo pou pigainame ta apogévmata tou Sawátou*." Which meant "Taylor is fine. Don't say anything. Come to the place we used to go on Saturday afternoons."

Jack had looked at her with confusion. "He knows how to read Greek?"

Taylor nodded. "When he and my mother were first married, they lived in Athens. He was a foreign correspondent. He became fluent, and since my mother had learned Greek as a child, they continued to speak it to keep it alive. They would talk in Greek when they were out to dinner and didn't want anyone around them to know what they were saying."

A siren wailed behind him.

He looked into the rearview mirror, then glanced at his speedometer.

"Crap!" He was going almost seventy-five.

The flashing lights got closer.

CHAPTER FIFTY-SIX

THE MAN STOOD IN FRONT OF DAMON CROSSE'S DESK, looking pleased with himself.

"We found his hideout."

Damon flashed a rare smile. "Where is it?"

"Vermont. A camouflaged facility in the Green Mountains."

"How long ago did you discover it?" Damon asked.

"Our aerial surveillance spotted it just now. I've dispatched a team. They'll arrive within the hour."

"Remember: treat her with kid gloves. I don't want one hair on her head harmed. And keep Jeremy alive. I want to talk to him."

"Yes, sir."

When the man left, Damon looked at Dakota. "You need to be gone when they bring Taylor here." She'd done well orchestrating the clinic bombing, but Dakota's usefulness was beginning to pale in comparison to her elevated opinion of her importance. In fact, he was quite displeased with her attitude of late. She had demanded to be kept apprised of the situation with Jack and Taylor. He had gone along, not wanting to disrupt the clinic plan by upsetting her—it had been in motion for too long, and she was the only one Nathan trusted. Dakota had always been a volatile asset.

She made a face. "As you wish. Imagine, Jack going back to *her* after he'd had me. I suppose his tastes really are as banal as I thought."

Damon had no interest in discussing her sex life. She was a loose cannon that needed to be capped. That was the problem with sociopaths—they were incapable of true loyalty and one never knew what they had hidden up their sleeves. It was a pity, really. She was interesting and held a certain fascination for him. But it was time to say good-bye.

He depressed the red button and his men appeared. "Please come collect Ms. Drake."

Her eyes narrowed, and she gripped the sides of her chair. "What do you think you're doing?"

"Saying adieu."

He nodded at his men, and they grabbed her and carried her, struggling and screaming, from the office.

He smiled. How he did enjoy tying up loose ends.

CHAPTER FIFTY-SEVEN

JACK PUT DOWN THE WINDOW AND LOOKED UP AT THE police officer looming above him.

"Do you know how fast you were going?"

"No, Officer. I'm sorry. I was lost and looking at my GPS instead of paying attention to the speedometer."

"Then you should have pulled over. It's dangerous to be distracted while you drive. You were going seventy-two. The speed limit is sixty. License and registration."

Jack leaned over and pulled the registration from the glove compartment. He fished in his pocket for his wallet and pulled out his license.

"Here you go."

He took them from Jack and returned to the police car to run them. Jack tapped the steering wheel and watched him in the rearview mirror.

He returned ten minutes later with his ticket pad in hand. He handed Jack a slip of paper.

"I'm only giving you a warning since you have a clean record but make sure you're more careful in the future, Mr. Morris."

Jack nodded. "Thank you so much. I certainly will be."

He waited until the cop had driven away before starting up the car again. He exhaled the breath he'd been holding and took a long swallow from the can of Coke next to him. Boy, was he grateful for Jeremy's foresight. He had been surprised when he was presented with a new name for the trip and the credentials to go along with it. Still, he'd better observe the speed limit the rest of the way.

o o o

Jack arrived in Washington at six in the morning and headed straight to the meeting place, but he waited until eight to send the text. He got a response almost immediately—a simple *on my way*. He'd chosen a bench facing the water. The breeze blowing off the Potomac was cold, and he pulled his collar up against the frosty bite. His hand rested on the inside of his jacket, curled around his SIG. He wasn't taking any chances. He saw Parks approach and was surprised when he walked right past him. He guessed the beard and bald head had thrown him off.

"Mr. Parks," Jack called.

"Jack? Is that you?" Parks walked over and his eyes bulged. "Where's Taylor?"

"She's safe," Jack replied evenly.

"That's not what I asked."

"Sit down," Jack commanded.

"Don't tell me what to do. What have you done with Taylor?" His voice rose and people around them started taking notice of the two men.

"If you want to know, sit; otherwise I'm out of here."

Parks grunted and took a seat on the edge of the bench. "I'm sitting. Where is she?"

"With a friend."

Parks looked like he wanted to kill him. "What friend? Damn it, Jack, you break her heart, then come back all these years later and I'm supposed to trust you?"

"There's no time to rehash the past. I wouldn't be here right now if her dead husband hadn't dragged me into this. He's the one you should wonder about."

"What did Malcolm get himself involved in?"

"I can't go into all of it now, but Malcolm worked for a man named Damon Crosse. Malcolm turned on him and Crosse had him killed. Now, Taylor and her baby are in danger."

"What are you talking about? Murder? You're crazy! Malcolm died of an allergy attack. I think you're delusional and you've caught my daughter up in your fantasy world. Do you know there's a national manhunt for you? They say you killed a man."

He was getting nowhere. "I killed him in self-defense. Taylor will tell you herself when she comes out of hiding."

"I want to see her now."

"It's not safe. I'm trying to explain. The recent bill on the vaccine expansion was created for something more insidious.

Malcolm sponsored that bill until he discovered that Brody Hamilton was sneaking in a clause in the rider to mandate vaccinations for everyone. When he voted against the bill, they had him killed."

"Who had him killed?"

"A secret organization run by Crosse—he's got politicians, judges, all sorts of people all in his pocket."

"Jack, you sound terribly paranoid. Do you have any proof to back up your outrageous claims?"

Jack handed him the drive. "Take this. It'll explain everything. It's got the names of everyone on Crosse's payroll and all their illegal activities. We're counting on you to investigate the people on that file. See if you can tie them to Crosse's organization. Check their bank accounts, look at their phones. There has to be a trail leading back to him."

Parks looked skeptical, but he took the drive from Jack.

"Don't show it to anyone. And guard it with your life."

"What?"

Jack explained about the file properties. "The drive can't be replicated or it will self-destruct. You can't print it out either. You have to bring it up on your computer and take screenshots with your phone. Bring a witness you trust. Make sure your computer is completely disconnected from Wi-Fi when you do. It's the only way that Taylor will be safe. Once we can get some dirt on Crosse and expose him, he won't be able to get to Taylor." Jack gave him a card. "Here's the passcode to open it."

Parks nodded. "All right. I'll check it out. Where are you going to go in the meantime?"

"I don't know," Jack said.

Parks gave him a hard look. "I'd like to believe you. I've known you since you were this high." He held his hand to his hip. "But after what you did to her . . . I've hated you for a long time." He reached in his pocket and pulled out his key ring. "But you *have* kept her safe, and if what you say is true, that was no easy feat. I've got somewhere you can stay until I can verify this information. Our cottage on the Eastern Shore. Stay there until I contact you." He took a key off the ring, then scribbled something on a business card and gave both to Jack. "That's the address."

"Thanks, Mr. Parks."

Jack stood up. "You can reach me on the same number I texted you from. It's a secure phone. I'll wait to hear from you." He walked away then stopped and turned back.

"Mr. Parks?"

"Yes?"

"I'm sorry for everything."

Parks simply nodded.

CHAPTER FIFTY-EIGHT

WE'VE GOT TO GO!" JEREMY WAS POUNDING ON TAYLOR'S bedroom door. She hurried to open it.

His face was white. "They've found us. We have to leave now."

"They're here?"

"Yes. They came in a helicopter. We shot it down, but they must have radioed him. More of his men will be coming."

He grabbed her hand and she followed, running, down the long corridor.

"Where are we going?" Taylor panted.

"Maryland."

"Why? Isn't that the least safe area for us right now?"

He just shook his head and pulled her into the elevator, then grabbed her hand when it opened as they ran down another corridor, then through a large garage and into an open field. There was a small prop plane waiting for them.

"Come on. Get in."

Taylor got in first, and within minutes they were both strapped in their seats, doors locked, the plane beginning its taxi down the runway. Once they were in the air, Jeremy let out a big breath and turned to Taylor.

"I've texted Jack and he's arranged for your father to meet us when we land. Damon won't suspect that we'd go back to where you live, and your father can help us get somewhere safe. I can't risk contacting anyone outside of my facility, I don't know who's been compromised. Your father is the only one we can trust."

"Jeremy, something I don't understand. Why would Damon orchestrate your mother's kidnapping and impregnating my mother, all for some coins? It just seems too unbelievable to me."

"They give whoever has them the power to accomplish their greatest desire—if the person is on the side of evil, that is. I've told you. He wants to pervert society. To eradicate morality—to win souls for Satan."

"I understand that he was brought up to believe in all this occult nonsense, but he's a grown man now. He still thinks it's real?"

Jeremy looked Taylor in the eyes. "It *is* real."

"Come on. The devil made him do it? A little clichéd, don't you think?"

Jeremy shook his head, and a sadness filled his eyes. "Taylor, do you believe in God?"

She nodded. "Yes."

"Then how can you discount the existence of the devil? The

Bible is not fantasy. Adam, Eve—they were real. The fall was real. And ever since, there has been a battle for souls. Ephesians 6:12 says, 'For our struggle is not against flesh and blood, but against the rulers, against the authorities, against the powers of this dark world and against the spiritual forces of evil in the heavenly realms.' Some believe the thirty pieces of silver contain the power to call forth more of these demons to earth. Damon has ten. Whoever possesses all of them will command the power. Look how far he has gotten. If he ever gets all thirty, there will be no stopping him."

"Why not destroy the coins back then?" Taylor asked.

"I don't think they can be destroyed, only neutralized, but that's not easy and we have to take them back to Greece to do it. Just as the hands that channeled evil gave them a dark power, hands that have turned away from evil and toward God, hands of someone who has been redeemed, may be able to deactivate them."

"Do you mean someone like you?"

He nodded. "Once we bring Damon down, I'll explain it all. For now, if we find them, we'll have to focus first on hiding them again. If we can find a holy place to do it, the destructive power is said to be made inactive while there. That's why they were hidden in Saint John's cave, and in the Virgin Mary's house in Ephesus."

"Did you say a holy place?" All of a sudden, Taylor had a flash of memory.

He nodded.

"I think I might know where they are."

CHAPTER FIFTY-NINE

JACK ARRIVED AT THE SMALL WHITE COTTAGE AND WAS relieved to see that it was surrounded by woods and no other houses were in sight. He walked around the back to the wooden deck and took in the two rusty chairs and rickety plastic table. Cobwebs covered everything, and the top of the table had clumps of dirt on it. He could imagine how relaxing it would be to sit on the deck in the morning with a cup of coffee. But right then, it looked run-down and desolate, and it was clear that no one had been to stay there in months. Once inside, he had to try two lamps before he found a working bulb. His text tone sounded, and he swiped his phone to see a text from Taylor's father checking to see if he had arrived. He sent a quick text back.

Too full of nervous energy to sit still, he went back into the house, stripped down to his boxers, and began doing push-ups. It felt good to exert himself, and before long, perspiration covered his back and chest. He got in the shower and closed his eyes while the water beat on his head. He stepped out, pulled a musty towel from the rack, and dried himself. Grabbing some clean clothes from his duffel, he got dressed, then opened the refrigerator to see if there was anything to eat. An open box of baking soda sat on a bare shelf. There was a bottle of white wine lying on its side and some shriveled lemons. He grabbed the wine and looked through the drawers until he found a corkscrew. Foraging through the cabinets, he was able to find some crackers and a jar of peanut butter. He took the plate with his meager dinner and sat down on the worn chenille sofa. The wine was pretty awful, but he drank it anyway. He wanted something to slow his racing mind. He drained another glass and put his legs up on the sofa and was just dozing off when the glare of bright lights and the sound of sirens roused him.

The door burst open and a swarm of green-armored and helmeted FBI agents poured in. Before he could get a word out, he was slammed to the floor, a knee on his back. As he cursed, he heard the click of the handcuffs and felt their bite on his wrists.

"Push on through. Once the house is clear and safe, I want the entire place searched from top to bottom." The agent turned back to Jack. "Sir, you are under arrest for the kidnapping of Taylor—"

"I didn't . . ." He stopped, coming to his senses. He would call Arnie, his lawyer. They would sort it all out.

CHAPTER SIXTY

WHEN TAYLOR AND JEREMY LANDED AT POTOMAC AIR-field, a black Suburban was waiting for them. The driver's-side door opened and Taylor's father's deep voice rang out as he got out of the SUV.

"Taylor?"

"Dad!" She ran to him and his arms encircled her in a tight embrace. Jeremy said nothing and stood back until she pulled away.

"I've been worried sick about you," her father said. "Whose plane is that?"

She turned to Jeremy and he walked over. "Dad, this is Jeremy Crosse. It's his plane." Her father appraised him with a long look then shook his hand. Taylor went on. "The men who killed Malcolm showed up at Jeremy's facility looking for me.

We had to leave. There's so much I have to tell you. I assume Jack filled you in on what's going on?"

"Yes. I've got him stashed at the cottage. He'll be safe there."

Taylor got into the front and Jeremy into the back of the SUV. Parks started it and turned to look at her.

"You look pale. Are you okay?"

"Yeah, I'm fine. Listen, we have to go straight to Agape House." When Jeremy had mentioned a holy place, that's when it had come to her. The shelter had been founded by her grandmother and was run by nuns. Her mother took over its support after Taylor's grandmother had died and had even left an endowment in her will so that it would always have money to operate.

"Why do you need to go there?"

"I think Mom's mother may have hidden something very important there."

He turned to look at her. "What?"

Taylor hesitated, and Jeremy answered for her.

"It's something my father is looking for. Silver coins."

"Okay. Tell me then," her father said.

After Jeremy repeated the story for him, Warwick rolled his eyes. "That's the most ridiculous thing I've ever heard. And, Taylor, your mother never mentioned a word about any coins or silver pieces."

"Dad, trust us. Please?"

He sighed. "Fine."

"Did you have any problems with the file?" Jeremy asked.

Warwick cleared his throat. "No, it opened fine. We're

following all your precautions. Two of my top investigators are working on it."

"Dad, there's so much to tell you. Jeremy's mother and Mom were sisters! She had a sister. Did you know that?"

The color rose in his cheeks. "Yes, Taylor. It was something she didn't like to talk about. Her sister ran off with someone she met at a medical fellowship, never bothered to get in touch with your mother again. Eva searched for her for years and years. It was only when you were born that she finally let it go. She never spoke of her again. It was too painful."

"Her sister didn't run off, Dad. She was held hostage by Damon Crosse, the man Jack told you about. She gave birth to Jeremy and then Crosse let her bleed to death. Jeremy found this out when his father showed him a journal that he'd been holding on to all these years," Taylor said.

"Held *hostage*? How do you know?"

"It's a long story. We'll explain it later," Jeremy answered.

"Dad, you missed the turn."

"Damn." He made an abrupt left and drove around the block. A minute later, they were in front of the shelter, a worn, brick two-story building. "Now what?" He looked at Taylor.

"Let's go inside."

Jeremy and her father followed her into the building.

o   o   o

"Dad, Jeremy, this is Sister Carlisle. She was a friend of Mom's."

The slight woman held out her hand in greeting, then

looked at Taylor. "Your mother was a good friend to me and to Agape House. If she hadn't continued her support, we wouldn't be here right now."

Taylor clasped Sister Carlisle's hands in both of hers. "Thank you. I'm afraid I have a strange request. My mother had something belonging to our family that she left here."

Sister Carlisle raised her eyebrows. "Oh?"

"When she had the bathrooms redone, she inserted some special tiles into the women's shower. I need to remove them." Before the woman could respond, Taylor continued, "Of course, I'll have workers come by and repair it."

"Whatever you need, dear. Go ahead."

"Do you happen to have a tool kit?" Taylor asked.

The nun nodded and picked up a phone. "Can you bring your tools to the women's lavatory? Eva Parks's daughter, Taylor, will meet you there."

Jeremy and Warwick followed Taylor into the dark locker room. The entire wall in the shower enclosure was tiled and in each tile was a pattern of five coins. The maintenance worker came in a few minutes later and put the toolbox down. Taylor pulled out the hammer.

Jeremy looked at Taylor, disappointed. "There are hundreds of coins here; they're just decorative."

"Did your mother tell you that she'd put them here?" Warwick asked.

"No, but I think I know where they are." She walked to the farthest end of the long wall, sat on the floor, and ran her hand over the tile. "When I was little, I used to come here and pretend I was locked away in a castle. I remember these tiles, that the coins felt different from the others. They're so low, no one ever looks at them."

Jeremy crouched down and looked where Taylor was touching. "You're right. These are different." He pointed to the head on the coin. "See he's facing right. The heads on the other coins are looking to the left."

"My grandmother must have had the other tiles custom made to look similar, so no one would notice the real ones, but different enough so they could be found by my mother or someone in the family," she hypothesized. "Should we leave them here? They've been safe all this time and only we know about them."

Jeremy shook his head. "We need to take them. Now that the three of us know they're here, it could be used against us if the wrong people tried to interrogate us. Besides, I have a plan for them."

"All right."

Taylor used the claw end of the hammer to try to dislodge the first tile. The mortar began to crumble, and the ceramic material started to crack. She kept at it, until the first one was dislodged. The space left next to the second tile made it easier to pull it away from the wall in one piece. Taylor ran her hand over the silver coins and looked at Jeremy. "This *is* them, right?"

He took the broken tile from her and peered at one of the coins closely.

"Yes. They're identical to the other ones I've seen." He opened his satchel and they placed both tiles in it.

They returned to the car. Warwick looked at Jeremy and asked, "Now what?"

"I need to think. Ultimately we have to get them back to Greece."

"What?" Taylor's father asked.

Jeremy sighed. "I didn't want to get into it now, but we need to take them back to Patmos, to the monastery, where the priest can perform a ceremony to neutralize the evil of the coins. My hands are needed because of my redemption from evil to good, and Taylor and I together are from the same bloodline that has protected them over the centuries."

"How do you know this?" Taylor asked.

"When Damon told me about our great-uncle, the monk, I wondered if he was still alive."

Taylor's heart skipped a beat.

"Is he?"

Jeremy smiled. "Yes. He's still there. I tracked him down and spoke with him on the phone not long before you and Jack found me. We need to take them to him. The three of us, all with the same blood flowing through our veins, can do together what we can't do apart. He quoted from Ecclesiastes 4:12, 'A cord of three strands is not quickly broken.' But in the meantime, I think we go back to Carl's and find a nearby church or cathedral."

Taylor's father spoke. "Where does this Carl live?"

"New Hampshire."

"That's a long way to drive with people trying to kill you. We need to get you somewhere safe, fast, until everything hits the paper and we can put these guys away. Then you can do whatever you need to do."

"How about the cottage?" She thought of Jack.

Her father nodded, then looked at Jeremy. "That should work. Okay with you?"

"Sounds good."

Parks nodded. "It's settled then. It's nearly a three-hour drive. Let's stop and get something to eat on the way and you can both fill me in on all of it."

As they were getting in the car, Parks stopped to look at his phone.

"Everything okay?"

He looked up. "Yes. Just need to send a quick text and then we'll be on our way."

CHAPTER SIXTY-ONE

FBI RESIDENT AGENCY, SALISBURY, MARYLAND

JACK HAD BEEN SITTING IN A WOBBLY CHAIR, HIS HAND cuffed to the table, for what seemed like hours. He had a dull headache from the cheap wine, and his mouth felt like cotton.

He looked up at the agent sitting across from him. He wanted to tell him to quit wasting his time. He had done nothing wrong, but even so, he wasn't going to talk without his lawyer.

"We're trying to get in touch with your lawyer now," the agent said calmly. "But it's in your best interest to tell us where Taylor Phillips is. Now. If we find her now, and alive, things will go much better."

Jack said nothing.

"Suit yourself. But you'll be out of options soon."

Jack knew his rights.

"Aren't you supposed to take me before a judge?" Jack asked.

"You would think," the agent answered. "Things seem to have gone a little off script." He shrugged.

Jack wouldn't give him the satisfaction of a reaction.

The agent stood. "I guess I *am* going to have to let you go. The search gave us what we need, and I can't keep you much longer." Then he smiled, and Jack got a sick feeling.

The agent picked up his pen, his thumb clicking the top up and down. "When I say I'm going to let you go, I mean I'm going to let you go with . . ." The door opened and two men walked in. The agent made a sweeping gesture with his hand. "These nice detectives from New Hampshire. See, when we ran your name in NCIC before we came to get you, it set off some flags. These two have been driving nonstop from New Hampshire just to meet you. I guess they want to chat about a murder. Know anything about that, Logan?" The agent laughed. "You don't have to answer that. If your lawyer ever shows up, I'll tell him where you're headed. Enjoy the ride."

CHAPTER SIXTY-TWO

A S SHE SPOTTED THE FORD ESCORT PARKED IN THE DRIVE-way, Taylor's heart soared at the thought of seeing Jack again. She looked at the old clapboard house, where she hadn't been in years. Her father and Evelyn had bought it when they were first married and used it as their weekend retreat. She'd failed to see the charm, finding it isolated and barren, and she spent as little time there as possible.

As soon as they were out of the car, she knew something was wrong. The door was slightly ajar and when she pushed it open, she saw the chaos—drawers wide open, their contents strewn, the floor littered with papers and objects. The sofa cushions were scattered on the floor, and all the cabinets in the kitchen hung open.

"Jack," she called, as she ran to the bedroom, frantic. "Jack, are you here?"

"What the hell happened here?" her father yelled.

Jeremy looked around the room, taking it all in. "Looks like the house has been ransacked."

She ran back in the living room, out of breath. "He's not here. He's not here!"

Her father pulled out a gun and pointed it at her. "Sit down." He looked at Jeremy. "You, too."

"Dad! What are you doing?"

His voice turned cold. "I'm not your father, and I think you know that."

This had to be a joke. Was he actually pointing a gun at her? She moved toward him, and he cocked the gun.

"Stay back."

"What are you doing? I don't understand."

"Taylor, do as he says." Jeremy's hands were up, and he sat on the sofa.

She continued to stand. "Why are you doing this? I'm your daughter. I love you." Taylor was too devastated to feel any fear. "Dad, please!"

Parks shook his head. "I never wanted kids. I had a vasectomy before I married your mother. Then she went on and on about becoming parents. Drove me nuts. I finally went along with the IVF just to shut her up."

She felt as if she'd been stabbed in the heart. "You mean she wasn't infertile? You let her think that she couldn't get pregnant and all the while you'd had a vasectomy? I don't understand. I thought you loved me." She sounded pathetic, even to her own ears. He didn't love her. Her father didn't love her.

She had loved him. Still loved him. She felt her heart break into a million pieces and a cold lump take its place.

"He's not worth it, Taylor," Jeremy said.

Parks put his free hand over his heart and flashed a phony smile. "Aw. Your big brother coming to your defense." He looked at her coldly. "It all worked out. Crosse got an extra kid, and he provided me with more money than I could ever spend, plus no messy emotional attachments. My time at the Institute was well worth it."

"*You* were trained at the Institute?"

He laughed, a humorless, odd laugh. "Trained, raised, made."

"You were one of the *orphans*?"

"Yep. How many poor throwaways do you know who have the power and money I have?"

"But I thought that your parents had died when I was too young to remember them. That's what you said. I've seen pictures of them. Pictures of you with them. Even a few of them holding me."

He sneered at her. "I showed you my cleverly designed cover."

She sunk to the sofa. "Both you and Malcolm were raised there?"

"Poetic, no? You've belonged to Crosse forever. Before you were even born."

A surge of adrenaline shot through her. "I don't belong to him and I never will. You're evil, and you're going to rot in hell."

He narrowed his eyes at her. "Just like your mother, with

the fire and brimstone. How about you let me worry about my eternal soul? And by the way, thanks for finding the coins. Your useless mother couldn't tell me where they were. Even when my guy tortured her."

"I hate you!" she screamed.

"Don't you want to know why she died?"

Jeremy reached out and grabbed her hand.

"Crosse had me marry her so I could find the coins, but your grandparents wouldn't give them up. He figured after a while, she'd confide in me. All those years, she pretended to know nothing. Then one day I hear her talking to you. Right after your fourteenth birthday. Do you remember? You had just gotten back from Greece a few weeks earlier."

Taylor thought hard and a memory came to her, of her mother sitting on the edge of her bed, talking to her before she went to sleep. Yes, it was coming back. She looked at the man holding the gun. Not her father—a stranger, an imposter.

"How could I have forgotten? The family's sacred trust. She said we were guardians of the faith, that we had to keep a relic hidden and that when I was twenty-one, it would be my turn. But I had to have faith. It could only be entrusted to one with faith."

Jeremy gasped. "That's why they told your mother about them, but not mine. My mother had lost her faith."

Parks said, "I knew then she'd been lying to me all those years. I could pretend a lot of things, but going to church every week, pretending to be devout, that was beyond even *my* abilities. I wanted those coins. Why should Crosse have them? I'd researched them, figured if it was worth making me marry this woman and wait to find them all those years, they had to be something special."

"So you killed her?" Taylor asked.

"I wasn't going to wait anymore. I hired someone to interrogate her. To torture her if necessary. She wouldn't tell him anything." A scowl transformed his face. "I couldn't let Crosse know what I'd done, so I had the guy steal her jewelry and murder her, made it look random."

He extended the arm holding the gun and aimed it at Taylor. "And now it's time for you to join her. Crosse will think that you two are still hiding somewhere, and he'll never know that I have the coins. Then *I'll* have the power. Maybe even immortality."

Jeremy flew from his seat and knocked Parks down, reaching for the gun. It went flying, skidding over the wood floor. They struggled, rolling on the ground, and Taylor jumped for it. The gun was now a few feet from Parks's arm, and he was reaching for it, but she got there faster, picked it up with a shaking hand, and pointed it at him.

"Get away from Jeremy."

Jeremy was pinned on his back, Parks straddling him, a hand on his neck. She saw Parks reach into his pocket and pull out something shiny. There was a click and a blade popped out. He was going to kill Jeremy. His hand moved toward Jeremy's neck, poised to slice. Taylor got ready to pull the trigger when a voice made her jump.

"What in the world is going on here?" She looked toward the door. It was Evelyn. Her entrance had distracted Parks, too. Jeremy took the opportunity to knock the knife from his hand and push the older man off him.

Before they could stop him, Parks ran to the door, shoved his wife out of the way, and jumped into his Suburban and took off.

Evelyn ran out the door after him, but he was gone. She came back inside. "What happened here?" She started walking toward Taylor, but Taylor raised the gun to stop her from coming any closer.

She looked her stepmother in the eye. "I think you'd better tell us what's really going on."

CHAPTER SIXTY-THREE

YOU LET THEM GET AWAY AGAIN?" DAMON CROSSE WAS livid. He had a bunch of imbeciles working for him.

"They shot down the helicopter and took off. They landed a plane in Maryland but we lost them."

"Damn it to hell! I won't allow him to undo everything I've accomplished."

"We recovered the flash drive from Parks. We also swept Jeremy's facility. And Logan's been arrested."

That was one bit of good news. But Jeremy and Taylor were still free.

"Find them. Do you hear me? Find them and bring them to me. And remember: don't let anything happen to the woman."

"What about Jeremy?"

"Bring him, too. He has information I need."

The man continued to stand there, looking at him.

"If I have to repeat myself, you won't live long enough to hear it. Get moving!"

After he had left, Damon opened the center desk drawer and pulled out the large black book. He turned to the familiar page and began to chant. Enough was enough. He should have known better than to ever show Jeremy that tape of Maya. He was furious with himself that he had unwittingly played a part in helping her achieve her agenda. How was he to know she would turn to God? He had selected her so carefully, made sure that her position as an atheist was solid, her idolatry of science secure. She had reached out from the grave and converted his son. His *son*. He had been foolish to forget the power of prayer. He knew all too well what it could accomplish. He had devoted his life to convincing others of the absence of God, knowing full well God's power. He had believed Jeremy was cut from the same cloth as he and that he would assume his role. The insolence! Plotting against him. *Him!* Jeremy had been conspiring with those traitors. It would stop now.

Picking up a rubber ball, he squeezed it in his left hand over and over. Frustrated, he threw it against the wall. He had one more chance and this time he wouldn't squander it. Time was running out. At best, he had another twenty-five years left, unless he got more of the coins and could turn the clock back. Taylor had eluded him thus far, but she couldn't stay out of his reach for much longer. Her child would be his. And this child would never betray him or search for his mother. Damon would provide a mother for him, one who shared his own ambitions. He would grow up in a stable environment and be more than willing to take his place when the time came.

CHAPTER SIXTY-FOUR

EVELYN PUT HER HANDS UP. "DON'T DO ANYTHING CRAZY. I'm not here to hurt you. I came here to help you."

Taylor was skeptical. "Did you know he was bringing us here to kill us?"

"Not until a few hours ago. Taylor, you need to tell me everything that's happened since you went missing."

"Why should I trust you?"

She looked at the gun in Taylor's hand. "You've got me covered, at least, let's talk. Warwick duped us both."

"He did more than dupe us. He killed my mother!"

Evelyn's face filled with resignation. She shook her head. "I began to suspect it just a few weeks ago."

"Wait, why?" Taylor asked.

She looked up and gave Taylor her full attention. "He was in his study. I was about to come in when I overheard him on the phone with someone. He was arranging some sort of meeting, and I thought he was stepping out on me. He's done it before." Evelyn sighed. "I'm not proud of this, but I didn't want it to be true and I searched around for anything that would prove me wrong. Then I found a burner phone in his study. I saw that he'd texted someone from it to come to the cabin and 'clean up after him.' That sounded ominous to me. Then I thought back to the day your mother died. She and I were supposed to have lunch, but he called at the last minute, asking her to pick up his tux for an event that evening. The house manager always took care of things like that, and we both thought it was odd, but when she pushed him he told her that the woman was going home sick. Only, later that day, after your mother had gone missing, I went back to the house and the house manager was still there."

"So why didn't you suspect him back then?" Taylor asked.

"I was such a mess in my panic and grief that I forgot about it. And I would never have thought your father could be a killer! But when I saw the text about the cabin, I knew something was wrong. I cloned it and his regular phone."

Jeremy had a suspicious look on his face. "You cloned it? By yourself?"

"I had a friend help me. The point is, today I saw a text saying they'd taken Jack and the house was clear. The second text he sent an hour ago was to an unknown number, saying he had you and would need someone to come to the cottage and clean up after him."

"That still doesn't explain how you got here so fast. What aren't you telling us?"

Evelyn shook her head.

Taylor walked toward her until she was only a few feet away. "If I have to shoot you, I will. Tell us the truth. Do you work for Crosse, too?"

"Who?"

"Come on, Evelyn, cut the crap." Taylor wasn't playing her game. "Were you in on the murder of my mother? Just waiting in the wings to marry her husband? Maybe you're just pretending you just found out about your husband being behind the murder." Taylor would never again refer to Warwick as her father.

"Of course not! I loved your mother."

"Really? It didn't take you long to become the new Mrs. Parks. Did he tell you that Damon Crosse is my father?"

Evelyn's mouth dropped open. "Your what?"

"My father. He made sure his sperm was used when my mother did in vitro at one of his clinics so that my mother would have his child. Warwick had to have arranged it. Jeremy is my brother and my cousin—our mothers were sisters. Jeremy's mother was a medical student at the Institute. Damon held her hostage, impregnated her, then let her die after Jeremy was born."

Evelyn looked horrified. "I had no idea . . . about any of this. Taylor, I swear!" She looked up at Jeremy. "What was your mother's name?"

He narrowed his eyes at her. "Why?"

"Please, I have to know. Was it Maya?"

His eyes widened. "Yes."

"I thought she had left the program voluntarily. He told

me that she'd run off with another man—Brian, I think—who left at the same time she did. Are you sure about this? Held hostage? I can't believe Damon would do that." She looked like she'd seen a ghost, and in her eyes was the same shell-shocked look that Jack had had when he found out about Dakota.

"You knew my mother?"

"I was there when she came to the Institute. Damon hired me right after I got my PhD. I thought he was doing noble work. He said I was helping to shape the future. She was in the first group I worked with, and I was so sad when she left. There was something about her that made an impression on me. I can't believe he would do something like that. It's so counter to all the work he does, it just doesn't make any sense."

Jeremy and Taylor exchanged a look.

"Let her read it," Taylor said.

Jeremy retrieved Maya's letter from his satchel and handed it to Evelyn. "My mother wrote this. You want to know about all the good he does at that institute? You'll see the truth."

She took the letter, then looked up, panic-stricken. "We have to get out of here. Crosse's men will be here any minute."

"What? You called them?" Taylor asked.

"I thought I was doing the right thing. He made me believe that Jeremy was the evil one. He said he wanted the chance to talk to him again, work things out. And I didn't think Damon would hurt you. He told me he just wanted to make sure you were safe."

"That's because he wants my baby," Taylor yelled behind her as they sprinted out the door.

CHAPTER SIXTY-FIVE

HILLSBOROUGH COUNTY JAIL, NEW HAMPSHIRE

Jack, it's bad. They say your fingerprints are all over that cabin. How did you get so sloppy?"

Jack's eyes went to the ceiling.

"I wasn't expecting it. I let my guard down. I didn't realize until the guy showed up that I'd been set up."

His longtime buddy and trusted lawyer, Arnie Thomas, chewed his lip. Jack waited for him to say something. He frowned at Jack. "It doesn't look good. We're going to need Taylor to corroborate your story that it was self-defense. She has to testify that you didn't kidnap her and that this man threatened your life."

Jack shook his head. "No way. She can't come out of hiding. It's too dangerous."

Arnie sank back into his chair. "Are you serious? How do you expect me to get you out of this without her help?"

Jack leaned forward. "Find a way. I'm not about to hand her over on a silver platter just to save myself."

"We might be able to use a deposition from her, plead the case that she has to stay in hiding. Can you contact her?"

"Maybe. If Jeremy's still got the same burner, it's possible." Jack scratched his head. "Have you been able to find out anything about Craig?"

"No. Nothing. I'm sorry."

"What about the paper? Did the story get printed?"

Arnie reached into his briefcase and pulled out a newspaper. He handed it to Jack.

"That can't be," Jack sputtered.

"I'm afraid it is. There's nothing about the conspiracy. You're still front-page news, though. And Parks never went back to his office. When I called, they didn't know where he was."

Jack felt like he'd been punched in the gut. "They must have gotten him. Taylor will never forgive me if he's murdered." He hit the table. "Please, try to find out if he's okay. Hopefully he's still validating the story and that's why it hasn't printed yet. I have to know he's safe."

"I'll see what I can find out." Arnie stood. "In the meantime, if you think of anything helpful, let me know. I've got a bail hearing to prepare for."

CHAPTER SIXTY-SIX

"WE CAN'T TAKE MY CAR. WHEN THEY GET HERE AND WE'RE gone, they'll look for it. What about the Escort?" Evelyn said.

Taylor shook her head. "No, whoever was here and took Jack would have the plates, and Crosse might too."

"What are we going to do?" Jeremy said.

She had to think.

"About half a mile up the road there's another cottage. We know the family; they only come here in the summer and an occasional weekend. They used to leave an old Volvo station wagon there. If we're lucky, it's still next to their house."

"What about the keys?" Jeremy asked.

"There's a toolbox under the kitchen sink. Can you grab it?"

They followed Taylor down the gravel road and narrow

dirt driveway that led to the house. A blue station wagon was parked in a carport next to the cottage.

Taylor tried the door. It was unlocked. "Get in." She turned to Jeremy, seated next to her. "Screwdriver, please."

He handed it to her. She inserted the flat end into the ignition.

"Hammer?" She took it from him and used it to smack the butt end of the screwdriver.

"What are you doing?" he asked.

"Unlocking the steering column so we can start the car." She turned the screwdriver and the car started.

"How in the world do you know how to do that?"

She gave him a wry look. "Things can get boring at boarding school when you don't have your own wheels."

"You're full of surprises."

"Let's get out of here."

"Where are we going?" Evelyn asked.

"I think the only safe bet is to go back to Carl's," Jeremy answered. "He's a good friend of mine, and he lives completely off the grid," he explained for Evelyn's benefit.

"Where is he?"

"New Hampshire."

"That's over a seven-hour drive."

"Well, we don't have much choice. We'll drive straight through, taking shifts," Taylor said. "In the meantime, we have to figure out our next move. Now that the flash drive is gone, all we have is the letter. I'm not a lawyer, but I have to wonder how it would be authenticated with Maya gone and everyone in her family dead."

"Evelyn's met her. And I'm sure there are handwriting samples from tests or essays while she was in school," Jeremy said.

Evelyn was shaking her head. "It's not enough. He'll figure a way to get out of it. He can claim that she was delusional—she made it all up. We need more."

"What if I went public with what we know?" Taylor asked. "I have contacts in the press. Everyone knows Karen Printz; I was her producer for years. I'm sure she'd love to interview me on *Newsline*. Even if they don't believe us about the illegal things being done at the Institute, we could tell them of our suspicions that it was started and funded by a Nazi war criminal. It might be enough to get people looking into the Institute and Crosse. They could investigate his dealings, get people to come forward. Those stories always bring people out of the woodwork," Taylor said.

"Maybe," Jeremy said, "but his people are not your ordinary victim types. Remember, they're either very well compensated, or zealots doing what they believe is their calling. I'm worried that that kind of scrutiny would only drive him to get rid of any evidence of what he did to my mother and all his other illegal activity."

"I agree with Jeremy," Evelyn said. "Being on staff all these years, I've seen how very careful Damon is to make sure his key players have passed stringent psychological screenings."

Taylor looked around to make sure no other cars were in sight and swerved off the road into a wooded clearing and turned to face Evelyn.

"Give me your phone."

"What?"

Jeremy sensed what she was up to, and from the corner of her eye she saw him pull the gun out of the satchel where he'd stashed it.

"I want to believe that you're going to help us. But how do I know you don't just want us to lead you to Carl?"

"Fair enough." She handed the phone to Taylor.

"Now get out of the car."

"What are you doing?" Jeremy asked. "You're not leaving her here?"

"Keep the gun on her. I want to search her."

They both moved behind the car and Evelyn put her hands up while Taylor patted her down.

"Okay, you can get back in. Give me your purse as well." Taylor threw it to Jeremy. After Evelyn and Taylor got back in the car, Taylor put the car in drive as she said to Jeremy, "Take out her wallet, then throw the rest out the window. We don't have time to look for a tracking device."

"Taylor, you have to believe me. Now that I know the truth, I could never work for Damon again. He truly never showed me that side of him. All I saw was his educational programs, the research I thought he was doing for the good of humanity."

"Come on, you had to know he was up to no good. You were the one administering the tests. What did you *think* he was doing?"

"A lot of companies use psychological testing on their employees. I thought he was a visionary intent on improving the world, that his work with doctors and lawyers was progressive. I believed in what he told me, that he wanted to relieve suffering through euthanasia, improve health through genetic engineering."

"And what did you think he was going to do with Taylor?"

"Both he and Warwick told me she'd been kidnapped. Jack's face was all over the news. I had no reason not to believe him."

Taylor still wasn't completely convinced, but Evelyn's words had the ring of truth to them. She needed to figure out a way to be certain. "I want to believe you, but you can understand if I'm having trouble trusting people these days."

"Record me. Record me saying that I'm helping Jeremy get back at his father. I'll say that I'm going to testify that I knew Maya and that I believe Damon killed her."

"What will that accomplish?"

"An insurance policy. You can email it to whomever you want, and they can send it to Crosse if I double-cross you." She threw her hands up. "It's all I have."

"You could always say we made you do it," Taylor said.

"I know my father; that'll be enough for him to doubt her and have her killed."

Jeremy swiped to video and recorded Evelyn saying the incriminating words. "Done. I've emailed it to three of my people."

"All right. We still have to figure out a way to take him down," Taylor said. "I think we need to get back into the Institute and try to get his files."

"Impossible. The video surveillance would pick us up before we got close and his security detail would get us," Jeremy said.

She drummed her fingers on the steering wheel. "What else

can we do? We can't let him get away with all of it." She had an idea. "What if we don't sneak in? What if we're invited?"

"What do you mean?" Evelyn asked.

"I'll call him. Say I want to meet him. I'll go in, wear a wire, and get him to admit to everything." Even as the words left her lips, she realized she'd watched too many detective shows.

"No way," both Evelyn and Jeremy answered.

"You can't go near him. It's too dangerous. If anyone is going in, it's me. Problem is, he just wants me dead. After everything I've done to hamper his plans—turning Malcolm, finding you—he wants vengeance," Jeremy said.

"There's something he wants even more," Taylor said.

"What?" Jeremy asked.

"The coins."

"The what?" Evelyn asked.

Ignoring her, Taylor went on. "If you call and say you want to talk to him and use the coins as a bargaining chip, he'd have to let you in. He wouldn't risk losing them forever. You'd have to prove that you have them, though, bring some with you."

"I don't like that. If he gets his hands on them, it will only make him more powerful."

"He's not going to get to keep them. We have to figure out a way to get you in and then contain him while you download the file from the main computer."

"I think I can help with that," Evelyn said.

"How?" Taylor asked.

"The head of security. He started when he was so young,

I practically raised him. If I call him and tell him I need to get on-site undetected, I think he can rig the security cameras so that they play old tape—Jeremy could sneak whomever he wanted on-site to help."

"Are you sure he'd do that? What would you tell him?" Jeremy asked.

"If I tell him I messed up on a dossier, that I need to re-place it without Damon's knowing, he'll help me."

"What do you think?" Taylor asked Jeremy.

"I think it could work. I could have my men surprise his security and take them out. I also have a connection there, who will help me keep Crosse contained if necessary."

"Who?" Taylor asked.

"Jonas, his house manager. We've been working on him for the past few weeks. His granddaughter died. He blames Damon."

"What happened?" Taylor asked.

"Her boyfriend was one of the kids that died trying the choking game from that show. She killed herself."

Taylor looked puzzled. "I don't understand."

"He knew that Damon had fixed the Supreme Court case against the parents and blames Damon for his granddaughter's suicide." He nodded. "This might actually work."

CHAPTER SIXTY-SEVEN

BAIL DENIED. THE DEFENDANT WILL BE REMANDED TO THE custody of the Hillsborough County Sheriff's Department," the judge said as she slammed the gavel down.

Arnie's face went white, and the bailiff cuffed Jack and led him away.

Hillsborough County Jail—Valley Street Jail, as the locals referred to it—was no place for lightweights. The fact that it wasn't a prison, just a jail, made little difference. The worst of the worst started their journey in a jail before heading off to prison.

The cells were full of men on trial for murder, drugs, rape, and other assorted crimes. Arnie had assured him that, unlike Jack, most of them *were* guilty, and that Jack better show them he was more than a pretty face, or it would be a long month waiting to be processed and moved—if he made it that long.

The first night was the defining one. Jack had to make the transition quickly if he wanted to survive.

It was lights out, and as he lay on his back he knew some of the inmates would be testing his mettle. Arnie had told him there were lots of repeat offenders who'd have alliances formed. Jack figured it would happen in the next hour or so. He evened his breathing and completed a quick visualization. Every muscle in his body was tense, and he listened for telltale sounds. He pretended to be asleep. He was ready.

He heard Finley, his cellmate, first—the creak of the metal bed as he got up. Jack remained motionless, his eyes closed. The swish of coarse fabric—thigh against thigh—as others approached the cell. He estimated that there were three plus Finley, not counting the crooked guard who would be letting them in. The whining of the door as they entered was his cue.

He sprang up from the mattress and gave the first man a swift upward punch, smashing his nose. He went down. Jack shoved his fingers into the second man's eyes. He pushed until there was no more resistance, and the man screamed in agony.

Jack felt a searing pain in his leg and realized he'd been slashed. *Where did that come from?* He turned and saw Finley dancing in front of him, waving the weapon in the air.

"Come on, big shot. Come and get it." He was grinning at Jack.

The last man came up behind Jack and threw a meaty arm around his neck. Jack didn't resist but fell back against the man in surrender.

"Not so tough, now, huh, Logan? It's Miller time." He

recognized the voice. It was Albert Miller. He'd made himself known to Jack earlier in the day.

Jack bent his head forward, then snapped it back hard, gratified to hear the sound of cracking bone. Miller cursed as he released Jack and his hands went to his own face. It was now or never. Jack rushed in and grabbed Finley by the balls. He squeezed. Hard. Finley screamed as he swiped at Jack. He got two more swipes in, but Jack didn't let go.

"Get off me, you lunatic."

"Drop the knife," Jack said.

Finley opened his hand.

Jack leaned down and took it, releasing his grip on Finley.

"Tell your friends to get out of here before I finish them off and blame it on you."

CHAPTER SIXTY-EIGHT

DAMON CROSSE FROZE WHEN HE HEARD THE VOICE ON the other end of the phone.

"Hello, Father." The sarcasm was palpable.

Damon scowled. "Have you called to confess the error of your ways?" He couldn't wait to vent his fury on Jeremy. But first he would let him know that all his efforts at redemption were in vain. Yes, he would make him suffer for his betrayal.

A loud sigh. "I've no patience for these tiresome games. I have something you want."

"And that would be?"

"The ten coins my family has been protecting."

His body tensed. "What do you want for them?"

"My mother's cross. I presume you still have it?"

"You presume correctly," Damon answered.

Jeremy continued. "And to work out a peace agreement. I'll leave you alone if you'll do the same."

He laughed. "You take me for a fool. You cannot seriously expect any peace between the two of us. You have betrayed me and everything I believe in. There is no peace." He felt the anger rise again and resisted the urge to smash the phone against the desk. The insolence!

"Fine. Forget it. Taylor and I will deactivate them so they will never do you or anyone else any good."

He clenched his teeth. "All right then. We shall talk. Perhaps we can come to some sort of cease-and-desist agreement. As long as you bring the silver pieces." Damon was dying to get his hands on the silver pieces, but this was too easy.

"You are willing to give them up just for a piece of jewelry?"

"It's all that's left of her."

What a sentimental fool. "Fine." He hung up. He would have twenty of them, and only need to find the last ten to complete the set. And once he'd taken them from Jeremy, he wouldn't stop until he hunted him down and killed him. If his son understood the power he was handing over, he would never make such a deal. Not only would they unleash demonic power that would be in Damon's control, but they would also restore his youth. Some even said they could make you immortal. He wasn't sure if he believed that, but with another forty or fifty years and more supernatural help, there would be no stopping him. Everything would be accomplished so much more easily, and the access he would have, oh, the access—it was something he had only dreamed about. He thought of his beloved mentor and whispered, "Oh, Father, if only you were still with me. What we could do together."

CHAPTER SIXTY-NINE

THE FIRST THING TAYLOR DID WHEN THEY REACHED CARL
and Gilly's house was to sit on the floor and embrace Beau.
He licked her face as he jumped, delirious with joy.

"So good to see you, baby. I missed you so much." She
showered his head with kisses. He finally settled down and put
his head in her lap. She looked up at Gilly. "I can't thank you
enough for taking such good care of him."

Gilly shook her head. "Nonsense. It's been a pleasure having him. Truth be told, I hate to see him go."

Jeremy came into the kitchen. "Let's go find Carl."

Taylor and Evelyn followed Jeremy down the stairs to the
basement, where he led them to a bookcase on the far wall,
and pulled out a book. As if by magic, the bookcase swung in,
becoming a door.

"You're kidding?"

He shook his head. "Nope. Sometimes life does imitate art."

They followed him into the hidden room and watched as he replaced the book and shut the door. It was a tremendous space with lab equipment and computers.

"How have you managed to keep this place a secret? They found your hideout."

"They think Carl is dead. Knowing Crosse was likely to discover my connection to him years ago, I knew he'd have him killed. My people made it look like they were dead, that he and Gilly had a car accident. There were obituaries in all the national papers. This house is in a different name, and my people have made up new identities for them." He made a face. "Crosse is not the only one with abilities. And despite his delusions of grandeur, he's not omniscient."

Yet another door, this one at the end of the room, opened, and Carl walked in.

He embraced Taylor warmly and led her to a chair.

"My dear. I'm so glad you made it back safely. I'm so sorry to hear about Jack."

Taylor's face clouded. It killed her not to be able to go see him, to try to help him, but she knew it was too dangerous right now.

Jeremy put his hand on her shoulder. "You okay?"

She nodded. "What if he gets thrown into prison? He needs my testimony to prove he killed that man in self-defense. I really think I need to come forward now."

"You'll never make it to court, Taylor. Trust me. The best way you can help Jack is to stay in hiding and stay safe. When the time comes, you can speak on his behalf—that is, after we put Crosse away," Jeremy argued. He sighed. "I know you're upset, but if all goes according to plan, I'll get the evidence we need, they'll arrest Crosse, and you can come out of hiding. Once you come forward, I'm sure they'll drop the charges."

"I'll testify, too, Taylor," Evelyn added.

Jeremy put a hand on Taylor's shoulder. "Try not to worry. You're a credible witness—the wife of a senator. Your word will hold enough weight for them to release him."

She arched an eyebrow. "Really? How do we know what judges Crosse controls? I'm not convinced that it will be so easy."

"Well, we'll just have to do our best. Damon doesn't own the entire world."

She looked at Evelyn. "Everything's all set on your end?"

"Yes. Jeremy will have five minutes to get his men on campus. My contact will text me when the tape is replaced. Jeremy will take my phone with him."

"Is that long enough for your people?" Taylor asked.

"Yes. They'll be hiding in the woods, waiting."

Taylor looked at Jeremy, then at Evelyn. "Just to be sure, we're going to need you to stay here until Jeremy gives us confirmation that you've done what you promised."

Evelyn looked hurt. "You still don't trust me? Taylor, I've raised you since you were fourteen. I'd never hurt you."

"I didn't think Parks would either." She softened her tone. "I do think you're telling the truth, but I can't risk Jeremy's life or my baby's."

"There's a safe room here. You'll be locked in it," Jeremy said.

"If you *are* trying to double-cross us, no one will ever see you again," Taylor added.

Evelyn was studying her face, probably trying to psycho-analyze her right now. Taylor had to convince her that she was capable of carrying out her threat. "If I've learned anything, it's that the rules only apply to the weak," she said. "Don't forget, Crosse's blood flows in my veins. I don't want to hurt you, either, but if you're lying to us now, I'll know you were part of the plan to kill my mother. That, I won't forgive, and that, I will avenge."

"I guess we'll know by tomorrow night" was all Evelyn said.

CHAPTER SEVENTY

JEREMY PULLED UP TO THE IRON GATES AND FELT A SHIVER go through him. He pressed the button on the video monitor and held his hand up, showing one of the coins he held between his fingers. The heavy gates opened, and he drove onto the property. Reaching the door, he was escorted to Damon's office by one of the security officers.

"You've aged." Jeremy looked at the man who had been the center of his universe for most of his life and was surprised to realize that all he felt was a deep sadness. Where was his hatred? His anger? His thirst for vengeance? All he saw was a tired old man. Frail, almost. Then, his father blinked and Jeremy saw that steely glint of something otherworldly still there in his eyes. He recognized at last what had been there all along—the complete and utter absence of any goodness or humanity. His sympathy evaporated.

"Let me see them."

"My mother's cross, first."

Damon opened a desk drawer and brought out the cross. He pushed it toward Jeremy, on the desk. "You get the chain when I get the coins."

"Fine." Let him think he had the upper hand. Jeremy would take them all back from him once he took over the facility. He played along, giving Damon the sack of coins as Damon pulled out the gold chain and put it next to the cross. Jeremy scooped both up and put them in his pocket.

Damon grabbed the velvet pouch eagerly, clutching it in his fist, then opened it and pulled a coin out and held it up to the light. He studied one side of the coin—a Grecian profile wearing an aegis—then turned it over to look at the eagle on the other side.

He clutched the coins to his chest, his eyes shining with excitement. His lip curled in a sneer, and he looked down at Jeremy. "Thank you for the coins. You're still as foolish as ever. I can finally have you killed and exact my revenge for your betrayal. You chose the wrong side. You are weak. Just like your mother."

Jeremy laughed. "Your words don't have the power to hurt me anymore. I can't even summon enough feeling to hate you."

Damon laughed, a dry, mirthless sound. "Tell yourself whatever you want. You were never good enough, never came close to measuring up. I expected great things from you, but you're weak and soft."

Jeremy looked at him without flinching. "I suppose you think you're strong? Powerful? Were you powerful when your father killed your dog in front of you? Or when he beat you with his belt?"

Anger flashed in Damon's eyes. "You have no idea what you're talking about. My childhood is none of your business. It has nothing to do with who I am today."

"Oh, I disagree. I think it has everything to do with you. And it's not very original. The abused child grows up to be the abuser. Straight from the psychology books, a tired cliché. The only difference is that your second abuser turned out to be rich and adept at using the occult to his advantage. He manipulated you, and your entire life's work has been nothing more than the completion of another man's dream."

"How dare you! Do you know what I can do to you? What I *will* do to you? No one has manipulated me. I'm the one in control. It's my world, and don't you ever forget it." Spittle flew from Damon's mouth, and his face contorted like an ugly purple balloon. "I'll kill you myself."

Jeremy remained calm. "You'd like that, wouldn't you? You can't touch me. I belong to God now. It must kill you that my mother's prayers actually worked."

Damon leaned forward. "You belong to me. You are nothing, and your god has no power here. He couldn't save your waste of a mother, and he can't save you." He pushed the button on his desk and looked at the door expectantly.

Jeremy laughed.

His father whirled around and demanded, "What's so funny?"

"No one's coming."

"What are you talking about?" Damon's eyes blazed.

"Your security has been disabled. While we've been having this nice little father-and-son chat, my men have taken over your facility."

Crosse's face turned white. "How?" he finally managed to ask.

"Jonas. He tipped me off about the DNA sequence. I'll get your dirt file. That'll be enough to take you down."

"Jonas would never betray me."

"Wrong. He lost his granddaughter because of you. The reason she killed herself was because her boyfriend was one of the kids who died as a result of your disgusting show."

Damon ran to the door. It was locked. "What happened to my guards?"

"Oh, Evelyn helped us with that."

Damon shook his head. "It doesn't matter. There is nowhere you can hide. We will find you again. Go ahead and walk out the door."

"I want the tape of my mother."

Damon laughed. "You're insane if you think I'd ever give that to you. I'll kill you and add you to the collection."

"You're not going to kill me or anyone else. You're finished. You couldn't even produce an heir the right way. How ironic that your only two children are both on God's side now. We will fight you until our dying breath and do everything in our power to neutralize your insidious influences. I'll go through your files and prove what you've done. This time I'll take it to someone who will actually help us. You'll spend the rest of your pitiful life in a cell."

Damon laughed again. "You fool. Do you really think you

can undo decades of my seeds? Take a look around you. You've already lost." He pulled a black leather book from his center drawer and threw it toward Jeremy.

Jeremy looked at the first page, which was a table of contents. Subjects were listed in alphabetical order: abortion, alcoholism, depression, divorce, drug addiction, murder, pornography, prostitution, rape, suicide, and trafficking. He thumbed through and saw that the divorce rates by state were displayed in a bar chart by year. The bars went up every year. He thumbed through more of the book and saw the same trend in most of the other categories.

"There are also cross-referenced graphs. It's quite fascinating, Jeremy. As a scientist, you will appreciate the synergy. You see, as the laws governing pornography were eased, the depression and divorce rates spiked as well. There are correlations between so many of the laws and the corresponding consequences. And it's so easy to accomplish. In the beginning, it was more difficult. Especially the pornography. But now with the internet, we can get it to kids. We've yet to see what effect that will have on future generations." His mouth was a ghoulish slash. "Isn't it wonderful? You will never stop this train."

Jeremy's stomach lurched, and it took everything he had not to strike him. "We have stopped it. We'll be cleaning house in Congress and in the courts. You won't win. There are still good and decent people who don't want a world like this."

"My pawns in the government and business are icing on the cake. The real power is the media and entertainment world. They lead the cause and influence everything that happens. I have already won. Look around you. Turn the television on.

Those good and decent people love to sit down and spend the evening watching vampires, zombies, cheating spouses, serial killers; those are the heroes of today's shows. Websites promoting adultery grow in popularity every day. Drugs are legal in more and more states. Anything goes. It's only going to get worse. Only a fool would waste his time trying to save the witless wretches. Leave them to rot in their own filth. It's what they deserve. You have chosen the wrong side."

"No. I will fight this with all I've got. And I've got God."

"God?" Damon snorted. "Where was God when you were growing up? When I took you from your mother?"

Jeremy shook his head. "It's no use. I've met him. I've felt his power, and nothing you can say to try to deceive me will work anymore. I will spend the rest of my life working for him and trying to forget the horrible things I did when I was still under your control. I won't give up on humanity."

"Humanity deserves to be given up on. What does it tell you about humanity when a rape victim is better served by screaming *fire* than *help*? The instinct for self-preservation is immeasurably more potent than the instinct to help others. The selfish, amoral, ignorant masses care only for themselves. You are wasting your life on them."

Jeremy stood up. He knew what he had to do and he stood there, grappling with the truth of it, fighting against what he knew was right but felt was impossible. Offering a silent prayer, he forced himself to remember God's grace toward him. He swallowed hard, then spoke.

"I forgive you."

Damon's eyes widened and he said nothing at first, thrown

by Jeremy's statement. Then the surprise in his eyes changed
to fury. "You forgive *me*? You are the one who abandoned your
calling, betrayed your destiny. It is you who should be begging
forgiveness from me."

Jeremy had done his part. Even though he would never
have any sort of relationship with this man, his words were a
symbol of his faith, and he knew that he would have to continue to rely on God for them to become true. He had taken
a step toward what he believed was required of him in the life
he had chosen. Damon's reaction was of no concern to him.

"We are finished." He walked over to the desk and took
Damon's laptop. He knocked hard on the door and it was
opened. "Detain him in his office, until we find what we need
to turn him over to the authorities."

Jonas bolted the door and resumed his station just outside it.

Jeremy walked out into the ornate hallway to Damon's tro-
phy room, where Damon had taken him to show him the tape
of his mother. Opening the door, he was struck by the starkness
of the room. Nothing personal adorned the walls or the tables.
He walked toward the tall, mahogany bookcase, crouched
down and pushed the gold book of Grimm's fairy tales, and
the bookcase opened. A second bookcase stood behind it. His
breath caught in his throat. A long braid, held together with a
red ribbon, was lying atop a wooden box on the middle shelf.
He picked it up and rubbed it against his cheek. It had to be
his mother's. But why had Damon kept it? He lifted the box
from the shelf and opened it. A series of DVDs were inside. He
pulled out one of them. It was labeled 9/75–10/75. He looked
at the next and it was 11/75–12/75. He stood up and walked

over to the DVD player and popped one in. His mother. His beautiful, beautiful mother. And that monster tormenting her. He had recorded it all. Every conversation, every heartbreaking moment of their interactions. He picked up the last one. It was marked "The End." He wouldn't watch it now. He put the discs into the duffel bag and put the braid on top, then went to the business office in case he could find any files there that weren't on the laptop. He would make sure he had enough to implicate everyone in Damon's network.

CHAPTER SEVENTY-ONE

AMON FELL BACK AGAINST HIS CHAIR AND HEAVED A DEEP sigh. Now that Jeremy had free rein of the facility, he would find the DVDs. Damn his own foolish arrogance in keeping them. He'd known, of course, that Jonas's granddaughter had killed herself, but he'd no idea it was because of that damn show. Jonas had intentionally kept that from him. It was all unraveling now, and he was smart enough to know when it was time to cut his losses. It didn't matter; his work would continue without him. He might not be able to prevent Jeremy from proving his crimes, but Jeremy would never gain access to the files that would disband the network he had so carefully built. He pulled out his cell phone, punched in the code, and destroyed everything.

He opened the center drawer and took out a key. He rose and walked to the wall across from his desk, pushed on the panel, and inserted the key into the lock of the wooden box. The purple velvet pouch inside the box fit in the palm of his hand. He returned to his desk and took out a sheet of ivory stationery. With a trembling hand, he picked up the antique fountain pen and brought it to the paper. He would never be a prisoner again. He opened the pouch and pulled out the capsule. Closing his eyes, he started chanting. He opened his eyes again and let them take in the room. It would be the last time he would see it. Much had been accomplished here. He ran his hand over the rich wood, soaking in its sumptuousness.

It was time for Damon Crosse to make his final exit. He opened his mouth and swallowed the pill. Now all he had to do was wait. He clasped his hands and bowed his head, again chanting the soothing prayers he had learned so long ago. When his speech began to slur and his mouth to numb, he knew it was coming. His head swayed, and he had the sensation of floating out of his body. He was a balloon gliding up, up, up. Nice. Smooth. Easy. He tried to move but found he was rooted to the chair. His brain and his body were disconnecting. He felt like a rock, heavy and blunt. And then, he felt nothing.

CHAPTER SEVENTY-TWO

J EREMY SAW THE BODY AS SOON AS HE OPENED THE DOOR. He ran over to the slumped figure.

"Call 911," he yelled to Jonas.

He felt for a pulse. Nothing. Then he saw the letter from the corner of his eye and snatched it from the desk.

> *Jeremy,*
>
> *Don't congratulate yourself yet. You must have surmised that I would never allow myself to be imprisoned. I have no fear of death. I am assured of what awaits me and am eager to take my place. Peritas is to go to the shelter on Green Street. They're expecting him and will find him a good home. I will rely on your sense of morality to ensure he is delivered there.*

*Adieu for now. And, Jeremy, remember: you will
never be free of me.*

Your devoted father

Jeremy threw the letter back onto the desk. Even with
death looming, his father had had to get his last licks in. He
hesitated only a moment before putting his hand in Damon's
pockets to get the coins. They weren't there. He searched his
jacket pockets as well. *Where were they?* What could Damon
have done with them in that short amount of time? Frantic, he
ran to the desk and yanked the drawers open, pushing papers
out of the way and pulling everything else out of them until
they were empty. Nothing. He walked over to the bookcase
and began pushing different books, looking for an opening.
They had to be here somewhere.

Jonas came in and looked at the mess Jeremy had made
and then back at Jeremy.

"I'm looking for something he stole from me." He
straightened up as quickly as he could. Damon's black book
had fallen open and a white paper was sticking out, with
a list of names in Damon's handwriting. Jeremy recognized
some of them. Folding the paper, he put it in his pocket and
looked at Jonas.

"Will you stay until the police come?" Jeremy asked.

Jonas nodded.

"What will you do now?"

"If you'll have me, I'd like to work for your organization,"
Jonas said.

"Of course. I couldn't have done this without your help.

Please feel free to stay in your quarters until we iron out the details of the estate."

Jonas shook his head. "Thank you, sir, but I don't want to spend another night here. I'll go to my daughter's for now."

"Very well. Thank you so much for all your help. I'll be in touch."

Jeremy would have to come back later and look for the coins. He needed to leave before the police arrived, so he wouldn't have to answer any questions about what he'd been doing there, or about the things he had taken.

As soon as he had walked into the business office and seen the white screens, he had realized that all the data had been deleted. When he'd opened Damon's laptop, he saw that it had been wiped clean as well. It hadn't occurred to him that his father could access anything without his laptop. He must have used his phone. He felt like a fool, but he was a scientist, not a technology expert. He would bring someone in to try to recover the data on the computers. There had to be some way to retrieve it. In the meantime, he had the list of names. It was a start.

"You haven't won." He spat the words out.

He opened the ornate wooden door and walked through it. He was finally free.

CHAPTER SEVENTY-THREE

DAMON CROSSE WAS DEAD AND TAYLOR DIDN'T KNOW HOW to feel about it. On the one hand, she was thrilled that she and Jeremy were able to come out of hiding and that her child was now safe from Crosse's reach. On the other hand, she wanted him to suffer in prison, to have to atone for all he'd done. And a part of her had hoped for a confrontation where she could vent all her rage at what he'd done to her life. His suicide had left her in a state of emotional limbo.

Malcolm's funeral had been last week. Everyone had asked why her father wasn't there, and she and Evelyn had made up a story about his being down with the flu. How could they explain that they had no idea where he'd gone after almost killing Taylor? The masquerade was the worst, everyone saying such wonderful things about Malcolm—what a great man he was—the asset he had been to Congress. She had wanted to scream: *It was all a lie!* She was still angry and didn't want to forgive him, to feel any understanding about what he had done. It hurt much less to hate him. But then she let herself remember the good he had done. In the end, he had sacrificed his life for her and their child. Despite the lies, she believed that she *had* known him, a part of him, anyway—the part that hadn't been completely corrupted by Crosse and his brainwashing. Finally she was able to come to terms with Malcolm's betrayal and look upon his final actions as a sort of redemption.

Even with Taylor's testimony, it had taken Jack's lawyer almost a month to get him out. The kidnapping charges had been dropped right away, but that was in Maryland. The New Hampshire state's attorney was not so easily convinced to drop the murder charges, even with Taylor corroborating that it was self-defense. A few years before, she'd met Senator Polk from New Hampshire through Malcolm, and so she had gone to him for help with Jack. She didn't tell him the truth about Malcolm, of course. The story she and Jeremy had agreed on was that Malcolm had confessed to Taylor that he'd been harassed by Damon Crosse and had received death threats if he didn't vote the way Crosse demanded, and that Malcolm had asked Jack to intervene if anything happened to him. In their version, Malcolm was a hero, refusing to be bullied and paying the ultimate price.

She was scheduled to appear on the Karen Printz show next week, and that would be the story she would tell the world. Malcolm *had* made the right choice in the end, and she saw no reason for her child to have to live with a legacy of shame. She had no idea whether Senator Polk was in Crosse's pocket, too, but she had a feeling he would help her regardless, to make sure he came out looking clean.

She was waiting outside for Jack, thinking that the modern brick building looked more like a high school than a jail. She didn't want to think about what the inside was like. His release papers had been signed yesterday, and she had overnighted him some clothes so he could feel like himself again. She checked her watch, and movement caught her eye. There he was. As he walked toward her, everything seemed to slow down, and she was afraid that if she blinked, he'd disappear.

"Hey, you." He pulled her to him and covered her lips with his own.

She melted into him, feeling her body respond.

He cupped her face in his hands. "I love you so much it hurts. I am never letting you go."

She smiled. "You just try to get away."

She took his hand as they walked to the parking lot. "I have a surprise for you." She couldn't wait to see his reaction. She stopped in front of the car.

His eyes widened, and he smiled in delight when he saw the red Mustang.

"Sorry it can't be the original. But it's the same year and color," Taylor said.

He ran his hand over the hood.

"She's a beauty."

"We can't change the past, but I didn't see any reason we couldn't recapture the good memories." She threw the keys to him. "Just do me a favor, and don't get us killed. No faster than sixty-five."

He cocked an eyebrow. "Yeah, that's gonna happen." He got behind the wheel. "Where to?"

"Back to the old neighborhood."

"Put your seat belt on. It's gonna be a long ride."

CHAPTER SEVENTY-FOUR

B EEN A WHILE SINCE I'VE BEEN HERE," JACK SAID AS HE pulled into her driveway. Looking at his childhood home, he was jarred by the bright red door. His family didn't live there anymore, but in his mind's eye, it was still exactly the same. It felt like eons ago since he'd lived there. For a minute, he pictured his eight-year-old self bounding from that front door over to the house of his best friend.

"Evelyn's going to sell the house." Taylor interrupted his thoughts as they headed toward the Parks home.

He looked at her, surprised. "Really? How do you feel about it?"

"I'm okay with it." She shrugged. "Most of my memories are tainted now anyway."

He hoped that didn't include the ones he was in.

The door opened as they approached, and Evelyn welcomed them in. "Jeremy's waiting in the kitchen."

Jeremy stood and walked over to them. Jack held out his hand, but Jeremy was having none of that. He embraced him in a bear hug, then pulled back to look at him. "None the worse for the wear. Good to see you, Jack."

"I'm tougher than I look," he joked. *Things could have been a lot worse*, he thought.

"I brought Jack up to speed on the ride here. I just want to make sure we're all on the same page before the interview," Taylor said.

Jack already knew that Taylor was going to be interviewed live on *Newsline* this Saturday. Everyone had been clamoring for her story since she'd surfaced. A senator's widow coming out of hiding after a supposed kidnapping made for big news.

He spoke up first. "Crosse is dead, and he left no will. So everything goes to Jeremy, right? The Institute, the pharmaceutical company, the works."

"Yes," Jeremy answered. "His death eliminates the worry about the genetic testing research being used for his purposes. Like I told you before, I've already been working with the Alpha Pharma CEO, Sinclair Devlin—the one who financed my facility. When I went to him with evidence of Crosse's plan, he agreed to help me. He'll stay on as CEO. I'll bring Carl on as well." He looked at Taylor. "I've offered to split all the assets with my sister, but . . ."

She put her hand up to stop him. "I don't want any part of any of it. And I don't want my child to know he or she is related to Damon Crosse. We're going to go public with the fact that a Nazi founded the programs there. I was able to trace Friedrich to Operation Paperclip. Jeremy recognized a picture of him from Germany. His real name was Friedrich Dunst and he worked under Mengele. When they finally had the Nuremberg trials, no one could find Friedrich; he had managed to change his name from the alias the government provided. He was responsible for helping Mengele perform all kinds of horrible experiments. I won't go into the atrocities. But when the details come out, they're going to cast a long shadow over the work done at that institute."

Evelyn gasped. "I remember Dunst. A cold, cold man."

"When people find out, it's going to have them looking into the programs Crosse ran there. Even the main institute and its legitimate programs will be under scrutiny. It will turn things upside down for a while. Phase two, where his secret work was done, is most likely already shut down. With him gone, the professors will be running scared. The legitimate programs will continue until the semester completes, I'm guessing," Jeremy said.

"What about the DVDs, are you releasing them?" Jack asked.

"No," Taylor answered. "Here's the important part. We're not going to talk about Crosse's influence over power players. We're going to make it seem like Malcolm was a one-off. Nothing about Brody Hamilton. Nothing about Malcolm being in the orphanage. Nothing about the orphanage at all. Since it's been out of commission for the past twenty years, there's little chance anyone will discover it, anyway. Jonas has already pulled the paper records and Jeremy has taken them to Carl's."

"All the electronic files were destroyed when Damon executed the system delete," Jeremy added.

Evelyn cut in. "But if all you disclose is his training facility and nothing about how he's strategically placed his own people in government and business, no one will look any further than the Institute. There won't be an investigation."

"We have no proof, Evelyn," Jack replied. He and Taylor had discussed this on the way back to Maryland and been in agreement. "All that will do is make his people run scared, cover their tracks. Now that he's dead, they'll feel safe. He has nothing over them anymore. Then we can quietly begin to investigate the list of names Jeremy found in his office. And of course, we'll begin looking into Brody Hamilton's dealings. We'll also try to trace where some of the orphans came from and see if we can find where they are now."

"Don't forget that we have Jonas, too. He's overheard and seen plenty in all his years of service. He'll work with us," Jeremy said.

Evelyn nodded. "Okay. It just makes me sick that I enabled him all those years. I feel like I need to do something to make it right."

"You have. You helped us. If Jeremy hadn't confronted him, he would have kept going. He knew we had him, and he took the easy way out," Taylor assured her. She exhaled. "It may not be right, but I'm glad he's dead."

Jack steered the conversation back on track. "So, nothing about Malcolm's involvement. What about the letter he wrote to you?"

"I burned it."

"Good."

"The coins. They still haven't turned up?" Jack asked.

Jeremy's face darkened. "No. I don't know what he did with them, but they've got to be hidden in his office somewhere. I've searched and searched. There must a hidden compartment I haven't found yet. The only good news is that no one else there would know what they are."

"Could he have hidden them in his body?" Taylor asked.

"If he did, they would have been found after the ashes cooled from the cremation. I hired someone to be there when they manually inspected the ashes. Nothing."

"I guess that covers everything. We're not mentioning the coins, either. Everyone's on board, yes?"

Yeses all around. Jeremy thought of something else. "What about Parks? He's still missing?"

"Yes," Evelyn said. "He's disappeared into thin air. The paper hasn't heard anything either. He had money stashed everywhere. My bet is he's on an island far away from here."

"What are you going to tell Karen Printz if she asks?" Jack turned to Taylor.

"I'm going to tell her the truth: I don't know where he is but I worry that it's related to Crosse."

"Looks like we're ready." He looked around the room. Normally it would have made him nervous to be involved in a plan this complex with three other people, but he knew it would be okay. He trusted Jeremy and Taylor with his life. And Evelyn, well, she had proved herself by helping them. Once they got this interview behind them, they could get on with the real work—figuring out who Damon Crosse's puppets were and exposing them.

CHAPTER SEVENTY-FIVE

BRODY HAMILTON SAT IN HIS FAVORITE CHAIR, A PLUSH leather recliner, holding a glass of scotch in one hand while the other scooped up a handful of peanuts from the bowl perched on his lap. He loved being back in his Charleston home surrounded by all his comforts.

"Hand me that remote. Hurry up." His wife gave him an annoyed look but placed the remote in his outstretched hand.

"What are you so anxious about?" she asked.

"The interview. It's about to start. Sit down now if you want to watch, but hush up, you hear?"

His wife was an incessant chatterer and it drove him crazy. As his grandpappy would say, she could talk the hind legs off a donkey. He'd learned to ignore her over the years, but tonight, his nerves were raw and he had to stop himself from telling her to shut up. But of course, he didn't. There were fifty million reasons not to—all in her name right down the street at First Fidelity. Besides, she was a good old girl at heart. She knew when she'd married him that he was a hard dog to keep on the porch and she didn't mind. He could have his fun, long as he came home again when he was done.

She sat her ample behind down on the sofa and pulled a box of Oreos onto her lap. Just as the program started, she piped up.

"What a pretty thing. I didn't know the senator's wife was so young. She his second wife?"

"Quiet, Coralee! I can't hear what she's saying."

She gave him a wounded look and stuffed another cookie in her mouth.

Karen Printz was talking now.

"Taylor, thank you for agreeing to come on tonight. I know you're usually the one behind the camera." She favored the audience with a smile and explained, "Taylor and I used to work together. She was my producer." Here a tender look at Taylor. "Still miss working with her." Taylor murmured a thank-you and looked duly humble.

"So, Taylor. The whole country believed that you had been kidnapped. Can you tell us what actually happened?"

"My husband, Senator Phillips, made a powerful enemy. He was approached by a man named Damon Crosse who tried to bribe him in exchange for certain votes."

Printz was leaning in toward Taylor, shaking her head.

"When my husband refused, his life was threatened."

"Do you know what he wanted him to vote on?"

Brody felt his stomach drop and tightened his hold on the remote, then pushed the volume up. What had the damn fool Phillips done? How much had Phillips revealed before they killed him? Brody had been on pins and needles ever since he'd read about Crosse's suicide. He didn't need the world to know about his connection to Crosse and Alpha Pharmaceuticals. Alpha had generously lined his pockets through the years. He hadn't spent the last thirty years creating alliances and building his political career to have his own dirty laundry aired for the whole world to see.

"No. I don't think it was a specific bill. He more or less wanted someone he could control. I'm assuming for business interests. Malcolm didn't share the details with me; I guess he thought it was safer for me that way. When the threats didn't stop, he told me that if anything happened to him, I should trust Jack Logan."

Here Printz's expression turned mischievous.

"The same Jack Logan you had a relationship with for years?"

Taylor's expression remained neutral. "That was a long time ago, Karen. Malcolm knew that Jack was an old family friend. And he trusted him to help us."

Brody took a long swallow of his scotch and relaxed slightly. So far so good. Nothing about him. The interview went on, Taylor recounting the days in hiding, finding her half brother, and the incredible story about his mother being held hostage.

A look of horror came over Printz's face. "Are you telling

me that Damon Crosse imprisoned a young medical student and forcibly impregnated her?"

"Yes, Karen. That is Jeremy Crosse's contention."

Brody was flabbergasted. "Well, I'll be a monkey's uncle." His wife started to talk, but he put his hand up to silence her.

Maya Papakalos. She must have been part of the medical group during his training at the Institute. Crosse had kidnapped her? No wonder Jeremy hated Crosse and had defected. Now it was all making sense. He looked back at the television as the interview continued.

"An investigation has already begun. The FBI is also trying to determine if anyone was complicit in helping Crosse when he kidnapped and murdered Maya Papakalos," Taylor said.

"Are there any suspects?" Printz asked.

Taylor folded her hands on her lap. "I'm afraid I can't comment on that while it's still an ongoing criminal investigation."

"All right then, let's talk about the origins of this institute," Printz began.

Taylor took a sip from the glass of water on the table next to her, then spoke. "We believe that Crosse's adoptive father, Fred Crosse, was actually Nazi scientist Friedrich Dunst."

It was too much for Coralee. "Nazis! What the heck? Can you imagine? What in the world was going on at the place? I never heard of the programs there. You think that girl is touched in the head?"

Brody had never told his wife about his time at the Institute or anything about his dealings with Crosse. The way she ran her mouth, it would have been suicide. From what he could tell from the interview, Phillips had taken the same approach with his own wife. As the interview concluded, he relaxed. There was nothing for him to worry about. He looked at Coralee, her eyes huge with amazement and black cookie crumbs around the corner of her mouth. He winked at her and said, "Truth is stranger than fiction, darlin'. Stranger than fiction."

CHAPTER SEVENTY-SIX

SIX MONTHS LATER

HER SON WAS PERFECT. EVERYTHING ABOUT HIM EN-chanted Taylor. Their eyes locked as he suckled, and she was filled with a rapture so exquisite, she thought her heart would burst. It was as though the pain that all the losses in her life had caused was slowly being healed by this beautiful little boy she'd named Evan, after her mother, Eva. When he had had his fill, she laid him on her shoulder and rocked him, their hearts beating in concert. He was soon asleep and she stayed that way a long time, savoring his closeness and the peacefulness. Reluctantly, she stood and put him in his crib. Beau remained on the floor beside him like a sentinel, ever watchful and protective. He had been like that from the moment she'd brought the baby home.

She tiptoed out of the room, and into the kitchen, where Jack was going through emails. After the Printz show had aired, the station had been inundated with mail and email from people claiming to have been brainwashed by the Institute. She, Jeremy, and Jack had read each and every one, and none seemed legitimate. As journalists, they knew these kinds of stories brought out the cranks in droves. But they couldn't dismiss the possibility that now that Damon was dead, some of his graduates might come forward. They'd put up a website specifically for people with information about the Institute. So far, nothing concrete had come through, but they weren't giving up.

In the meantime, they were working with Jonas and Evelyn to try to find the churches and orphanages that had delivered children to the Institute. It was slow work, as so many years had passed, but they'd just gotten a call from Jeremy that he'd located a nun who remembered Crosse taking some of the children under her care. This was the first break they'd gotten so far. They were also looking into the backgrounds of the individuals on the list of names Jeremy had found.

Jack looked up as Taylor walked in.

"Is Evan sleeping?"

She smiled. "Like a baby. Any luck?"

He shook his head. "Nothing."

Pushing his hair back from his forehead, she leaned down and kissed him. "You've been at it for hours. Time for a break."

He yawned and nodded in agreement. "You hungry?"

"Starved."

"How 'bout I order some pizza and we watch a movie?"

"Perfect."

"What kind of thing are you in the mood for?"

She gave him a long look. "Anything that doesn't involve Nazis, conspiracies, or car chases."

"In other words, a chick flick?"

"Just for that, I get to pick." She walked into the family room and pulled out a DVD from the cabinet. "Here you go." She handed it to him.

He groaned. "*Gone with the Wind*?"

"That's right. And no falling asleep till the bitter end."

"Fine, but I'm getting anchovies on the pizza." He picked up the phone and ordered.

"Hey, what did you decide about the job?" Jack asked after he hung up.

Karen Printz had called Taylor last week. Printz had recently taken on a new job as the prime host of a weekly news show on the UBC network and wanted Taylor to join her team as a producer.

"I told her I didn't want to come back full-time. I don't want to take so much time away from the baby, and I can't get back into that crazy rat race."

"And?"

He could read her so well. She smiled. "And she countered with an offer to let me produce one show a month. I was going to talk to you about it tonight, see what you thought."

"What do *you* think?"

"I want to do it. One show a month is manageable, and

I love working with her. It would be good to get back into it. It will still leave me time to help you and Jeremy with our research, and it will keep me connected, so that when we're ready to go public, we'll have more allies."

He was nodding. "I totally agree." He grabbed her hand. "Come on, let's go see how Miss Scarlett's getting along."

CHAPTER SEVENTY-SEVEN

CROSBY WHEELER PERUSED THE CONTRACT BETWEEN Taylor Phillips and UBC while he reached under the desk and stroked Peritas's soft fur. It was all in place now. He opened the file drawer and placed the contract in the folder he had prepared weeks earlier.

He had been in the studio audience the night her interview was recorded, had been sitting in the very wheelchair that his beloved mentor had graced. His arms hung limply at his sides, his right hand curved like a claw, useless and slack against his stomach. He'd watched through thick glasses as everyone averted their eyes, avoiding looking directly at him. A "nurse" sat next to him, glancing over at him occasionally to make sure he wasn't in need of anything. He suppressed a smile, congratulating himself on his disguise. He may as well have been invisible.

Predictable—the shallowness of human beings. As if by acknowledging him, they might embarrass him or themselves. Better to pretend he didn't exist than to confront the fact that he was a cripple while they walked around able-bodied. Never mind. It all worked in his favor. He had to remind himself not to move. Most likely no one would notice, but one could never be too sure. Crosby Wheeler was used to personas. After all, no one had yet figured out that he was the same elusive gentleman otherwise known as Damon Crosse.

It had been risky but he was used to risk. He had to use the precise dose. The good thing about tetrodotoxin was that if one recovered from the poison, it had no lasting effects. The bad thing about it was that it was highly lethal, and any miscalculation would result in a quick death. Its ability to mimic death to the degree that it fooled even EMS personnel made it the right choice. It was referred to in some circles as the "zombie drug"—those who were dead suddenly and inexplicably resurrected. The concept had a certain poetic irony. Of course, he didn't wait days to wake up on his own. He needed only to fool the people transporting him to the morgue. The medical examiner had received a text alerting him to Damon's imminent arrival. The ME administered the necessary antidote as soon as his body was brought in. His body was soon replaced by that of a nameless unfortunate, then sent on for cremation after the autopsy had been completed.

And the coins were now safely in his possession. Peritas had been the ideal courier. It hadn't been difficult to get them down his throat—they were small enough. A quick text to his connection at the dog shelter assured that they would be retrieved at the other end. Now he had twenty—only ten away from the full set and then he really would be invincible. With everyone thinking he was dead, it would be that much easier to track them down.

He had watched Taylor, curious as to what she would reveal. She was quite good-looking, he had thought, appraising her as he would a piece of art or fine furniture, but he felt nothing for her. She'd made Malcolm out to be a hero. And why not? It would only reflect badly on her and her child if the truth came out. She was smart to protect herself. The apple didn't fall far from the tree. Pity he hadn't raised her. Her portrayal of Friedrich and the Institute had infuriated him, though. She had reduced him to a stereotype, had said nothing of his brilliance, his dedication to science and progress. But what did he expect? She was a victim of her own mediocre upbringing. But his grandson would be different.

He would wait and watch, see what his interests were, what his passions became. When the time was right, he would use those interests to bring his grandson to him. It was what he did best. Let them have their false sense of security and believe that his threat had died with him. He could wait as long as he had to. After all, he was a patient man.

As for his fortune, it was safe. He kept most of his money in Wheeler's name. And no one knew that Catherine Knight was only a figurehead for his own vast media empire—he had owned it all from the beginning. Omega Entertainment was the only outlet he ran publicly, under his Crosby persona. How

he would love to tell Taylor that when she accepted the job
with UBC, she had become his employee. Oh well, she would
find it out eventually.

Damon Crosse had left no will, so the Institute would go
to Jeremy, as would Alpha Pharmaceuticals, which, he supposed, would continue to finance the Institute if Jeremy so
desired. He hated walking away from Alpha, but he could
woo his key scientists away in a few years when he opened a
new lab. As for his political connections, they were all through
Wheeler anyway. His work would continue. It was a shame
that he had to walk away from the Institute, but it had already
succeeded in its mission and nothing would stop what he had
started all those years ago when Friedrich and he founded it.

He pressed a button and remotely engaged the lock on
his office door. Pulling out his smartphone, he tapped an
icon to access the camera he'd had the real estate agent install
in the nursery. Damon watched as Taylor rocked her child.
He was a beautiful boy, with curly, black hair and smooth,
ivory cheeks. His eyes were closed and he sucked his thumb
while his mother sang a soft lullaby.

"Sleep soundly, young master. One day, you will hold the
world in your hands. Until then, sweet dreams."

ACKNOWLEDGMENTS

BEHIND EVERY ENDEAVOR IS A GROUP OF SUPPORTERS WITH-
out which the journey would be much more difficult and
lonely. I have been blessed with an abundance of encouragement and help from dear family, friends, and subject matter
experts generous and willing to share their knowledge and
resources.

Thank you to my fabulous agent, Bernadette Baker-
Baughman, for finding the perfect home for the Jack Logan
series and for her continual support and encouragement. The
journey is so much more enjoyable with you by my side.

To my brilliant editor, Emily Griffin, deepest gratitude
for your expert guidance and tireless efforts in reshaping and
refining the manuscript into a finished book. I'm continually
amazed by your keen insight and talent.

The feedback from beta readers was a key component in

improving the story. Thank you for reading and often rereading the manuscript with enthusiasm and providing valuable feedback: my husband, Rick Openshaw; my sister, Valerie Constantine; my sisters-in-law, Lynn Constantine and Honey Constantine; my nephew, Christopher Ackers; my in-laws, Dorothy and Dick Openshaw; my dear friends: Eileen Arndt, Tricia Farnsworth, Lia Gordon, Deb Nygard, Michele and John Perkins, Kim Torre-Tasso, Rivers Teske, Rich Schneider, and Diane Vara. Thanks to Tracey Robinson and Valerie Constantine for invaluable proofreading assistance. Special thanks to Marie Diven for being my first reader and editor. To my good friends and authors Anthony Franze and Sandra Brannan, thank you for reading, encouraging, and providing me with endorsements for the book.

I continue to be humbled by the generosity of experts in their fields who were willing to take the time to answer my questions. Thank you: Anthony Franze for your legal expertise, Chris Munger for FBI authenticity, Lori Cretella, MD, and Fady Sharara, MD, for medical advice, Lynn Drasin for television production information, Stanley Constantine for technical advice on escape hatches and hot-wiring cars, Lieutenant John Thomas for information on Hillsborough County Jail, and Tony Burke and Slavomír Čéplö for information on the history of the thirty silver pieces used to betray Christ, and Tony in particular for advice on elaborating on what could have happened to them. Any errors are solely my own.

To the master of the thriller, David Morrell, heartfelt thanks for taking the time to work with me on perfecting the synopsis and for your encouragement and advice along the way.

My deepest appreciation to Jaime Levine, my first editor, who, in addition to the extensive time she spent editing, sat with me at my kitchen table for fifteen hours straight refining story lines and plot issues. Thank you for helping me to find the story within the story and for making it shine. I will always be grateful for your wholehearted partnership.

To Nick and Theo, you inspire me to want to make the world a better place.

And finally, I would be remiss not to acknowledge the inspiration, empowerment, and grace from the divine Author without whom none of it would have been possible.

READ ON FOR A SNEAK PEEK AT

L. C. SHAW'S

UPCOMING BOOK,

COMING FALL 2020

FROM HARPERCOLLINS PUBLISHERS

CHAPTER ONE

THE DARKNESS WAS THERE BEFORE MAGGIE RUSSELL WAS aware of it—the gentle May breeze whispering evil in her ear. When she arrived at the field, she was still in a good mood, eager to cheer on her son and his team during the last Little League game of the season. She took a seat next to a friend at the top of the bleachers where she had a good view of the entire field. It was cool for a spring day in Baltimore, and she slipped her arms into her pink cardigan and pulled it tightly around her. Maggie generally thought of baseball as boring, but she got a kick out of watching her nine-year-old son, Lucas, his face scrunched up in concentration, as he tried to make the bat connect with the ball, and she faithfully attended all his games. But today he hadn't been played yet, and her mind started to drift to the long list of things she still needed to accomplish over the weekend. There was the Sunday school lesson to prepare, dry cleaning to pick up, and a meal she'd promised to make for her neighbor who was down with the flu. And she still had to finish her notes from her nursing rounds last night. At least she'd managed to get her roast in the oven so dinner would be ready when they got home from the game. Her husband liked for the three of them to have dinner together every night. She turned to her friend Agatha, whose son Phillip was pitching, watching as she carefully quartered apples and oranges on a cutting board resting on her legs.

"Run out of time?" Maggie asked. Agatha was always late, forgetting appointments, or misplacing things—one of those perpetually out-of-breath people. But she was funny, and her charm made it easy to overlook her scatterbrained tendencies.

Agatha rolled her eyes. "We were walking out the door when Phillip reminded me it was my turn to bring snacks." She shrugged. "Oh well, at least this fruit will get eaten. I don't know why I bother trying to feed my family healthy food. All they want is junk."

Maggie didn't understand why Agatha allowed a child to dictate what she bought at the grocery store. Phillip's eating habits were appalling. She was getting restless now and glanced at the scoreboard again. Only one more inning to go, and they were still tied up. She caught sight of Lucas sitting on the bench and felt a slow burn begin. The new coach hadn't played him at all. Her son was looking at the ground, his shoulders slouched, looking as if he might cry, and she began to get angry. Okay, maybe he wasn't as good as the other kids. But how was he supposed to improve if he didn't get enough playing time? She and her husband didn't have the extra money to hire the private coaches like some of these families did, and these kids were only nine years old, for goodness' sake. Wasn't this supposed to be a team-building exercise—a bit of fun for kids and a way to get them off their phones? Getting more annoyed by the moment, she turned back to her friend.

"What's up with this guy? Isn't he supposed to play all the kids?"

Agatha shrugged and gave her a sympathetic look. "I think so, honey. But this game will determine if they go on to the playoffs. Try not to get upset."

That was easy for Agatha to say, Phillip was always put in first.

She couldn't just sit here and do nothing. Almost without being conscious of it, Maggie sprang up and yelled out to the coach, "Everyone's supposed to get a turn!" The coach ignored her, but she received plenty of dirty looks from the other parents. Agatha put her hand on Maggie's arm and whispered. "Honey, try to calm down." Maggie shook free and was about to answer her when a dad sitting in front of her turned around and shook his head.

"It's tied up. If we want to win, we have to play our best." He looked disgusted as he turned his gaze back to the field.

Three big fat red words rose from his head. *You stupid bitch.* She could see his thoughts as clear as day.

Maggie's temples began to pound and she suppressed the desire to grab him and tell him to shut up. How dare he use that kind of language with her? Suddenly she had the urge to push him off the bleachers and watch his head crack open on the cement below. She wanted to put her hands around his neck and squeeze until he couldn't speak and watch the breath drain from him so he could never talk to anyone like that ever again. But instead, she rose from her seat again.

Agatha tried to get her to sit down. "Maggie, it's just a game. Sweetie, you're making a scene."

She pushed Agatha hard. "Leave me alone!"

"Coach! Coach!" she yelled again, louder this time.

The coach looked up at her and threw his arms up in exasperation.

"Put Lucas in the game. Now! I didn't come here to watch him warm a bench."

The coach shook his head and whispered something to the umpire who was now walking toward the stands. Maggie wasn't going to let him ignore her or send his lackey to placate her. She began to march down the bleachers toward the field, then stopped, as both her arms began to itch with an intensity she couldn't ignore. She glanced down to see a swarm of angry bugs biting her. She tried to push them off her skin but they wouldn't budge. "Get off me!" she shrieked. A dull roar in her ears began to grow, like the sound of crashing waves getting closer. Heat worked its way up her chest again until she felt like she was on fire. She turned to Agatha, grabbed the knife out of her friend's hands, and started stabbing at the bugs, though she kept missing and piercing her skin instead. She ran straight down the bleachers, causing everyone to move out of her way. Once she reached the field, she stood in front of the coach, who was looking at her with hatred. It was obvious that he was out to get her and her son and had been from day one. Maggie felt as though she'd been infused with a superstrength as she plunged the knife deep into his chest over and over, and the blood began to pour out of him. That would show him. She felt hands pulling at her but they weren't strong enough to stop her. When he slid down to the ground, his body lifeless, she suddenly felt cold. What had just happened? The roar was gone and in its place she heard the screams of people around her. Lucas was yelling, trying to get to her as a sea of arms held him back.

"Mom! Mom!"

"I'm sorry!" She called to him, tears streaming down her face. What had she done? She looked down again at the man on the ground. A loud voice boomed from the sky. *Look what you've done. The only remedy for this evil is to turn the knife on yourself.* Yes, that was only fair. She looked at the bloody knife still clutched in her hand. One swift slice to the jugular was all it would take. Before she could change her mind, she raised her hand to her neck and cut. The last thing she saw before she lost consciousness was her son's heartbroken face.

L. C. Shaw is the pen name of internationally bestselling author Lynne Constantine who also writes psychological thrillers with her sister as Liv Constantine. Her husband wonders if she is actually a spy, and never knows which name to call her. She loves to procrastinate by spending time on social media and, when stuck on a plot twist, has been known to run ideas by her silver Labrador and golden retriever who wish she would stop typing and play ball with them. Lynne has a master's degree from Johns Hopkins University and her work has been translated into twenty-seven foreign languages.